C000254770

A BODY OF WATER

A DCI EVAN WARLOW THRILLER

RHYS DYLAN

WYRMWOOD
BOOKS

COPYRIGHT

eBook ISBN - 978-1-915185-14-3
Print ISBN - 978-1-915185-15-0

Published by Wyrmwood Books.
An imprint of Wyrmwood Media.

EXCLUSIVE OFFER

OTHER DCI WARLOW NOVELS

THE ENGINE HOUSE
CAUTION DEATH AT WORK
ICE COLD MALICE
SUFFER THE DEAD
GRAVELY CONCERNED
A MARK OF IMPERFECTION
BURNT ECHO

CHAPTER ONE

SUNDAY

Detective Sergeant Catrin Richards stood next to her partner, Craig Peters, a traffic control officer in the same Dyfed Powys Force that policed the whole of Mid and West Wales. In front of her knelt Detective Constable Rhys Harries, a member of Catrin's Major Crimes Team, and next to him, giggling, his partner, PCSO Gina Mellings. They were four of a group of eight off-duty officers on a charity hike up to the Drygarn Fawr summit at six hundred and forty-five metres above sea level in the Southern Cambrian hills of Mid-Wales.

Also known as the huge 'gap-in-the-map' because of its uninhabited inaccessibility, other than on foot.

Catrin had grabbed a fellow walker and asked him to take the snap which she'd circulate to the group. They posed in front of the beehive cairn at the top of the craggy ridge in what was one of, if not the most, remote spots in this empty part of Mid-Wales. Rhys Harries had challenged them all to do the seven-mile charity trek; a linear walk up from the bottom end of the Caban-Coch reservoir in the North, and then down parallel to the river Gwesyn to the south. Rhys had done the walk before and promised them all that it would be a hike and a half, but that they wouldn't regret it.

And neither would Macmillan Cancer Research.

It was not a particularly long nor steep ascent to the cairn, but there were no marked paths to help indicate the way. The weather remained dry; a blessing on these boggy moors, but every one of these fit officers found it difficult because of the tussocks of purple moor grass that made walking an aerobic challenge. Molinia, as Rhys explained to them all, had become the dominant upland grass. On Dartmoor, they were experimenting with covering the stuff with salt lick to make it more attractive to ponies. But in the meantime, on the Drygarn Fawr, it made for hard going as the tussocks were too big to stride through and required stepping over, resulting in a variety of individualised silly walks as they hiked. A cause of much amusement to each and all. They'd all been blowing like freight trains by the time they reached the summit.

The volunteer photographer handed Catrin her phone back. She checked the image and thanked the walker. Glancing up, she brought the phone back to head height and took a panoramic shot. Rhys had been right; it was worth it. She'd seen prettier views of parts of Mid-Wales but here, at the summit, a three-hundred-and-sixty-degree scene presented itself. One that she knew she'd never forget. The autumnal day remained bright, with patchy high cloud. The view, as a result, was astonishing, with the lakes and Pumlumon to the North and to the South, the distant misty-blue outlines of the Brecon Beacons dominated by Pen Y Fan. But what struck her, and, from the look on their faces, everyone else, was the scene's emptiness.

No buildings. No habitation. No one as far as the eye could see.

Rhys, the history nerd, explained that the older cairns were Bronze Age. Astonishing to believe that people congregated here for any kind of purpose, let alone carried metre-long blocks of stone across the moors. It made for an oddly poignant setting. Eerie even.

'Right, last one down buys the beers,' Rhys said, breaking the spell for Catrin.

'That's not fair because you're our guide and are supposed to know where we're going.' Catrin sent him one of her trademark scathing looks.

'Where the hell is the nearest pub, anyway?' Craig asked.

'Probably best we wait until we're back in Llandovery.' Rhys looked at his watch. 'It's a three-mile meander down to Abergwesyn from here.'

He was right. Once they got out of the Molinia, the path became clearer and rougher but easier going than the tussocks. The narrow river meandering alongside provided distraction with pools and little waterfalls that seemed to encourage the troop. An hour after leaving the cairn, they emerged onto a road towards the community hall at Abergwesyn where a minibus would pick them up and take them to their cars parked at Llyn Brianne Dam. Rhys had planned it such that, should the weather turn,, they could walk around the Brianne Reservoir. But the rain stayed off and so they hiked the Drygan.

———

A FEW MILES AWAY, as the crow flies, John Finny was delivering parcels on this Sunday afternoon. He hated this route. His sat nav didn't even show the lane he navigated, but he'd delivered to George Marsden before and was well aware of how to get to Cuckoo's Nest. He'd met a postman up here once and that had been an invaluable half an hour lesson on lane geography. In the winter, when it rained non-stop for days, the road flooded and once he'd even had to wade fifty yards to get to the gate.

Thankfully, today wasn't winter, and it wasn't wet. Another three stops after this and he could call it a day. Three stops out here, though, could mean twenty miles. He glanced down at the seat next to him. Judging by the size and weight of the parcel, another book. John referred to George as GM. Not to his face, but to himself. He spent so much time alone in the van he'd got used to chatting away to the eyes he saw looking back in the mirror. John didn't fret over his little one-way chats. There was only so much Radio bloody Two you could take, and the local station played such a load of poppy crap he'd given up on it. And anyway, out here, reception could be patchy at best. But John knew all too well that GM liked books since he drove up here at least once a week. Sometimes twice or more.

But at least the remaining two deliveries were, mercifully, on the way back to civilisation. Cuckoo's Nest was remote. There was no other word for it. There were three other properties on this stretch east of the dam, but largely the area contained bugger all. That was okay. That suited John Finny well enough. God forbid there should be more places he needed to find.

This was wild country. Exposed to the elements. GM's house was at least hidden by some trees, judiciously planted to provide some protection from the howling south-westerlies that sometimes strafed the landscape.

Finny used the turning space in front of the gate, reversed and got out. GM rarely bothered shutting the gate, but he had today. No matter. Finny grabbed the parcel, opened the side gate and walked in along the curving drive. He'd got halfway when he saw something strewn across the way. Black and brown, like an old carpet or… he stopped, all the moisture disappearing from his mouth in a dry swallow.

The lumpy carpet possessed a head and legs.

George Marsden was a nice old bloke. On the odd occasion he happened to be around when Finny called and not pottering around somewhere in the big garden, he'd have a few words to say. About the weather, or the Russians, or some other thing in the news. But the good thing about George was that they were few words. Never enough to delay Finny. Not like some of the poor buggers for whom the delivery man's visit might be the highlight of the week. Not only because he came bearing gifts in the form of Amazon parcels, but because he might be the only person they'd see for days. He had a strategy for the worst offenders. He'd press a button on his phone that bleeped a tone and put a hand up to take a call. He'd hold the silent phone to his ear and pretend that someone at work was hassling him to get on because a punter had waited in for his arrival.

They never had.

But he'd hold up the phone with a little apologetic shrug and a muttered, 'Duty calls'. A little white lie that got him away from the chatterboxes.

He'd never used that ploy with George. In fact, Finny quite enjoyed his chats with the articulate octogenarian. A man still fit and bloody amazing for his age.

But there'd be no quips today. Not from the look of it. These random thoughts flashed through Finny's brain as he stood, open-mouthed, staring at the crumpled lump in the drive. Maybe the old bloke had suffered a stroke or a heart attack. Christ, where the hell was the nearest defibrillator?

Then Finny saw the open front door and the strange black liquid line that led from it to the man lying on the ground. Reality kicked in and Finny moved. He ran forward.

'George, George? you are you okay?'

Silly question. George lay face down. Or, more accurately, face to one side, the flesh distorted by the pressure of the hard ground that forced the mouth open in a goldfish pout, and Finny knew straight away that he was looking at a dead man. No living thing had skin that grey and lips with no colour at all. Still, Finny put his hand in front of the open mouth.

He felt no breath.

Oh shit, shit, shit. What should he do? CPR? How the hell did that song go again? Staying alive, ah, ah, ah, ah.

But there'd be no staying alive for old George. That ship had upped anchor and left the dock a while ago.

Finny reached out a trembling hand and placed it on the dead man's shoulder, meaning to turn him over. He'd shifted the heavy weight about six inches from the prone position when he saw the handle of the knife sticking out from George's sternum.

Finny let out a noise that came from somewhere deep in his throat. He fell back and scooted backwards on his rear, kicking up stones and dirt into the dead man's face. His eyes went back to the black line leading from the body to the open front door.

George hadn't pissed himself.

The line was congealing blood.

Finny got to his feet, his breaths shallow and quick. George Marsden's parcel, along with his body, stayed on the ground.

What Finny wanted to do more than anything was light up a fag.

But he didn't. He did the decent thing and ran back to his van and, with trembling fingers, hoped to God he'd get at least one bar as he dialled nine-nine-nine.

CHAPTER TWO

As so often was the case with police officers, you were never truly off-duty. When the bus pulled in to the Llyn Brianne car park and disgorged its human cargo, someone hailed Craig as he headed for his vehicle.

'Like bloody buses, mun,' said a male voice. 'Never around when you need one and then eight of the buggers turn up at once.' All delivered in a loud and challenging basso profundo, but with just the right amount of faux aggression to make everyone aware that the voice's owner meant no real offence.

Catrin looked across to a large bronze four-by-four and its driver, a burly older man with a round face the colour of bricks, who'd wound the window down to stare belligerently at Craig. The traffic officer stared back for a moment before grinning broadly and striding across the car park.

'Danny,' Craig said. 'I thought the golf course more your thing than a dam.'

The four-by-four driver shrugged. 'Visitors.' He pointed a banana-sized thumb towards the back seat. 'Wife's relatives from the Midlands. Thought I'd show them a few sights. A bit of what Wales is about now they're fed up with McArthur Glen.'

Mention of the designer outlet mall brought another grin to Craig's lips. 'You should come here tonight. They've promised clear skies. This spot has a dark sky status. If you want to see the stars, that is.'

'All I'll be wanting to see is a pint of best in the rugby club.' Danny looked across and waved at Catrin, who was busy putting her backpack in the boot of Craig's car. 'That your better half, is it?'

'By a long chalk,' Craig said loud enough to ensure Catrin heard. He threw her an over the shoulder glance and got a little curtsy in response.

'And I'll put money on all of this lot being cops, too?' Danny asked.

'How can you tell?'

'Maybe something to do with those hats with Police written on them.'

Craig laughed. 'No flies on you, Danny. You well?'

'I am, but I wasn't joking about a police presence, mind. These country roads are supposed to be quiet, mun. Christ, we were up at that chapel half an hour ago, uh, that chapel on the mountain, Zoary Mynydd—'

'Soar ar y Mynydd,' Craig corrected him.

'Yeah, you know, most isolated chapel in Wales, blah-di-blah. Anyway, I'm on the way there when a red VW comes haring up towards the turning for the dam right in front of me. I swear to God, another ten yards and they'd have been scooping me and the rest of us up with a trowel.'

'Boy racer?'

'No, that's the weird thing. Middle-aged woman racer. Screamed around that one-hundred-an-eighty bend she did. I didn't get the number, or I'd tell you. Too much mud, though I caught a glimpse of her. Not bad looking but… not very happy, like.'

'Sounds like it could have been an emergency if she looked anxious and needed to get somewhere in a hurry.'

Danny nodded. 'You're probably right.' He gestured at the others in the car park. 'What's this? Manoeuvres.'

'Charity walk,' Craig said.

Danny used both hands to dramatize a count. 'Eight of you? Christ, the Llanelli burglars' union will be having a field day. I mean, who's looking after the shop?'

'Someone will be. Don't worry.'

'Yeah, well. Look out for a red maniac driver up here. And give my best to your dad.'

Danny wound the window up, and with a last wave at Catrin, pulled out.

Craig joined her at his car.

'Trouble at 't'mill?' she asked.

'Who knows? Danny's one of those who always has something to say. Likes a bit of drama. Worked with my dad for years at the steel works in Trostre.' Craig threw in his backpack and walked to the driver's door. 'Right. What pub did Rhys say again? I could murder a pint of lemonade.'

'You boozer, you.' Catrin threw him a grin as she slid into the passenger seat. The drive to Llandovery was not that far, through Ystradffin, along the upper reaches of the steep-sided Towy Valley.

'Aren't we near whatsisname's cave here?' Craig asked a few miles later.

'You mean Twm Siôn Cati?'

'That's him. The highwayman bloke. Weird name, I always thought.'

'We should have Rhys here. He'd tell you all about him. All I know is that the 'Sion' came from his father,

'Cati' from his mother. That was fifteen hundred and something, though. That's all I remember.'

'Won't be in his cave now, then. But he stole from the rich and gave to the poor like that other bloke?'

'There is that. These days he'd probably be labelled a marauding terrorist.'

'Is there really even a cave?'

Catrin pointed west. 'There is. It's on an RSPB reserve. We ought to go up there one day. Great place to hide out, I'm sure. Between here and Tregaron, there's a big space on the map. A bit like where we've come from. The roads go around, not across.'

'Who'd want to live up here?'

'People who want to get away from other people, I expect.'

'That's very profound, Sergeant,' Craig said, using the epithet to tease.

'I have my moments, Constable,' was Catrin's pithy reply.

When they got to the Bluebell, they ordered sandwiches and sat with the others in the beer garden in their fleeces to recount the day's adventure. Craig was halfway through his lemonade when both Catrin and Rhys's phones beeped at once. That could really only mean one thing since they were both, and the only two, members of the Major Crimes Unit present. Both read their texts and exchanged knowing glances.

'Oh, no. Don't tell me I'm eating alone again tonight?' Craig let his shoulders drop. Catrin knew he was teasing, but the little whine in his voice added the merest touch of sharpness to the "not again" sentiment and brought a regretful twitch to her lips before her phone rang. She took the call. It came from her fellow sergeant, Gil Jones. When he'd finished, she turned to Craig.

'It's up here. More or less back the way we came, would you believe?'

'Nasty?' Craig asked.

'Sounds like it. Stabbing. Delivery driver found it. Knife still in the chest.'

'Shit,' Craig said, and promptly put down his half-eaten bap.

'Are we doing it now?' Rhys asked, his mouth full of egg mayonnaise on granary bread.

Catrin's gaze flitted from Gina, to Rhys, to Craig, and then back again to Rhys. 'Would it be okay to take your car and get Craig to run Gina home?'

Four faces displayed a variety of expressions. From resignation to excitement and with a little soupçon of disappointment evident in a couple.

Rhys shrugged. 'Seems silly not to.'

'Especially since the Wolf has given us permission… If we're up for it.'

Impressed, Craig nodded. Approval from the Wolf, aka DCI Warlow, wasn't ever a thing to be sniffed at.

'I'm game,' Rhys said.

'I knew you'd say that.' Craig shook his head with a wry smile.

Gina moved over and claimed the seat Catrin had just vacated, addressing Craig. 'Well, if these two are off on a jolly, I'd say we deserve some fish and chips in Llandeilo on the way home. Better than sarnies. What say you, Constable?'

'I say yes, definitely. Serves the buggers right.'

If stares were daggers, both Craig and Gina would have ended up pinned to the wall.

CHAPTER THREE

MONDAY MORNING at Ffau'r Blaidd. the Wolf's lair, a place named many centuries before, when it was a shepherd's outpost and surrounded by forest. A name from a time when there really were wolves roaming the lands. There were none now. Except, perhaps, for the man making coffee from a bean-to-cup machine. An expensive little foible that remained one of his more extravagant indulgences. Evan Warlow got called the Wolf by friends, and, occasionally, inevitably accompanied by a four-letter-word prefix, by enemies. He had more of one kind than the other. Both stemmed from his work as a Detective Chief Inspector. A job that encouraged both loyalty from colleagues, and vitriol from the perpetrators and criminals he put away.

But today, as the coffee percolated through into a heated cup, he had another role to play as host to a guest, who at this moment, was making a fuss of Cadi, Warlow's black Labrador. A dog well into post-feeding gratitude mode. A state of grace she attained twice a day; when all she wanted to do was thank the humans looking after her for providing food. These periods were always accompanied by a great deal of tail wagging and the pushing of a stuffed toy, currently and almost permanently held in the dog's soft mouth, into a thigh, or if you weren't careful and happened to be looking the wrong way, a backside or a crotch. An activity which almost always elicited a human squeal of embarrassment and surprise, or an acknowledgement of her presence at the least, and a ruffling of the fur on top of the head if she was lucky.

But today, there was much more in the way of tactile response from Warlow's guest. Molly Allenby and Cadi had already established a relationship which, in Warlow's mind, made them part of the same pack. The dog knew who the leader was. That pecking order with Warlow at the head had been set up from when the dog was a pup. But in Molly, Warlow suspected, Cadi saw a playmate and an equal. And from the way the two of them sometimes behaved when they were together, he was hardly surprised.

'Right, breakfast, what can I get you, Molly?'

'Coffee'll be fine,' Molly said, looking up from where she was squatting low on her haunches to be on nose level with the dog.

'No Rice Krispies? Toast? Scrambled egg?'

Molly gave a dismissive shrug. 'I don't really do breakfast. It's not that I can't be arsed, I'm never that hungry in the mornings. But I'll have something at break time. I'm starving by then.' She smiled at him with a hint of apology. She'd lost only the sharper edges of her Mancunian accent. Unless she was angry, when she sounded like her mother, Jess; a Detective Inspector and colleague of Warlow's who was, as of this moment, about to begin her residential Hydra course to allow her to be certified as a Senior Investigating Officer.

All SIOs needed that certification, even though Warlow was aware Jess could do the job with her eyes shut. But the Dickensian levels of bureaucracy still plaguing law enforcement in the UK demanded that bits of paper were required, and so Warlow had encouraged Jess to attend with Molly the only major stumbling block.

'She's flatly refused to stay with one of her school friends,' Jess had said over a glass of wine one night a few months ago. 'She says she's not a baby and doesn't need to be looked after. I relented and got her the run-around that she drives now so she can commute to college, but I will not leave a seventeen-year-old girl on her own. Not even in Cold Blow.'

The well-named hamlet the Allenbys rented a house in had one crime in every ten years, but Warlow knew exactly where Jess was coming from.

'She could stay with me if she wanted to,' he'd said. A throwaway remark done with little thought.

Jess hadn't answered right away and left Warlow wondering if he'd put his foot in it. For no other reason than the vaguest of anxieties about how it might be construed. Jess was an attractive colleague, recently divorced from her husband. Molly, whom Warlow had known ever since Jess moved down from Manchester to West Wales, was already a pretty girl. Anyone looking in from the outside could put two and two together and come up with a hideous number at the end of that equation.

'Are you serious?' Jess had asked.

Again, the faintest twinge of anxiety made him wonder if he'd overstepped the mark, in case her response expressed how ridiculous he sounded. But he'd persisted with the offer. 'Of course. Cadi is there.' He had no idea why he'd added that.

'She'll jump at the chance if I know Molly.'

Warlow'd blinked. 'But only if you're sure. You know…'

Jess's brows had gone up and she'd replied with her usual northern candour, 'Are you asking me if I am worried about leaving my seventeen-year-old daughter alone with a much older man and his dog? A man who I have known for only two years, but who is a Chief Inspector of police and who has already once saved my life?'

'Well, if you put it like that,' Warlow had replied, a little sheepishly.

Jess had texted Molly there and then. The reply had taken fifteen seconds to come back.

'It's a yes. Let's both hope you don't live to regret the offer.'

Then it had been Warlow's turn to raise his eyebrows.

'I'm thinking of you,' Jess had said, adding a wry smile.

Warlow had that conversation on speed dial in his head as he contemplated the girl, dressed for college in jeans and T-shirt. As if on cue, Molly's phone rang, and a moment later, Jess's face appeared on its screen, pointed in Warlow's direction.

'All set?' Warlow asked, seeing Jess's grey eyes in a face blessed with good skin, staring back at him.

'Just about. The place wins a prize for the worst hotel coffee I've ever had, but otherwise, I'm fine.'

'Just nerves, Mum,' Molly chipped in. 'I'm like that before an exam.'

'It's not an exam—'

'Got your pencil case and two pens?' Molly persisted with the teasing.

Warlow snorted. National SIO murder week was a five-day course. Not cheap once you factored in the accommodation. But travelling up and down to Cardiff every day was a good hundred-and-fifty-mile round trip and two hours each way in traffic. Staying over was the best way.

'I see you're missing me,' Jess said as Molly turned the camera back towards herself. 'Evan feeding you, is he?'

'We had salmon en croute last night, so I am stuffed.'

'Sounds fantastic,' Jess said.

'It's only fancy sardines on toast if you think about it.' Warlow took the coffee from the machine and poured in some frothed almond milk which he'd bought for Molly.

'Cadi says hi.' Molly swivelled the camera down towards the smiling dog.

'Hi Cadi,' Jess called through the speaker. 'Right, I'd better go. We have a briefing at eight and it's ten-to. Wish me luck.'

'You won't need it,' Warlow said. 'And anyway, it's you who should be wishing me luck. We got a shout last night. A body up in the wilds near Llyn Brianne.'

'Brianne? That's a new one on me.' Jess shook her head.

'Yes, well, it's not a sort of just-passing-through kind of place. North of Llandovery and Rhandirmwyn.'

'I've never heard of either of those places,' Molly muttered.

'More Gil's neck of the woods if it's anybody's,' Warlow said.

'What sort of shout?' Jess asked. Warlow could tell she was intrigued.

'Isolated cottage. Owner attacked. Catrin and Rhys were already up there on some charity walk thing, would you believe? They've already been to the scene. It's nasty. Eighty-year-old recluse, stabbed through the chest.'

'Oh, no. Not more "out into the wilds" stuff?'

'Looks like it. So, count your lucky stars that you will be in a comfy hotel with half a dozen other officers doing a mock investigation without even getting your feet wet.'

Molly stood up and swung the phone back around so Jess could see Warlow's face. 'Fifteen love to Evan, Mum,' she said with a hefty dollop of smug.

'I'm not playing today.' Jess shook her head. 'It is what it is. I wish I didn't have to do this, but…'

'You'll boss it, as Rhys would say,' Warlow said.

Molly swung the phone back to put her face in the frame. 'Have a good one, Mum.'

'You too, love. What time's your first lecture?'

'Half-nine.'

'Okay. Well, take care driving in.'

'Aww. I was going to see if I could get the car up to ninety.'

'Not funny.'

Molly's eyes rolled up. 'I'm a careful driver, Mum.'

'I know. But you've only been doing it for three months. So, keep up the good work is all I'm saying.'

'Bye, Mum. Speak to you later.'

Molly ended the call with an enormous sigh. 'I swear she still thinks I'm ten years old.'

'It's called unconditional helicoptering. We all do it with our kids.'

'Nah. I bet you were the cool dad with yours.'

'Not when they came home drunk and vomited on the stairs, I wasn't.'

'My dad was worse. When I was fourteen, he'd be in the street waiting for me to come home, so I'd have to vomit in the bushes.'

Warlow handed her the coffee. 'That is a lie.'

Molly's smile was playful. 'So, what are the arrangements for Cadi?'

'I'm dropping her off with the sitters. The Dawes. I'll say that you'll pick her up when you come back. You're going to a mate's, right?'

'Yep. Straight after college. I'll probably eat there.'

'Okay. Can't say what time I'll be back, but I will.'

'No worries. I'll feed Cadi and myself if I need to.'

'And tomorrow I've got some tuna pasta bake I'm defrosting if you fancy that?'

'Sounds great.' Molly's phone buzzed. She glanced at it

and didn't respond. But whatever it was triggered a little shake of the head from her.

'Problems?' Warlow asked.

'There's this bloke in college. He's…' Molly stopped and smiled beatifically. 'No, no problem.'

'Isn't Bryn around?' Warlow had seen a lot of Molly's boyfriend over the summer.

'Yes, he still is, but he isn't in college anymore. He's packing for Imperial and the bright lights of London in two days' time.' Molly let out a big theatrical sigh.

'When does his course start?'

'Two weeks. But there's fresher's week and all that stuff.'

'So, this other bloke…'

'Is a pain in the backside.' Molly sipped her coffee and her brows crumpled. 'This is so good.'

'If there's anything I can do. Regarding this nuisance bloke…' The words were out of Warlow's mouth before he had time to analyse them.

'What, you going to arrest him for having too high a testosterone level?' Molly shook her head. 'I can deal with it.' She bent her head to sip more coffee and murmured as an afterthought, 'Deal being the operative word.'

Warlow picked up on that. 'Is he a pusher?'

'Let's just say he's the go-to source if you're after something for the weekend.'

Warlow nodded. 'As I say, if there's anything I can do.'

'You can be my secret weapon of mass destruction. Only to be used as a last resort. But I think I can handle Zac.'

Warlow washed his coffee cup at the sink. He glanced through the window. Outside, next to his Jeep, sat a yellow VW Up. Molly's run-around.

He turned back and put a set of keys on the counter-top. 'These are yours, Molly. I'll let you lock up.'

She followed him to the door, while Warlow coaxed Cadi into the boot.

'*Cadwa'n saff,*' she said as he walked to the driver's door. That made him turn back with a grin.

'Stay safe is what Mum always says to me,' Molly explained. 'Bryn did the translation.' She hesitated. 'It *is* right, isn't it? It's not some horrible homonym swear word. That would be just like him to prank me.'

'No. It's spot on. And I will do my best, as I'm sure you will.'

Molly, arms folded across her chest, was still in the doorway as Warlow drove out.

CHAPTER FOUR

ONE HOUR LATER, Warlow walked through the doors of Dyfed Powys Police HQ on the outskirts of Carmarthen. They'd built the place on a greenfield site outside the town. That meant no trouble parking and easy access to the A48 and all points east via the M4. But it also meant no easy access to the town for a quick coffee or a bacon bap at Vio's.

September still had a hint of summer about it, even if the light was leeching out of the sky earlier each evening with the depressing thought of a winter solstice to come in a few months' time. But there'd been no need to switch on the central heating yet, and given the surging cost of energy, the people of Wales sighed in relief. A mild climate, albeit a wet one, had its merits. But this morning, rain clouds were already gathering in the west and a fresh breeze would bring them in by lunchtime. Same *caca*, different day, as Sergeant Gil Jones might say.

Upstairs in the space that doubled as an Incident Room for the team, that same Gil Jones was holding court, perched on the edge of a desk and addressing DC Rhys Harries and DS Catrin Richards; both of whom had their arms folded across their chests, as sure a sign of wanting to debate what they heard from Gil's mouth as any Warlow had seen. He watched them through the half-open door and lurked unseen to listen.

It made for better entertainment than TV any day.

'Hang on, not every monk is evil like Paul Bettany in the Da Vinci code, sarge,' Rhys protested.

'I'm not saying that. All I'm saying is there's a lot going on with them and you never know which bit of the whole monkish thing it is that they're into.'

'Monkish thing?' Catrin made a puzzled face.

'What they wear for a start. I mean, those robes. *Arglwydd*, come on. I get the simplicity and detachment from worldly things vibe. All the same material and colour et cetera, I get that.'

'But?' Rhys asked.

'It's a dress.'

'I doubt the Cistercians are all cross-dressers,' Catrin said, her patience waning.

'Did I say all?' Gil argued. 'And who on earth knows what's going on underneath that robe. Could be anything. Could be an explosive device. Ideal for a concealed weapon IMHO.'

'Oh, my God. Monks are not terrorists,' Catrin replied.

Warlow smiled. He'd sussed Gil's technique a long time ago. Throw a grenade into the conversation and wait for the fallout. In Catrin, he had a willing sparring partner, too.

'Never said the word terrorist,' Gil corrected her. 'But old Henry saw through them, didn't he? Got rid of almost the whole lot.'

'Who the hell is Henry?' Catrin asked.

'The eighth. Tidy Welsh boy. Liked his mead.'

'And beheadings,' Catrin muttered.

'The reformation was political suppression and a land and wealth grab, sarge,' Rhys said.

'Exactly my point.'

'How is that your point?' Catrin said, a tad too loudly.

Warlow decided to pour oil on troubled waters and walked through the door.

'Fascinating as the history lesson is, I can't wait to hear how it pertains to our case.'

'Good morning, sir. And to answer your question, it doesn't.' Catrin levelled her eyes at Gil.

Rhys was more conciliatory. 'I suppose it does a bit. In that we were talking about the area where the body was found, sir. Doethie Valley and all that. We were discussing who wanted to live out in those wilds, sir. It's not that far from Soar Y Mynydd, the chapel, either. But then Sergeant Jones went on to talk about Strata Florida and the Abbey further north, and—'

'That's where I came in. I get it.' Warlow nodded. 'How about we all have a cup of tea and start from scratch?'

'DI Allenby isn't here yet, sir,' Catrin said.

Warlow shed his jacket. 'And she will not be. Jess is on murder week, part of her Hydra course. We're down to just the four of us. I'll be expecting you to act up, Sergeant.' He gave Catrin a pointed stare.

'Doesn't she always?' Gil muttered and got a half Gorgon stare in response.

'I forgot,' Catrin said.

'Lucky I'm here to remind you all of who we are and what we're about, then. Right, tea?' This time, Warlow's gaze strayed pointedly towards Rhys. The DC sprang up and left the room. 'And as for you,' he turned to Gil, 'stop goading the youngsters.'

Gil looked anything but sorry. 'All I'm trying to do is expand their horizons.'

'Yes, with a sharp stick, it sounded like.'

Gil grinned and pointed to the Gallery: a whiteboard for images. 'Would you like to see where they found the body?'

Warlow wandered over to a pinned-up map which had a red circle drawn on it.

'The cottage is called Nyth Y Gwcw or Cuckoo's Nest by its owner, who was not a Welsh speaker.'

The map was a blown-up ordnance survey map and the most notable thing about it was the absolute lack of roads and trails surrounding the spot.

'To the east, Soar Y Mynydd Chapel, also sometimes known as Soar ar y Mynydd, because it is, as you can see, a chapel called Soar on a mountain, i.e., *mynydd*. Further out is Llyn Brianne Dam, to the northeast, Tregaron, and Strata Florida. In between, bugger all. Except for Cuckoo's Nest.'

'Do you mean that? Nothing?'

'No. We have three other properties within a three-mile radius, and that's all.'

Warlow shook his head. He let his eyes stray around the perimeter of the circle. 'Strata Florida is one of your dissolved monasteries, if I'm not mistaken. Why were you discussing that?'

Gil shrugged. 'Gives you an idea of the sort of place we're talking about here. A place where people go to get away from it all. Monks to start with back in the day.'

Warlow accepted the point. 'Is Povey up there?'

Gil nodded.

'She must be loving it.'

Warlow went over the access roads with Gil. None of them looked very promising. A yellow marker pen showed the way. Towards the south end of the dam along a fire road, and west around the dam's lower arm, then branching east through forestry along an unpromising track, before branching north again through open moorland.

Rhys came back with the teas, and they did their usual round-up. Warlow insisted every member throw their two penneth into the hat.

'Right, Rhys, you went up there. What do we know?'

Rhys, mug in hand, stood in front of his colleagues.

'The dead man is George Templeton Marsden, aged eighty-four. Born 15th May 1938. He retired to Wales after leaving the civil service twenty-seven years ago. His wife died eight years ago. Since that time, he's lived alone.'

'Civil service?' Warlow asked.

'Still digging into that, sir. Seems he worked abroad for much of his time. Germany mostly. And then London before retiring.'

'Links to Wales?'

'His wife, sir. As I say, she passed away. Born and bred in the valleys before getting a job in London. The delivery man who found him said they used to keep animals out there. A few horses, some llamas, and chickens.'

Rhys pointed to an image of a man in his mid-seventies next to a woman roughly the same age, both dressed formally and posing for a photographer. 'Fiftieth wedding anniversary, sir, about nine years ago. This was taken off the photographer's website. George Marsden didn't have a social media footprint.'

Both George and his wife looked happy in the photograph. 'We'll need a more recent one than that. Children?'

Rhys shook his head.

Catrin didn't stand but spoke from behind her desk. 'I have footage of what we found when we arrived, sir. There were some Uniforms there, and they'd sealed everything off, not that there were any visitors. We got there before the crime scene techs, so I thought I'd shoot a video.'

The team crowded around her desk as Catrin scrolled

with a practised finger and clicked on a file. The video showed the delivery van and the response vehicle parked outside the gate of a whitewashed cottage. Accompanied by the sound of crunching feet on gravel, the image wobbled as Catrin walked through onto the curving drive, but after thirty steps, the body came into view. She provided the voice-over.

'The body is face down. We didn't move him, but the driver had tried to and he told us that the knife had a black handle. Beyond, there's a blood trail to the open door, but we didn't contaminate the scene by going in. This was at six pm yesterday evening. The crime scene vans arrived at seven.'

Warlow watched the video with grim attention.

'Outside, to the side and a little beyond the house, there's a vegetable garden and a big chicken coop with maybe twenty chickens. Beyond that are a couple of paddocks with no animals. The fields beyond that end at a planted conifer forest and open upland moor beyond.'

'Did he have a car?'

'Yes, sir.' Catrin moved the video on at double speed until she showed the side of the house and an open timber-framed carport, big enough for two cars. One side looked half full of neatly stacked logs. Next to the pile sat a small compact SUV, reversed in. A Kia with a white body and a black roof. The number plate showed a 2021 registration.

'Who's the pathologist?'

'Sengupta, sir,' Rhys said.

Warlow tilted his head. 'No shits and giggles from Tiernon this time, then?'

'No, sir,' Rhys said, fighting a grin.

The Home Office pathologists shared responsibility for the examination in cases of unlawful deaths. The last few involving the team had seen Dr Tiernon attend, a lugubrious Irishman with almost no sense of humour.

Sengupta, like the others, was thorough and knew her stuff with far less in the way of hubris than her three male colleagues. Together, the four of them made up the forensic path department in Cardiff.

'Another visit to the butcher's shop for you, then, Rhys, eh?' Catrin said.

'I'd be happy to go if no one else wants to.' Rhys's grin this time was broad. His interest in all things post-mortem and forensic-related had earned him a 'ghoul' badge. He wore it willingly and with a touch of pride.

'Has Povey moved the body?' Warlow asked.

'They're doing it now. I said you were happy for them to do so, having had us look first.'

Warlow nodded. The video Catrin had taken was invaluable. 'Best get a shift on before the rain comes. Gil, what do you have?'

'Not much.' The big sergeant scratched his head. 'I'll try to establish a timeline, sort out a next of kin. The usual.' He nodded towards the others in the room. Four people had so far been recruited for the jobs of indexing and research. 'Timeline might be a problem.'

'What about the delivery man? Is it his usual route? Did he see Marsden regularly? Does a postman call?' Warlow fired off the questions as they came to him.

Catrin answered, 'The delivery bod was on his usual route. He last delivered to Marsden four days ago. As for the post, I'll get on to the post office.'

'Good. I need to get up there. Take a sniff around. Gil can run the office as usual and it looks like you have enough to do at your desk for now, Catrin, agreed?'

She nodded.

'Right, Rhys, you drive since you know the way. Let's see what this is all about. But it looks like you two will need to do some of the legwork with Jess missing.' He looked from Gil to Catrin.

'Watson and Holmes,' Gil said with a nod to his fellow sergeant.

'Chalk and cheese, more like,' muttered Catrin under her breath, and with just enough volume to ensure everyone heard her.

CHAPTER FIVE

THEY WERE TAKING a new Audi RS6, the latest addition to the carpool, and Rhys was looking forward to driving it. A fact which he had relayed both to Warlow and Gil three times already. Rhys went to fetch the car like a kid on his way to the tree on Christmas morning with instructions to wait for Warlow outside the main entrance. But, as the DCI left the Incident Room, a strange hissing noise accompanied him. He did an about turn, half expecting to see an adder, but confronted, instead, by something much larger.

'For God's sake, Gil. You sound like a bloody punctured tyre. Or is that your impression of the racing snake you're always trying to convince us you are?' He looked his colleague up and down, taking in the round face, the too-tight shirt and the belt holding up his trousers nestling an inch or two lower than it should have been.

'Oh, come on, we both know that I've lost a few pounds already. And the road to Damascus was ever one fraught with potholes.'

Warlow lifted his eyebrows. 'Did they have potholes in the Bible?'

'Must have. I'm sure there's a passage about Nazareth

council workers leaning on their shovels, too. But that's not why I was hissing. I was trying to attract your attention to remind you of this evening. In my own subtle way.'

Warlow's face comprised itself into a Wallace-and-Gromit-style grimace.

'Don't tell me you've forgotten?' Gil's admonishment still triggered nothing in Warlow's desperately thinking brain. Gil added an exasperated, 'Meal? This evening?'

The light came on in Warlow's head. 'Ah yes. A quick kitchen supper at yours, right?'

'Indeed. The Lady Anwen just texted me to remind you.'

'Just as well you did. Heart healthy, I hope?' This time, Warlow kept his eyes on Gil's.

'Of course. And just the one glass of vino. It's a school night, after all.'

'You have told her there's no need for a fuss.'

Gil shrugged and slapped his ample belly. 'She's grateful that you are leading me towards the straight and narrow. The walks and stuff.' Warlow had taken Gil on a few hikes with Cadi. Since the scare with Gil's blood-stained urine, which turned out to be nothing but beetroot-stained urine courtesy of a genetic quirk, Gil was attempting to get fitter.

'So, not a big night, then?'

'No. You have Jess's girl at home with you.'

'She's out, anyway. But I'll text her. She has her own key. That reminds me, you know Dai Vetch? He's a DS based in Aberystwyth.'

'Our go-to expert on everything drug related? Yes, I've known Dai since he was a spotty DC.'

'Great. Can you run a name past him? Nothing to do with this case, but a name has come up in relation to something else.'

'Anyone I know?'

'No. A CHIS dropped him into a conversation.'

Gil's nod was patient, but the closing of his eyes told Warlow said patience was strained. 'Remember the days when all you had to say was informant? Covert Human Intelligence Source my arse. What's the name?'

'Not that much to go on. It's a first name but unusual. Zac. He'd be seventeen or eighteen, based in Pembs, Haverfordwest or maybe Pembroke Dock. Not much, but—'

'We've worked with less,' Gil nodded and finished Warlow's sentence. 'Oh, and no need for a dinner jacket tonight, in case you were wondering. It's come as you are.'

'Just as well, because I can't come as anyone else.'

Gil looked at his watch. 'Way too early for philosophical quandaries, if I may say.'

'Since we're heading up your way now, I'll take the Jeep and leave it at yours. Rhys can then drop me off when we come back.'

'Good idea.' Gil beamed. 'Let's hope you and Rhys don't get lost up in the wilds.' He huffed out some air. 'I'm not sure I'd want to be all the way out there when I'm eighty-four. I've told Anwen we need an upstairs flat with a lift, above a doctor's surgery, with a bus stop outside and a post office cum pharmacy across the road. Covers all the bases.'

Warlow shrugged. He sympathised. 'Dream on. Right, best be off. I can hear Rhys revving the engine as we speak. I think I'll make him follow me up to Llandeilo to keep him in check.'

Gil grinned. 'Oh yes, that'll rain on his parade.'

'Keep me in the loop about any findings,' Warlow added.

'You'll be lucky to get a signal up where you're going. Christ, you'll be lucky to get electricity and running water.'

Warlow grunted.

He left Gil to it and met Rhys outside, explained quickly about the change of plan and walked over to the Jeep. He'd known about the supper, of course, but he'd put it on the back burner. Yet, he had no excuses since he would be, for once, in the right neck of the woods and on his way back from 'the wilds' as Gil had so neatly put it. And Anwen, Gil's wife, was a superb cook. But he couldn't quite rid himself of the slight niggle that persisted. Anwen was a mother hen and Warlow certainly did not feel the need to be taken under anyone's wing.

'Don't be such an ungrateful grump,' he mumbled as he pulled out onto the road that led down into the Towy Valley. He stayed on the Capel Dewi B road south of the river. His mind drifted back to Gil's OS map, and he realised that he and Rhys would be following this river to its source today. Up to the open spaces of the Doethie Valley and beyond. But, so long as the rain held off, there were worse places to spend an afternoon in.

———

CATRIN HAD George Marsden's history up on the screen in front of her. George had not been on Facebook or Instagram. At least there was no sign of him in any of their searches. But she had accessed his military record. Marsden joined the army when he was twenty-two after attending university in Bristol in 1960 and almost immediately was seconded to Berlin. Catrin knew little of the Cold War, except for what she'd learned since Russia invaded Ukraine, and the whole thing seemed to be on every newscaster's lips.

But it was into this 'war' zone in Berlin that Marsden had gone, and seen the actual Wall go up, physically and symbolically dividing east and west in 1961. Marsden had a degree in mathematics and Catrin wondered if he'd made use of this somehow as a codebreaker. She had no idea if any of this was in any way relevant. A doubt that grew bigger following the phone call she took from Povey some half an hour after Warlow and Rhys had left.

'Alison,' Catrin said when she answered the phone in the SIO room.

'Catrin? No Jess?'

'I'm sort of being Jess while she is away on her Cluedo course, as Gil calls it.'

'Oh yes, she's doing the Hydra thing. She'll sail through that. Meanwhile, you are holding the fort?'

'Attempting to.'

'Okay, well, hang on to your hat because we've just found something that I'm definitely going to file away in my weird drawer.'

'Really?'

'I'm sending this through to the group email.'

Catrin waited for a little circle to stop going around on her screen and opened the image. What she saw was the back surface of a wooden door with wooden braces diagonally in both upper and lower halves.'

'It's in the lower section of the upper half of the door,' Povey said.

Catrin blew up the image. The rear of the door had been stained a dark brown. And there, in white chalk, someone had drawn a symbol. 'What exactly am I looking at, Alison?'

'It's a rough chalk drawing. Difficult to be sure exactly what it is, but to me it looks almost like a crown sitting on a triangle or a mountain, with the peak of the mountain poking through the crown.'

'Is it recent?'

'There's chalk dust on the horizontal brace beneath it. So, I'd say yes.'

'Did Marsden do that, you think?'

'Either Marsden or whoever killed him.'

Catrin peered at the drawing and took a screenshot. 'I don't suppose you have any idea what this is?'

'No,' Alison said. 'No idea. We've had a good look around, but there isn't anything remotely like it anywhere else. On the walls or behind any other doors.'

'That is odd,' Catrin agreed.

Povey growled. 'I hate spooky crap like this.'

'You think it's spooky, then?'

'It's odd. It's disturbing.'

'Any sign of a struggle inside the house?'

'Not as far as we can see. You said Evan is on his way up?'

'He is. I'll make sure he gets this.' She paused before adding an afterthought, 'He won't like it.'

'No, I'm sure he won't.'

Catrin toyed with not telling Gil immediately, but relented when he called over to her. 'Seen this thing Povey's posted?'

'I have.'

'What do you make of it?'

'I'm having a Google about. Nothing so far.'

'Weird as hell, isn't it? Is that a crown? And is that the number 24 next to it? Now if this isn't Dan Brown territory, I don't know what is. Told you.'

Catrin didn't take her eyes off the screen. 'Told me what, exactly?'

'It's that neck of the woods. There's a bit of otherness about it up there.'

The derisive laugh that wanted to emerge from her lips died when she realised the same thought had occurred to her when she'd stood on top of the Drygan Fawr. She realised that she could have seen the hills surrounding the spot where George Marsden died from that beehive cairn they'd posed at. An echo of that vague sensation of uneasiness when she'd stood there and looked out returned now and sent a little shiver through her. Gil was right. There was something about that neck of the woods. Something old and wild and untamed.

Catrin sighed. 'I'd better get all this WhatsApped to DCI Warlow while he's got a signal. Forewarned is fore-armed and all that.'

'Good idea.' Gil paused and then said, 'The more I look into George Marsden, the more I'm convinced he was a bloody spy.'

Once more, and against her better nature, which was to argue tooth and nail with Gil, she had to agree. 'How do we go about contacting MI6 to find out?'

'We don't,' Gil answered. 'They'll contact us if there's anything. Once this stuff gets uploaded to HOLMES 2, they'll know.'

Catrin nodded. The security services had alerts set up via The Home Office Large Major Enquiries database that set off an alarm on anyone of interest to them. That may have included ex-employees.

'Meantime, I'll tell Rhys to be on the lookout for Russians,' Gil added.

'How will he spot one?'

'They wear fur hats and are always squatting with their arms folded, ready to kick you in the knees, aren't they?'

'That is pure casual racism,' Catrin objected. 'You're talking about Cossacks.'

'There's no need for that sort of language. Personally, I think we're better off concentrating on the weird stuff. And come on, you love all that.' He started humming the theme tune to The Twilight Zone.

Catrin narrowed her eyes but resisted the urge to turn around and look at Gil who, she suspected, would be grin-ning. Instead, she simply muttered quietly to herself, 'This is going to be a very long day.'

CHAPTER SIX

JUST AS WELL RHYS HAD MADE THIS journey once already because as soon as they reached the dam, neither the sat nav nor Google Maps were of any use. They had to revert to a copy of Gil's OS map. The Audi's tyres rumbled over the hard-stoned fire road and when they hit a larger dip than usual and the suspension jerked alarmingly, Rhys apologised and slowed down.

'Sorry, sir.'

'No, that's fine. My spine could do with the odd shake-up now and again. Does that dodgy lumbar disc of mine the power of good.'

Rhys glanced over with a look of pained horror on his face.

'I'm kidding, Rhys. Let's just get there.'

The dam was on their right. Its shape on the map was that of a splayed-out legless lizard with its head in the north and arms extending west and east. For now, they were parallel with the body.

'Do the roads get any better?' Warlow asked.

'Not really, sir. At least it's dry, though.'

'For now. But the rain is coming later. You're going to

get their nice new Audi well and truly mud-spattered. The boys in the garage are going to love you.'

'I could run it through the carwash, sir.'

'You'll do no such thing. Not our fault we're out here in the *anialwch*.'

Warlow chose the Welsh word for wilderness. And wild indeed it was. To their left was forestry land, with clearer swathes that had been cut down and replanted, the stumps of harvested trees like tombstones. To their right, the land fell away towards the huge expanse of the flooded lands that made up the dam.

Rhys ignored the first turning they came across and travelled further north to a 'T' junction and took a left, away from the dam and through mature forest until they emerged onto the open moor. Here, the road branched and, after half a mile, the fork going north revealed the surprising sight of a cottage nestling in the shelter of a shallow valley. Pillowed hills at the northern end formed a backstop, the fern and bracken mottling their surface already dying back and losing colour. Even more surprising was to see the response vehicles and crime scene vans parked up on the side of the road, many of them tilted up at angles with tyres on the banking to allow movement of other vehicles as needs be.

'Best you park here, Rhys. If we go in there, we might never get out.'

Rhys pulled in and Warlow exited the vehicle and arched his back. The wind grabbed at him immediately and he reached for his rain jacket, more to ward off the gusts than the rain, which was yet to arrive. He stood and studied his surroundings. The cottage looked as if it had been dropped in by helicopter. All he could see of the building from where he now stood was a roof that had the look of a traditional farmhouse about it: oblong in shape, with a chimney at each end.

The gate stood open, and as Warlow approached, a uniformed officer got out of a car, clipboard in hand. Warlow signed in and walked around the curving drive to be met with the usual sight of half a dozen white-suited techs on their knees or examining some patch of ground. He counted three white Tyvek shelters making up the 'Apache' village, as Gil liked to call the temporary SOC tents. Two were off to the side, but one, the biggest, stood over the middle of the drive, twenty feet from the front door.

'That where the body was?' Warlow asked Rhys with a nod towards the tent.

'Yes, sir.'

They slipped into the nearest tent and put on their snowsuits and overshoes.

Suitably dressed, Warlow headed for the front door. With no body on site, there seemed little point in wasting time on the drive, though he noted the blackened trail of blood marked by yellow numbered flags stuck into the ground.

The two officers came to a standstill to the left of the half-open doorway. 'Was this how you found it? Partly open?'

'Exactly like this, sir,' Rhys replied.

From around the side of the house, a white suit appeared, hood up, mask on. But Warlow recognised the senior crime scene coordinator's gait and the trademark look of disappointment that haunted her eyes. A look not caused by Warlow, but by her constant exposure to the consequences of what some people could wilfully inflict on others. There was only one Alison Povey.

'If you want a look at the door, best you come in through the back. We haven't quite finished with it yet.'

Warlow complied. They were here because someone had been brutally slain. They followed her without discussion around the edge of the house, its whitewashed wall showing signs of flaking. Warlow peered in through the small windows, but the rooms beyond were too dark to see anything. At the rear, the lean-to's door was open, and they stepped into a kitchen with an old-fashioned wood-burning range, free-standing cupboards, square sink and a flagstone floor. But, unlike many of the places Warlow had to visit as part of his job, the place looked clean and tidy.

'Spic and span,' Povey echoed his thoughts.

She led them on into a dim passageway, the only light coming in through the half-open front door where a Tyvek'd tech stood examining the door jamb.

'Len, switch the floor light on and show Mr Warlow the back of the door, will you?'

Len nodded and pushed the door so that it remained open by an inch and no more before leaning down to switch on a free-standing lamp. Light flooded the space and Warlow stepped forward to examine, in real life, the image Catrin had forwarded to him. No one would describe it as a careful attempt at art. The crown had four pinnacles with round circles at the top representing gems. The triangle poking through the crown had uneven sides. Even the number 24, too, had been scrawled.

'What's interesting, though, is a more faded-out message to the right and above, in the other half of the door. We didn't see it at first, but in the right light, it's visible.' Povey stepped forward and picked up the floor lamp, angling the light until something became apparent.

'What does that say?' Rhys squinted his eyes.

'16/9, Craf, 6. I've asked a few of the team to look at it and that's what most of us see. It's been crossed out, too. And then an attempt made to rub it out.'

'The date is two days ago?'

'Agreed,' Povey said.

'No sign of a break-in or struggle?' Warlow asked.

'None. If you ask me, it looks like the attack took place at the front door. There's blood spatter there. Then a blood trail to the point of collapse.' She pulled the door open and pointed to the large tent. 'There.'

'Murder weapon?'

'Still in the chest. Looks like a kitchen knife. Sengupta will have more detail as we left it in situ.'

'Anything matching it from here?'

'Not that we've found. And curiously, the utensils here all match. Global knives and Robert Welch cutlery. All in the drawer. A complete set.' Povey shrugged.

'Okay,' Warlow turned away from the door, 'what else have you found?'

'The simple answer is not a lot.' The passageway led to the lean-to kitchen, which left another two rooms down-stairs on either side. One held a table and a couple of chairs, and an old-fashioned dresser complete with plate rack and hanging cups. All matching bar a couple of mugs on each end.

'This looks pretty spartan.' Warlow looked at the draw-ers. 'Okay if I…'

Povey nodded.

Warlow opened a drawer. Tea towels and coasters. In the next, fuses, a screwdriver set, spare plugs, two torches, everything you'd need in an emergency. In the third, a chequebook, an old out-of-date passport, two credit cards and a hundred and fifty pounds in cash. He held up the chequebook in a gloved hand and flapped it at Povey. 'Not a robbery, then?'

'Everything looks in its place.' Povey stood in the door-way, leaning against the frame while the two men studied the room. 'No sign of drawers being turned out anywhere.'

They crossed the passage to the other room, a sitting room which, judging by the number of books, doubled as a library. A wood burner with logs in a basket had ash in the grate. One entire wall was a shelving unit. The floor had rugs on the flagstones to take the chill off bare feet on cold winter mornings, before the fire got lit, Warlow presumed.

'No TV?' Rhys asked, unable to mask the implied horror that such a statement suggested. 'I thought I saw a dish on the roof.'

'Just the hi-fi.' Povey nodded to the other wall behind the door; at a black speaker-amplifier-deck system under a purpose-built shelving unit stuffed with vinyls to head height. The whole thing looked neat. Warlow was no hi-fi buff, but the system appeared expensive. He got closer to look at the titles. Classical, mainly, but also some fifties and sixties stuff he recognised: The Stones, The Beatles, Neil Young, Jefferson Airplane. It looked like two collections mingled in the one place. His and hers? He knew from his own stuff how difficult it was to get rid of music you'd accumulated over the years, whatever the format. These days, it had become so easy to download anything you wanted.

He'd tried explaining to his boys what it had been like in the days of tapes. The thrill of waiting for a song you loved to come on the radio and trying to record it while avoiding too many of the disc jockey's inanities. It had sounded impossibly complicated and hit and miss to their ears. The priceless look on their faces said it all.

But here, in front of him, was the soundtrack to a man's, and possibly a woman's, life. It gave him a moment's poignant pause. One thing was certain, the vinyls were worth the money.

'Definitely not a robbery if these are all still here,' he said.

'My thinking exactly. These would be easy to shift on eBay,' Povey agreed.

'Upstairs?'

'Much the same.' She led the way up some wooden

stairs. A small bathroom, completely tiled, with a combined shower and bath unit in white and blue. Everything in it shone and sparkled. Two bedrooms. One obviously doubling as a box room with an unmade bed, the other with the best views, had a bed and wardrobe.

'Looked after himself, this chap, didn't he?' Warlow said.

'There is one thing…' Povey led the way to a small set of drawers. A round portable mirror on a wooden stand dominated the centre, but to the left was a framed photograph. Two people, mid-thirties, with two babies, twins possibly. The adults looked proud and happy. Warlow picked it up. The Marsdens. George, Beryl, Georgette, and Jack. Dated June 1964.

'This them?' Warlow asked.

'That would have made George Marsden and his wife twenty-six and twenty-four, respectively. It fits.'

'I thought Catrin said there were no children?' Rhys frowned.

'She did,' Warlow said and snapped an image of the photograph for his phone. 'We'll get this back down to her. See what she can come up with. Right, Rhys, let's you and me go for a little drive.'

CHAPTER SEVEN

LUCY PARGETER HAD STOPPED CRYING. For now. Across the
room, she could make out the slumped form of her friend,
Nola. She'd woken up once and moaned a few times but
had said nothing.

Not that either of them could physically talk. Not
through the duct tape stuck over their mouths.

Lucy had no idea where she was. Not as an address.
She doubted this place, this hovel, had an address. They
were still in Wales, about half an hour from where they'd
been staying. She'd monitored the time as she'd driven the
car to this prison. So, they were still in the mountains
somewhere and near to the dam because it had been there
on both sides as they crested the track before descending.
Before the man told her to stop, dragged them out, and
locked them in here. Wherever the hell here was.

And hell would be about as good a term as any to
describe it.

She shivered. Partly from the cold, mostly from fear.

How could this have happened? How could she and
Nola have got themselves into this mess? Another surge of
panic flooded her, squeezing her gut, threatening to bring

up her breakfast of muesli and coffee. But she couldn't. She wouldn't. The very idea of vomiting through the gag was beyond disgusting. She'd have no option but to swallow it all back down or risk inhaling it… the thought of that made her feel even more queasy.

Stop it.

Stay in control.

But she hadn't been in control from the moment Nola had waved to him as he'd stood outside their little cottage. Him with the carton of eggs and the smiley face. They'd made a joke of it. Nola, as usual, coming up with a name.

Humpty Dumpty.

Of course, it made no sense. She'd said it only because he was carrying a carton of eggs.

'Eh up, Humpty Dumpty's arrived.'

So, it had been Nola who opened the door. Nola who'd engaged him in conversation. Nola who'd called back over her shoulder and asked, 'Luce, do we want these eggs?'

Eggs. The last words Nola had spoken before he'd punched her full in the face and barged in. He'd knocked Nola to the floor with that punch. Stunned her. She'd moaned, confused, maybe even half conscious, and she, Lucy, the sensible one, the smaller one, had stood in paralysed horror and done nothing because she did not know what to do in the face of such sudden and vicious violence. Until he'd screamed at her and she'd jumped.

'Get back. Get fucking back or I'll stomp on her head.'

And so, Lucy had retreated, watching as he dragged Nola in behind him like a sack of vegetables. Shock or pain or concussion or all three rendering her inanimate. Until they were in the tiny kitchen and he'd grabbed a knife out of the block and stabbed her in the arm.

She'd screamed. Then Humpty had the knife to her throat.

It had happened so fast. They were dressed for a walk.

About to go when Humpty turned up. They both had coats on and that, under the circumstances, was a blessing. The smallest of consolations as he'd issued orders. 'Get the keys. You're driving.'

And all the while, poor Nola only moaned and whimpered. He'd hit her again then, snarling out a, 'Shut the fuck up.'

What choice did she have? Lucy asked herself a thousand times. She'd done what he'd asked. As he'd ordered them to the car, she'd stupidly felt for her phone in the pocket of her coat. He'd seen her do that, made her produce it and tossed it away. He'd sat in the back with Nola, that knife still at her throat, and Lucy'd done exactly what he'd told her to do. She'd driven along the crappy, empty roads where they'd seen not one other car for two days since their arrival. He'd told her where to go. Grunting out the instructions in between telling her to do like he said or Nola would lose an ear or an eye.

But they had seen one person. A mile after leaving, there'd been a man in a field. He looked stooped, a scarecrow figure. He must have been intrigued because seeing any vehicle out here was a novelty. He'd stood up, no more than a hundred yards away. Stood up and stared. She'd thought about winding down the window and screaming.

But she hadn't. Of course, she hadn't. Not with Humpty in the back with a knife at Nola's throat.

Behind her, in the seat, *he'd* ducked down and hissed out an angry curse. 'Do not stop. Keep going.'

She'd kept going. Even though their passage took her closer to the man. He'd looked old. Standing stock still and staring. But then he'd raised a hand. So, not a scarecrow. But a man watching them hurtle past. They'd gone east towards the dam. Humpty warned her about the turn, but she wasn't thinking straight. And she wasn't expecting any other traffic. When he yelled at her to 'Turn, you stupid bitch', she did, but another car was coming down along the forest road and he'd had to break hard as she took the corner.

Humpty yelled at her to be more careful.

He yelled a lot.

Another fifteen minutes went by with the car bumping along worsening tracks until they'd pulled up at a ruin. An old, abandoned house with a tin-roof outbuilding. Rotting and rusty but still present in parts. Inside, the place stank of standing water pooled inside metal and concrete feeding pens, filthy from the day they were abandoned half a century ago. He'd chained the both of them up to those metal posts. Chained them and gagged them and taken the car. And now here they were, getting colder and thirstier, with Lucy urging herself to stop crying. But the awful, creeping realisation of their predicament would not go away.

She'd seen too many Netflix movies to not imagine how this was going to end.

'Nola? Nola?' Lucy called out once more. But all that emerged was garbled, muffled 'Oo-fee, oo-fee',,'

But Nola didn't answer. A sense of hopelessness crept in.

Although there were two of them, Lucy Pargeter had never felt so alone as she did in that old outbuilding that had once housed animals. She wondered if the animals were kept here, ready for slaughter.

She wondered if she and Nola were too.

Her shivering ramped up at the thought.

———

THE NEAREST PROPERTY to Nyth Y Gwcw was Foynw House. Only three miles in a straight line on the map. But to get there, Rhys drove back along the track to where they'd turned off, went north for a mile, and then turned back south at a forty-five-degree angle. Whoever lived at Foynw House had not skimped in the renovation. Locked steel gates barred the way and an expensive-looking dry-stone wall provided a barrier against the sheep and ponies that roamed the moor, and, from the look of it, anyone else who called.

Rhys pulled up and pressed a button on a conveniently placed post.

'Bit different to where we've just come from, sir,' Rhys observed.

Warlow didn't answer because an electronic bleep came through the little intercom on the post.

'Yes?' Not quite the greeting they'd been expecting.

'Morning, I'm Detective Constable Rhys Harries and in the car with me is Detective Chief Inspector Warlow. Sorry to bother you. There's been an incident at one of your neighbour's properties and we wondered if we might ask you some questions?'

'What kind of incident?' The voice was female, cigarette ravaged, and not possessed of the local lilting accent.

'A serious incident.'

'Nothing to do with us.'

'We're not suggesting it is. We'd like a few words, that's all.'

'I don't have to let you in.'

'No, we know that.' Rhys looked at Warlow for guidance.

The DCI leaned across and said, 'We're investigating a suspicious death, madam. And you're right, you're under no obligation. But we'd appreciate your cooperation since we're here.'

An electronic hum was the only reply to this statement.

'Hello? Is there—' Rhys said but didn't go any further because the gates had begun to swing open.

The gravelled drive opened to reveal a stone barn converted for modern living with extended wings, a slate roof and stone walls. A parked Porsche Cayenne looked in need of a power wash and a couple of quad bikes stood at an angle to one another in front of the door. Solar panels covered the southern half of the barn roof with the U-shaped building enclosing the courtyard. Beyond were paddocks with healthy-looking horses curiously observing the approach of the Audi.

No one came out to meet them as they pulled up. Next to the paddocks, a narrow strip of planted conifer forest marched up the hill and Warlow wondered if this was the same forest that bordered the Marsden property a mile away. He turned back to look at the barn. Wooden shutters held open by iron stays told the story of how exposed to the elements this place might be in winter. But the glass and wooden door had been painted a National Trust aquamarine.

There was a touch of taste here. An aesthetic that carried over to the woman who stood in the doorway, po-faced, to greet them.

'You have identification, I take it?'

Both Rhys and Warlow held up their warrant cards. The woman studied them both.

'What's this about?'

'Nice place you have here,' Rhys began.

'Please. Let's just forget the small talk palaver if you wouldn't mind.'

Rhys nodded, looking admonished.

Warlow stepped forward. If that was how she wanted to play it, fine by him. 'Thanks for seeing us, Ms…?'

'Thorley. Angela Thorley.'

Warlow gave her one of his quick smiles, designed to

let her know that no one here needed to worry, but that cooperation was always appreciated and a good idea. She was a well-preserved forty-ish. Thin, from the cigarettes, he suspected, and perhaps long walks over the moors, judging by the boots and expensive-looking mauve wellies visible on a rack inside the door.

'Who else lives here, Ms, or is it Mrs?'

'It's Mrs. My husband and son live with me. My husband works from home.'

Rhys's eyebrows went up as the implication of that statement sank in. 'You have internet access out here?'

'Satellite broadband.' She pointed towards the dish on the roof of the corner of the building. Her fingernails were shellacked pink, but the adjacent skin looked rough and stained.

'So, your husband works from home. Are you the horse-rider?'

She nodded.

'What does your son do?'

'We're here so that he can enjoy the environment.'

Not an answer. The environment? Moors and open space?

Warlow filed that away.

'Okay. Plenty of that out here,' Warlow said. 'Are you familiar with the property known as Cuckoo's Nest?'

'I am. There's a path through the forest that takes you past the place.'

'And do you know its occupant, George Marsden?'

'Of course. We buy eggs from him. George is lovely…' She paused and frowned. Her blonde hair had been tied back and her hand now fiddled with a little pendant hanging around her neck. 'It isn't poor George, is it?'

Warlow didn't answer. 'Are your husband and son in?'

'No. They've taken the dogs out.'

'How old is your son, Mrs Thorley?' Rhys asked.

'Nathan is seventeen.'

'How long do they take the dogs out for?' Warlow asked.

'Depends on the weather. On a day like today, they might go out for an hour, maybe two.'

'What kind of dogs?'

'Two Springer Spaniels. They need the exercise.'

Warlow nodded. Springers needed much more running about than Labs. 'When was the last time you saw George Marsden, Mrs Thorley?'

She stood in the doorway, arms folded. Warlow sensed she would not ask them in, no matter how long they stood there. She shook her head slowly. 'We usually collect eggs on a weekend. A dozen will last us a week. So, Saturday.'

'And is it you who collects them?'

'Either me or Nathan.'

Warlow sensed the guarded defiance in the way she held herself. He smiled. 'Never your husband.'

Mrs Thorley shook her head. 'Hardly ever.'

He could have asked why then, but he didn't. Something made him hold back on that.

'Lovely place you have,' Rhys said again, his delivery full of admiration and not a little envy as someone yet to get a foot on the property ladder.

'We like it. We've rebuilt it to suit our purpose.'

Warlow pondered those words, too. Remodelling an old property always meant putting your own stamp on things. He should know because he'd done the same thing with Ffau'r Blaidd. But her choice of words was odd. Dissonant somehow.

'So, was it you or Nathan who picked up the eggs on Saturday?'

'I did. On the quad. It was a dry day. I only go on the dry days.'

'And when you picked the eggs up last Saturday, you noticed nothing different about Mr Marsden?'

Angela Thorley's puffy eyes narrowed. 'No. Nothing at all. As I say, he's a lovely old chap. Loves his chickens, and he has bees, too.'

'I didn't know that,' Warlow said. He looked around. The quad bikes appeared well kept as opposed to the four-by-four. And the house looked in good nick. There was money here. 'Okay, well, if you remember anything, please give me a ring.' He handed her a card. 'That is, if you can get reception out here.'

'It's patchy and weather dependent sometimes. But we manage.'

'Good. We may need to follow this up. I'll be in touch. Perhaps you could let Rhys have your number?'

Mrs Thorley looked at the card and then up at Warlow. 'Is he dead? Is that why you're here?'

'He is,' Warlow said. And for a few brief seconds, the veneer slipped away from Mrs Thorley like sand blown across a pavement. She squeezed her eyes shut briefly, but then jerked herself out of it before folding her arms tight across her chest as if something cold had suddenly taken hold of her.

'Poor George.'

Rhys gave her his card and a pen, and she wrote a number on the back and returned both card and pen to him.

'Perhaps you can pass the message on to your husband and your son,' Warlow said. 'They can ring me if either of them can remember anything... odd.'

Angela Thorley did not acknowledge having heard him. Instead, she waited until the officers turned away and then slipped into the house, like an animal retreating into its hide.

CHAPTER EIGHT

By now it was approaching lunchtime and Warlow knew full well that Rhys would require sustenance to remain useful in any functional sense for the rest of the day. He studied the map and traced a route with his finger.

'To get to the other properties, we need to go around this unpopulated area, yes?'

'Yes, sir. They're no further away than the Thorleys' place, but it's accessible only from the west. That means going back south of the dam.'

Warlow's phone rang. He answered it with no frills.

'Catrin, what do you have for me?'

'George Marsden is registered with a local GP in Llandovery, sir. Since there's so little information on him, I thought she might be a good source?'

'Good idea,' Warlow replied. 'Is the GP there now?'

'Not until 2pm, sir. She's agreed to have a chat at 1.45.'

'Right. We'll be there. And see what you can dig up about the Thorleys who live at Foynw House.'

'Can you spell that, sir?'

Warlow did.

'That's unusual. Is it an old Welsh name?'

'The property probably had an old Welsh name, but Foynw isn't it.'

'How do you know, sir?'

'Because I've met Mrs Thorley. And I've come across the name before when I worked in the Met. The DI I worked for was a curmudgeonly cove. When he didn't want to be disturbed, he put a notice on the door. F.O.Y.N.W.'

'What does it stand for?'

'Fuck off, you're not welcome.'

Next to him, Rhys let out a loud guffaw.

'No red carpet, then, sir,' Catrin said.

'Not even a scruffy door mat. I'd be interested to know the background, though.'

'I'll have a root around.'

Once Catrin had rung off, Warlow gave Rhys instructions. 'It's almost eleven thirty. We need to get to Llandovery, so I suggest an early lunch.'

Rhys brightened. 'Good idea, sir. Where to?'

'Let's try the Old Moat.'

'Pie and a pint, sir?'

'Not for me. At least not the pint. And you're driving.'

'Never drink on the job, sir.'

'Wise words, Rhys. Wise words.'

They parked in the Llandovery town car park near the castle, under the shining statue of Llywelyn ap Gruffydd Fychan, a Welsh martyr executed by Henry IV. People came from miles around to see it, but Rhys had seen it before. So had Warlow, yet he lingered a moment to wonder at this piece of public artwork. A reminder of the country's bloody past. And this county's especially.

'The Old Moat is this way, sir.' Rhys had already begun walking towards the town.

'Okay, I realise you're starving, but hold your horses. Those legs of yours are longer than mine.'

The Old Moat had changed hands since Warlow had last been there. Like so many establishments, Covid had done for the last owners. So, new management had brought in a new name. Previously, it had been called *Yr Hen Ffos*. But at least the incumbents had kept to a literal translation. Llandovery was an old agricultural town, and at one time, two hundred years before, had seventy pubs, the Old Moat being one of them. It had seen significant change and would, no doubt, still be serving weary travellers long after Rhys and Warlow had come and gone.

They found a corner table. Rhys ordered a goujon sandwich, which, in Warlow's vernacular, was a dressed-up fish finger butty. The DCI searched in vain for something lighter and ended up with a ham and lettuce sandwich which he transformed into a smørrebrød by discarding one slice of brown bread.

'So, how are things with the lovely Gina, Rhys?' Warlow asked once the food arrived.

Rhys, his mouth full of North Sea cod, chewed and nodded. 'Good, sir. Very good.'

'You're thinking of sharing a house now, I heard. Spreading your wings and flying the nest, is that right?'

'Yes, sir. Big plan—' Rhys tried swallowing, but the bread stuck in his throat, triggering an eye-watering cough that ceased only after he'd turned crimson and cleared the blockage with a swallow of orange and lemonade.

'Something I said?' Warlow asked, eyebrows raised.

'What? Oh. No, sir,' the DC squeaked. 'Crumb went down the wrong way. That's all.'

'So, no qualms about the moving in thing, then?'

'Qualms, sir? Absolutely not. No qualms at all. It's a qualm-free zone I'm in.'

'Right, well, we're both perfectly clear on that score.'

Warlow waited, in case Rhys felt like saying qualm once more, or even explaining what any of those qualms, which he clearly did have, were. But the young officer deflected the conversation by taking another bite of his sandwich and another sip of his drink, spending an extremely long time with the glass bottom up in front of his face, pretending not to stare at Warlow over the rim.

'Good for you,' Warlow said to put him out of his misery. 'Be sure to send Gina my regards.' He'd worked with the charming Gina Mellings more than once in her role as a Family Liaison Officer. She was bloody good at it. Rhys was a lucky boy.

'I will, sir. She'll appreciate that.' Rhys picked up the sandwich, ready for another bite, but hesitated, obviously keen to redirect the questioning. 'How do you see this case, sir? It's early days, but what do you think?'

Warlow wiped his lips with a napkin and sat back, clinking the ice in his glass of soda and lime. 'Good question. But that isn't how this works. Give me your thoughts first.'

Rhys's mouth twitched to the side. 'I knew you'd ask me that.'

'Part of the job, Rhys. Every day is a school day, as Sergeant Jones would say.'

The DC put his sandwich down. 'I suppose the main feature is the remoteness. Who and why would anyone be out there?'

'Exactly. And that's a valid point. No passing traffic. No drunks on the way home from the pub who decide to confront a passer-by. No addiction-driven burglary by a user looking to make a quick few quid for a fix.' Warlow could have reeled off another half dozen common scenarios from an urban setting. 'So, what does that tell you?'

'From where the body was found, I'd guess that George Marsden opened the door to someone.'

'I agree.'

'And that someone might have been a stranger or someone known to him.'

'Agreed again. Now, given the location and having done due diligence by travelling that access road, which of those two scenarios do you think is the most likely?'

'I can't see someone stumbling on Nyth Y Gwcw, sir. Not unless they were hopelessly lost. I mean, there's lost as taking the wrong turning at a busy junction and there's lost out here. Pretty much lost in space. What I'm saying is that you'd have to make a genuine effort to get out here. You wouldn't be here by chance.'

'So?'

'So, whoever did this was someone George Marsden had knowledge of.'

Warlow nodded slowly. 'We keep an open mind, but constantly weigh up the likelihood and give more emphasis to the best explanation. Occam's razor.'

'Sergeant Jones told me to use Occam's razor, too, sir. But then he said to be careful not to cut myself with it.'

'Yes, well, he would say something like that.' Warlow glanced at his watch. 'Right, we have fifteen minutes. Get that down your neck. I don't want to be late for our doctor's appointment.'

When they'd finished eating, Warlow excused himself for a comfort break and told Rhys to get hold of Catrin and ask her what she'd learned of the Thorleys and if she had anything else useful.

By the time he'd got back, the DC had made the call.

'Well?' Warlow didn't bother to sit, but sank the last of his lime and soda in one swallow.

'Catrin said that the Thorleys have previous. At least the son does. They moved to the property a couple of years ago. William Thorley has an e-commerce business selling hunting and fishing gear. There are warehouses in Bristol and Swindon, but he works from home. It's the son that's been in trouble. Permanently excluded from two private schools, Kingsbirton in Gloucestershire and Stonecastle in Dorset. In both cases, police were involved when Nathan turned violent and attacked a teacher.'

'No wonder Mrs Thorley seemed overjoyed to see us,' Warlow muttered.

'She must understand we'd find out.'

'Indeed. But if I was cynical, this way buys them a little time and a chance to make sure of a watertight alibi.'

'Of course.' Rhys shook his head.

'It'll mean another visit. This time, we'll make an appointment so they'll have no excuses.'

———

THEY GOT to the surgery with five minutes to spare. It shared a block with the community hospital, a couple of hundred yards from one of the few traditional boarding schools in West Wales. Warlow and Rhys went to the reception area, and ten minutes later, they were sitting in front of a female GP by the name of Donna Hadden. The receptionist rustled up some tea for the officers, but Hadden sipped from a large aluminium water bottle.

'No tea or coffee after mid-day for me, I'm afraid. Anything after that and I'm awake half the night. I am so sorry to hear about poor George. What happened?'

Warlow made a judgement call. Hadden was late thirties, short hair, and pale from too many hours spent indoors. Her ears stuck out a little through her pixie-cut hair, but her smile was good and welcoming. Warlow had a doctor son and was well aware what long hours and worry did for you. And being a doctor was all about both. But he needed information from the woman. No point pussy-footing around.

'We don't know, other than he was stabbed.'

Hadden's hand flew to her mouth, and she sat back in the chair. 'That's awful.'

'We're trying to find out as much as we can about a recluse. That's why we're here. Mr Marsden was a patient of yours. Am I right?'

Hadden nodded. 'I've been in the practice for eight years. George came to see me shortly after we lost Beryl, his wife. He was such a stoic. There was no denying how much of a blow it was, but he remained determined to continue at Nyth Y Gwcw. It had been their retirement plan, and he wanted to honour Beryl by staying there.'

'What was his health like?'

'He had a few issues. At eighty-four, who doesn't? Hypertension, some thyroid problems we were treating, an enlarged prostate, and glaucoma.'

'When did you last see him?'

'Two months ago. We discussed his eye drop medication. There'd been a manufacturer's delay, and we needed to switch him to some generics.'

'You managed his chronic illnesses here?'

'We had to. Post Covid, hospital clinic follow-up times have been awful.'

'Like the rest of the country.'

'I'd say a lot worse.'

Warlow nodded. 'We're looking to contact his next of kin. Do you have any record of that?'

Dr Hadden shook her head. 'Not necessarily. Let me call him up.' She turned to her keyboard and clicked the keys. After two minutes of searching, she came up blank. 'There's a name and address in Australia.' She clicked her mouse, and a printer whirred somewhere.

Warlow tried another tack. 'We found a photograph in his house. Of him and his wife, I assume. With two children. Babies.'

Hadden's expression became tight-lipped. 'Yes. A tragic

history, I'm afraid. They had two children. Unfortunately, the twins were born with a rare genetic disorder. Both died within twelve months of birth.'

'Both of them?' Rhys shifted in his seat next to Warlow.

'Within two weeks of each other. I read their notes when Beryl got ill.'

'How do you get over something like that?' Rhys asked.

Hadden considered the question before answering. In the end, she merely shrugged and said, 'You don't. But perhaps you deal with it by moving to an isolated cottage in the middle of a remote area so that you don't have to face the world.'

'As good a reason as any, I suppose,' Warlow said, trying, and failing, to imagine a scenario like that. 'You know that for a fact?'

'George never mentioned it. That's me surmising.'

'Did he mention any tensions? Any issues with neighbours?'

Hadden shook her head. 'No. George was well but getting increasingly fragile. You don't get to that age without some determination.'

'Compos mentis?'

'Very much so. He was a bright man.'

A bright man living alone. So, why was he killed?

They left Dr Hadden shortly after that. A little wiser about their victim, but not a lot.

Warlow settled into the passenger seat and Rhys glanced across.

'Where to now, sir?'

'Let's get this Airbnb looked at before the day runs away from us. Head for…' He scrolled on his phone to the name Catrin had given them. 'Cysgod Y Mynydd. In the mountain's shadow.' He waved two fingers forward Picard on the Enterprise. 'DC Harries, make it so.'

Next to him, Rhys grinned and gunned the engine. 'Warp factor three, sir?'

'Warp factor in one piece, if you please. Never mind the dilithium crystals. Think of the poor Audi's suspension.'

Rhys still wore a grin as he pulled out into traffic. 'Didn't realise you were a Star Trek fan, sir.'

'I go way back to the Shatner/Nimoy days.'

'Sergeant Jones says they should name a GPS navigation device after Shatner. One that would automatically take you on the crappiest route. They could call it the shat nav.'

Warlow chuffed out a wry laugh. 'Just drive, Rhys, while I sit here and cringe.'

CHAPTER NINE

THIS TIME, Rhys took a left at a signpost about halfway to the dam. The tarmac ended with the hills on their right, half a mile after passing a farm on their left. At right angles to a steel gate, a rough track curved left over a rise.

'It's this one, sir.' Rhys eased the Audi onto the track.

'You say that as if we have any choice.'

They'd gone half a mile when a small hand-printed sign announced Cysgod Y Mynydd with an arrow pointing right along an even less well-travelled track.

'Not that easy to find, is it?' Warlow commented.

'Probably why people come up here, sir.'

Rhys was right. Type in secluded Welsh cottages and this place would probably feature in the top ten. The track wound through gulleys and over hillocks parallel with the river until they crossed it and turned north.

'Are we heading back towards Marsden's place now?' Warlow asked.

'According to the map, yes, sir. But there's no road across. There may be paths. Trouble is the big patch of bugger all in between.'

The track twisted around one last bend and came to a stop in front of a small, steel-profiled building with a black stove chimney poking out through the roof. This was more a hut than a cottage, but stone slabs laid in front acted as a patio and the hard-standing parking space was nothing more than grey chippings.

'The rustic touch,' Warlow said.

'Nice, though. Gina would love a weekend here.'

'Alone away from you, you mean?'

'Ha, good one, sir.'

Both officers exited the Audi. 'No one here by the looks of it,' Warlow said.

Rhys walked across to the wooden steps leading up to a triple-glazed glass double-door. The curtains had been drawn, but he cupped his hands around the glass and peered in through a small chink.

'There are some clothes scattered on the bed, sir. Looks like whoever's staying here has gone out.'

'Hmm,' Warlow muttered. He joined Rhys and looked for himself.

The hut had a curved roof of the same metal profile as the outside walls, but inside, the space was very modern, with white painted matchboard, grey laminate flooring, and grey kitchen units. He made out a barrel bag next to a sofa, and a rumpled sweater on the made-up bed.

'Very nice,' he said, and stepped back to examine the surroundings. 'Only one way in and out, though.'

'And definitely no CCTV, sir.'

Warlow circumnavigated the hut. A gate led to a path winding up towards the hill nearby.

'Did we find out who owns this?'

'Uh, it's an address in Swansea, sir. Not local.'

Warlow wrinkled his nose. Often, getaways like this were owned by local farms who'd seen the diversification light. But clearly, this had been bought as a ruin by someone with the foresight to spend a bit of money without increasing the footprint. The Airbnb mantra of "If-you-build-it-they-will-come". It was early autumn, and the weather was not too bad. But he wondered what on earth this dot on the landscape would be like in mid-December.

Warlow took out his phone and glanced at it. No signal. Hardly surprising. This really was a get-away-from-it-all spot. No point loitering on the off chance that the occupants would come back. They'd get more information by talking to the owner.

'Come on, let's find out where this path leads.' Warlow strode along a narrow line of tamped-down vegetation leading away from the building and climbed up over a rise. After a hundred yards, there were no properties in sight. After a hundred more, they were in a wide-open wilderness. To the northeast, the inevitable caterpillar curve of planted forest offered lower ground.

'According to the map, sir, there's a logging road in that forest. It doesn't quite go all the way to Marsden's house, but it ends up half a mile north of it.'

Warlow gazed around. There were not even any farms visible from where they now stood. The surrounding hills would all have names, but that was for another time. The important thing to note was that it might be possible to trek across to Nyth Y Gwcw from here if you were energetic and determined enough. But would you, in all honesty, risk being out in the open like this? Admittedly, the chance of you meeting someone would be slim. Still, if you did, it would be memorable.

'Right, let's get back to civilisation, aka a phone signal. There's one other property, the Retreat, but I'm guessing that's even less accessible than this one?'

'Go much further east and head in from that direction according to my map, sir.'

Warlow checked his watch. 'I said I'd meet up with the Amazon driver who found Marsden in the dam car park at four-thirty. The Retreat will have to wait another day.'

They headed back to the Audi and Rhys drove them out the way they came in. Warlow, though frustrated, didn't consider it a total waste of time. At least now he had a mental image in his head and a rough idea of the lay of the land. It all helped.

———

THE AMAZON DELIVERY van turned out to be a rental. White with no markings. Rhys parked next to it. A man leaning against the railings took one last drag on a cigarette before stubbing it out and turning towards the two officers as they approached.

'Mr Finny.' Rhys held up his warrant card. 'Thanks for meeting us.'

Finny wore shorts and a thin polo shirt. Not exactly appropriate garb for the brisk wind whistling up the valley. That might have been a cause for shivering, then again it might not be. But even as Rhys put away his wallet, the first spots of rain began spitting at them.

Rhys introduced Warlow. Finny nodded, and his lips twitched a half smile.

'Why don't we sit in the Audi,' Warlow suggested. 'This rain is only going to get worse.'

'Fine by me,' Finny said.

Warlow took note. No hesitation there. Getting into a vehicle with two police officers had its own fear factor. But Finny showed no sign of reticence. That meant either he had nothing to hide, or he enjoyed double bluffing. Some of the worst recidivists he knew could lie through their teeth and swear that day was night.

With the three of them in the car, Warlow asked the driver to run through exactly what he'd found. When he'd finished and it tallied with the report Warlow had read, the DCI continued with the questions. 'How often would you call?'

'Once, maybe twice a week. Books mainly, judging by the packaging.'

'Hang on.' Rhys frowned. 'How did he order stuff from Amazon? I didn't see a computer at his place.'

Warlow threw him a glance. 'Good point. Let me text Povey. We need to find that out.' He sent a message while Rhys continued to quiz the driver.

'Did you see any traffic on the tracks?'

'No, nothing. It's rare that I see anyone out there.'

'It can't be a straightforward route.'

Finny shrugged. 'You get used to it. Do you have any idea what happened?'

Warlow glanced up from his phone. 'We're in the process of finding out.'

Finny grimaced. 'I can't stop thinking about George, uh, Mr Marsden. He was such a nice old bloke. Always had the time of day for you, but not clingy. I can't be doing with clingy. We're always on a deadline, you know? Bloody apps tell people how far away we are. They know if we've been dawdling.' Finny didn't seem to know what to do with his hands. 'Will you? Find out, I mean?'

'It's what we get paid to do, Mr Finny,' Rhys said with admirable reassurance.

Finny nodded.

Warlow read the signs. Finny had been traumatised by events. 'Any chance they could give you a day or two off?'

The driver let out a single derisive, 'Huh,' and his expression became long-suffering. 'Fat chance. I'm their man in the mountains. Take forever for someone to learn this route.'

'And you've seen nothing odd since, or before? No new vehicles? No one hanging around? Nothing suspicious?' Rhys asked.

'I've been racking my brains, but I remember nothing odd. Not until I rounded that bend in the drive and saw…' Finny sucked in a breath. 'I've never seen a dead body before. I haven't slept much since…'

'Do you have a partner, John?' Warlow asked.

Finny nodded.

'Kids?'

'Two. Both girls.'

'When you go home tonight, surprise them. Take them out for an ice cream. Do something different with them and the missus. They're your best antidote to this.'

Finny blinked, confused by what he was hearing, but then he thought about it and his brows cleared. 'You could be right.'

'He usually is,' Rhys said.

'But I want to help if I can. Help you get whoever did this.'

Warlow thought about the offer. 'You can. You'll be up here over the next few days in a white van. You might as well wear an invisibility cloak. So, you can be our eyes and ears out here. If you notice anything odd, anything at all, give us a ring.'

Rhys gave Finny a card which he looked at carefully before regarding Warlow with a focussed expression of intent. 'I'll do that.'

The officers watched him return to his van, and he waved to them as he drove away.

'Think he's genuine, sir?'

'What do you think, Rhys?'

'Is this going to happen every time I ask you a question now, sir?'

'What do you mean?'

'You, returning my question with one of your own.'

'Who knows?'

'You just did it aga—' Rhys caught himself. 'That was a mickey take, sir.'

'Indeed. But come on, your impression of John Finny. I want to know.'

'Seems like he's genuinely upset by what happened.'

'Agreed.'

'So, can we tick him off as not a person of interest?'

'Not yet. You know I like to keep an open mind on these things until we have our perpetrator. But if John Finny killed George Marsden, I will eat Sergeant Jones's sou'wester.'

'Ugh, that's not a pleasant image, sir. He showed me the sweat band on that once. It's almost turned black.'

'Put you off the idea of a cup of tea and a cake at the Cawdor in Llandeilo, has it?'

Rhys's reply came back in an instant. 'Are you buying, sir?'

'Don't I always?'

'Then Sergeant Jones's sweatband is already forgotten, sir.'

'Funny that, isn't it? Let's go.'

An hour later, Warlow contented himself with the tea and watched Rhys devour a carrot cake the size of half a brick in the cosy courtyard of the hotel. At six-thirty, Rhys took his leave and Warlow waived the offer of a lift to Gil's house.

'It's a ten-minute walk from here. Get going,' Warlow said.

'See you tomorrow, sir.' Rhys hurried off to the Audi.

'And don't break the car on the way back to HQ,' Warlow warned.

'No chance, sir.' Rhys dangled the keys and grinned.

Warlow shook his head. He paid at the desk and made his way down the busy Rhosmaen Street, acutely aware of the articulated lorries playing touchy-feely with his shoulders on a pavement that could not have been more than a couple of feet wide at some points on this busy high street that doubled as a trunk road from north to south. Despite its love affair with the Sunday supplements as a destination town and one of Wales's most desirable places to live, Llandeilo was an angina town: in desperate need of a bypass. A plan much talked about but one which, like a sperm whale, came up for air now and again, only to dive into the depths whenever costs were discussed. No doubt it would take some giant transport vehicle's catastrophic brake failure and the destruction of property, or, God forbid, lives before someone in authority grasped the nettle and approved the bloody thing. Warlow feared he would not be alive to see it.

He'd turned up the much quieter Carmarthen Street on his way to Gil's house on the Pencrug Estate and was passing the Gin House when his phone rang and Povey's number flashed up.

'Alison, what have you got for me?' he said without missing a step.

'An explanation for the Amazon orders. There was a laptop hidden in a false floor of a trunk and a modem linked to satellite broadband.'

'What? That's a bit cloak and dagger, isn't it?'

'No cloak, just dagger. We're taking it to the lab. See what the digital forensic techs can do with it.'

'Good idea. Any chance you can get a push on it?'

'Do my best.'

'You always do, Alison. And I, for one, appreciate it.'

'You say the nicest things, Evan. When you want something, that is.'

'Ooh, that hurt.'

'Good. I'll be in touch.'

Smiling to himself, Warlow pocketed his phone and headed to Gil's, knowing that a couple of dominos had toppled in the case. Whether they were the right ones was yet to be seen. But it was progress of a sort. And progress was never to be sniffed at.

CHAPTER TEN

He'd arrived at the Jones's property and been let in by a nervous-looking Gil, and a beaming Anwen. Warlow muttered, 'Quick word with your husband before supper, if that's okay?'

Anwen, quite used to having work plod in through the door, usually in her husband's size tens, shrugged her understanding. The two officers walked through to the kitchen where a tantalising aroma of cooked meats and steaming vegetables shot right up Warlow's nose and made his salivary glands go into overdrive.

'Smells fantastic,' he said.

'She's an alchemist with food,' Gil replied.

'Can't wait. But this is about tomorrow morning. I'm shooting up to Cardiff early. Sengupta's got Marsden scheduled for 09.30. With a bit of luck, we'll be out of there by eleven. So, I'd like a pow-wow no later than 1pm.'

'Right you are.'

'But there is one spot we didn't get to today. The Retreat. So, if you and Catrin can pop up there first thing, that would be great.'

'I'll get her to pick me up here.' Gil was all smiles. 'Good. Anything useful from your road trip?'

'Just the news that Marsden had a laptop hidden away at his place. Explains the Amazon orders. But it might explain a lot more once we get access.'

Gil's eyebrows crawled up. 'You're not asking Rhys to do that?'

'No, Povey's taken it straight to the techs.' Warlow's eyes strayed to a cooling tray. 'Are those vol au vents?'

'Anwen puts a spicy spin on them. Chicken with a dash of chilli sauce.'

Warlow moaned. Anwen appeared in the doorway. She'd made an effort, as always. Hair done, nice dress, apron on so as not to get the dress marked. Anwen was nothing if not pragmatic about these things.

'Right, come on, you two. Drink, Evan? We have some non-alcoholic lagers.'

'I'll try one.' Warlow was not a huge fan of pretend alcohol. But he'd be driving back to Nevern later and one glass of wine with food was his limit.

'Okay. Gil, you heard the man. Bring it through to the living room.'

'You've gone to a lot of trouble, Anwen. Gil said we were having a quick bite.'

'We are,' she said, but turned away before he could read her expression.

One glance into the dining room as they passed revealed a table laid with four settings. That should have given the game away. But the realisation that he'd been ambushed only truly solidified when he walked into the living room and Anwen introduced him to the other supper guest.

'This is Dee Sanderson, my good friend. Dee, this is *the* Evan Warlow.'

The woman who stood up to shake Warlow's hand was,

in Warlow's rough estimation, a few years younger than he was, but a lot fitter. Her arms were bare under a loose-fitting, white, short-sleeved shirt tucked into jeans with white canvas sneakers on her feet. The arms on display looked toned and her short, blonde hair showed off her blue eyes. Eyes that looked amused by the world around her.

'Nice to meet you, Dee,' Warlow said.

'Nice to meet you, finally.'

'That sounds ominous.'

'So it should.' Dee's smile was quick. 'You're a frequent source of discussion in this house and polite company.'

Warlow threw Anwen a glance. 'Gil only tells us the funny bits. Don't worry,' she explained.

'Not too many of them, unfortunately.' Warlow leant forward and picked up a crisp from a bowl.

'Oh, you'd be surprised,' Dee said. 'Gil is a hoot.'

'That's one word for him, certainly.' Warlow popped a crisp into his mouth and chomped down. A hint of balsamic vinegar filled his mouth.

'I'll let you two chat for a minute. I don't know what Gil is doing.'

Anwen left the room. Warlow looked around at the nicely painted walls and new curtains. 'They've done a good job with this place,' he commented.

'They have.'

A few seconds of silence threatened to stretch out between them. Eventually, Warlow succumbed to the pressure. 'So, how do you know Anwen, Dee?'

'Same ramblers' group. She's been very active since she moved down here. I think she takes pity on me because I'm… unattached.'

'And is that by choice?'

'I'm divorced if that's what you mean. I know you are too, but that your ex-wife died a few months ago.'

'These things happen,' Warlow said, surprised at how much the reminder stung. Especially since he and Denise had been apart for years before she passed.

Dee dropped her voice. 'Do you think Anwen is playing matchmaker here?'

Candid this one.

'One hundred percent.' Warlow grinned. 'She sees me as a lost soul. Not sure what label she's stuck on you.'

Dee smiled. It made her look younger. 'Confused middle-aged woman in need of partner. But she doesn't know me that well yet. If she did, she'd realise the reason I left my husband was because of irreconcilable differences.'

'Differences tend to be that way inclined.'

Dee appraised Warlow and seemed to come to a decision. 'You're an easy man to talk to, Evan. That's a dangerous trait in a police officer. So, though I don't broadcast it, I might as well tell you I'm gay.'

Warlow nodded. Unusual to see cards on the table this early, but he appreciated it, nonetheless. 'And Anwen doesn't know?'

Dee shook her head. 'Few people do. My partner's choice. She's in the sort of job where that sort of thing makes for awkwardness.'

'In this day and age?'

'You better believe it. She's an educator and negotiating that with a cultural identity at odds with a traditional mindset is problematic. She's opted to keep all of that private. We live apart for now, but together in every other sense. She prefers to remain in the closet.'

Once the relief of not *having* to dance to Anwen's tune had washed through him, Warlow nodded. He understood better than most about keeping secrets, though he felt for Dee. And not every gay person he'd ever met wanted to join a parade. 'To tell you the truth, I am not in the market for a relationship, either.'

Dee smiled again. It was a good smile and Warlow warmed to it, even though he was slightly shocked by the words he'd just spoken. Normally, he didn't voice these things. But Dee's openness had dragged those words up from the depths. God alone knew he had reason to believe them of himself. Still, it surprised him at how easily they'd tripped off his tongue. 'How about we play Anwen's game?' A wicked sparkle glinted in her eyes.

'You mean, pretend we're getting on like a hut in a forest fire?'

'Why not?' Dee grinned.

The atmosphere in the room lifted.

'You look fit,' Warlow said. 'Rambling suits you.'

They chatted amiably. Warlow learnt that Dee still lectured part-time at the university in Lampeter. The philosophy of theology, no less. There was probably a joke in there somewhere, but he couldn't think of one there and then. Drinks were served, canapés eaten, and a supper of chicken chasseur with crisped roasties consumed. As the evening wore on, Anwen's little smile of gratification grew ever wider at seeing how well Warlow and Dee Sanderson were getting on. And the truth was, they were, now that Anwen's little scheme had been exposed and dealt with. When, at nine, Warlow looked at his watch and excused himself, it was with some regret. He'd enjoyed the evening. He thanked Anwen with a hug.

'Nice to meet you, Dee,' Warlow said as he slid on his jacket.

'And you,' Dee replied.

Gil walked Warlow to the door with an anxious expression. 'Sorry about that. I knew bugger all about Dee coming until Anwen announced it at six o'clock.'

'No bother, she's good fun.'

'Even so, I understand you don't need any hassle. I did try to explain.'

'Don't worry about it. And anyway, Dee and I understand each other perfectly.'

'Really?' Gil cocked one eyebrow.

'Yep.' He glanced at his watch. 'Okay, I'm off. Molly's picking Cadi up. I don't want them to be home alone. I'll see you at lunchtime tomorrow.'

Warlow waved his goodbyes and made for the Jeep. Before he set off, he texted Molly.

> You at Ffau'r Blaidd?

>> Been back half an hour. Took Cadi into the field to play ball in the twilight. She's happy.

> See you in an hour.

Dog and guest were okay. Good. Warlow's mind had reset thanks to the diversion that Anwen had provided. His subconscious, meanwhile, had been processing the day's information on some other level. And he was aware of how important such processing was. As he drove, he gave his thoughts free rein. He wasn't hungry, nor thirsty, and the road now was quiet. Ideal for cogitation. He wondered how Jess was getting on in murder week. He could give her a ring but remembered enough about his Hydra course to know that they'd be on downtime now. Probably in the bar having a swift half before catching some sleep and another day's sweat in a mock Incident Room. Yet, his mind never strayed very far from Povey's message about Marsden's laptop and the fact that it had been secreted away. Not that they had any proof it was Marsden's. Not yet. He might have been keeping it for someone.

Secrets and lies were Warlow's stock-in-trade. Everyone had them. Dee Sanderson for one. Trouble was, not everyone was as open about them as she had been. More often than not, you had to dig down through the layers of

BS people had smothered over their inner selves in order to survive. How much easier would it be having a lid on everyone's head you could unzip? That way, you might peer inside to see the truth of their existence.

That's a bit Hannibal Lecter, Evan.

He snorted. He didn't even like fava beans. Though he was partial to a drop of Chianti now and again.

Warlow reached for the radio and found something to listen to on the BBC World network about the price of avocados. Anything to get his brain away from Lecter.

When he got back to Nevern and his cottage, Cadi came to meet him at the door. Molly sat in the kitchen with stripey socks on her feet and a sweatshirt hanging over her jeans, laptop and books open.

'Hi,' she said.

'Evening. Sorry I'm late.'

'Hard day at the office?'

'Harder evening fending off a determined matchmaker at a colleague's supper date.'

'Ooh, sounds interesting. But no trouble for you. You're a born fender.'

'One does one's best,' he replied, not sure if Molly's statement was a compliment or a criticism. Judgement calls on Molly's pithy banter were often tricky. But he was too tired to spar, so he parked the thought and asked, 'You okay?'

'Fine. I'm just finishing reading through an essay and then I'm off to bed. I'm in tomorrow at nine-thirty.'

'Mind dropping Cadi off at the Dawes, then? I'll be off before that.'

'No problem.' She grinned at the dog and her enthusiastic tone brought Cadi over to her for a neck rub.

'That dog is being spoilt.'

'Totally.'

'Heard from your mother?'

'She's fine. I think she's sneakily enjoying it. She says there are one or two clueless twerps there.'

Warlow nodded. 'Nothing changes.' He meant it as a throwaway remark and was surprised to see Molly run with it.

'I don't know about that. Stuff changes all the time. I mean, look at us Allanbys. Five years ago, we're buying Happy Meals for me in Stockport and now my mother is on a mission to become top-dog and my dad thinks he's…' She searched for a reference and Warlow sensed her struggle to find one she considered Warlow-relatable. She finally plumped for, 'Jason Bourne.'

'As in the Ultimatum and Identity?'

'The same. Matt Damon's rogue spy trope. And to cap it all, my best friend in the world is a black Labrador. Talk about dysfunctional.'

'Poor you,' Warlow replied, not meaning a word of it.

'Imagine what I could do with that sort of sob story on Britain's Got Talent or whatever heart-string yank-fest floats your TV boat.'

Warlow eased out a quiet chortle. In this mood, Molly was excellent value. 'Have you heard any more from your dad?'

'I got a text. Good luck with year twelve. It was signed 'R'.' She shook her head. 'You couldn't make it up.'

'If there's anything you need to talk about…' Warlow let the words drift into the ether.

'You'd lend a paternal ear?'

'I'm not your father, Molly. I was actually suggesting you whinge into Cadi's ear so she can tell me all about it later.'

This time, Molly's grin spread over her face. 'Nicely done, Mr Warlow.' She turned her gaze back to her laptop. 'I'll bear it in mind. Now, much as I'd love to chat, this essay is not going to proofread itself.'

'Tea?'

'Not for me. Too much caffeine.'

'I've got some caffeine-free, sleep-friendly stuff.'

'Ooh, go on, then.'

'Right. Let's get the kettle on.'

CHAPTER ELEVEN

SLEEP CAME QUICKLY to Warlow that night.

The same could not be said for Lucy Pargeter and Nola O'Brien. Their prison, because that was how Lucy thought of it, felt inhospitable, cold, and dank. What little natural daylight filtering in through the holes in the roof had long gone. Darkness had arrived to engulf them.

Lucy had managed to get to her knees. Her wrists were tied behind her with tape and the chains prevented her from standing up fully. She was most comfortable lying on her side. He'd been rough and quick in applying the tape over her mouth, winding it several times around the back of her head and it cut into her flesh.

And now, worst of all, she wanted to pee.

In fact, she'd wanted to pee for hours. She'd held off only because a ridiculous thought had popped into her head that he might come back and let them use a toilet.

But there was no toilet in this decrepit ruin.

And him coming back would be the last thing she wanted. She dare not think of what he was planning to do when he did.

But oh God, she was bursting for a pee.

For the last twenty minutes, the pressure in her bladder had grown to enormous proportions. No chance of jogging on the spot to distract her brain. An ache had spread up her back. Lucy wasn't a nurse, but she knew tubes joined bladder to kidneys and the pain spreading up was deep and uncomfortable. Was that ureteric pain? Or even kidney pain? Could you get that from holding your pee?

She moaned. Again. Thoughts of passing water consumed her. From somewhere across the room came an answering moan.

Nola.

Nola!

Lucy tried saying her name, but all that emerged were two muffled syllables. After three goes, Nola finally responded with her own blunted moan.

Lucy would take that as an acknowledgement. Tears of relief coursed down her face. There'd been nothing from Nola for hours. Lucy had feared that Nola might even be dead.

She sniffed and shook her head to get the tears away, but the movement brought on another spasm in her bladder. A desperate, unstoppable urge overtook her.

She wailed through the gag in pain and protest. But there was nothing for it.

She squatted, her head hanging down, and let go. The wet heat spread like a warm hand through her underwear and her jeans and dripped onto the floor beneath her. But the shame and misery of all got buried under the total relief.

For a moment, anyway.

At least Nola had not seen her do that. Or heard her do that.

Wet from her own waste, Lucy shuffled over to find a drier patch of ground to sit on. The chain yanked against the post. She hunched there, disgusted with herself, trying to become as small a ball as possible to keep what heat there was in her body. Neither she nor Nola were religious, though Nola sometimes went to midnight Christmas services for the singing. But now, in this desperate, hopeless situation, Lucy had no hesitation in praying to whatever god might listen for help.

But no one answered.

All that was left to do was await the morning light.

———

WARLOW GOT UP EARLY and took Cadi out for a quick walk along the lanes, enjoying the sunrise over the freshly cut hedgerows. There was no sign of Molly when he got back, but vague noises from her room suggested she was awake. He showered and changed and got ready for the day. When he emerged from his bedroom, Molly was in the kitchen, tousle-haired and bleary-eyed in chequered pyjama bottoms and an oversized sweatshirt.

'Morning,' she said, shuffling towards the coffee machine.

'Sleep okay?'

'Mm-hmm.'

Warlow had already worked out that Molly did not do mornings. Not until at least two cappuccinos had crossed her blood-brain barrier.

'The dog's been fed, watered, and toileted. I can drop her off with the Dawes if you like?'

Molly shook her head and pouted. 'Haven't had our morning cuddles yet, have we, Cads?'

The dog's tail thumped up and down on the mat.

Molly looked up, studying Warlow as if seeing him for the first time. 'You're off early?'

'Slice and dice in Cardiff first thing.'

'Nice.' Her pained expression belied the sentiment.

'You won't be wanting much breakfast, then.' Her phone vibrated, and she picked it up off the table, glanced at it, and swiped the message away.

'Unwanted?' Warlow asked.

Molly nodded.

'Zac?'

'How do you know?'

Warlow tilted his chin down.

Molly shook her head. 'No, don't say it's what you do. Mum does that all the time. It's irritating as hell.'

'I thought you said you could handle him.' Warlow fished out the Jeep's car keys from the bowl he kept them in.

'I can. But he's persistent, I give him that.'

'Like an angry wasp?'

'More like an irritating horsefly.'

'Sometimes they need swatting.'

Molly sent him a narrow glare. 'Or, you can just wait and they always go away.'

Warlow opened the door and a fresh breeze wafted in. 'Take care, Molly, I'll see you later. I should be back at a reasonable time tonight. I'm defrosting that pasta.'

'How many times have I heard that one?' Molly spoke with her back to him, busy at the coffee machine.

Warlow didn't fight the smile. *She's a copper's daughter alright.*

———

CATRIN DROVE. She'd weighed up the options in her mind and decided that she'd be better off in the driving seat. Sometimes, she preferred to be a passenger because she had no problem working on her laptop while someone else drove, though it gave some people seriously bad motion sickness.

Not her.

But there'd be no opportunity for working this morning because she'd have to navigate from the map. In that instance, she preferred to drive.

The huge downside to all of that was that it gave Gil ample opportunity in the passenger seat to be… Gil. They were halfway to Llandovery, and he had the map and the report on the 'third' property within striking distance of Nyth Y Gwcw on his lap.

'Bryn Encil,' he said, reading the name for the fourth time and pronouncing the c as an English k, as it always was in the Welsh alphabet. 'What odds would you give me that when they first bought it they pronounced encil like pencil?'

'People would, wouldn't they? They'd assume that.'

'When you assume, you make an ass out of u and me. They teach you that at school?'

'No, I read it in a Christmas cracker.'

Gil opened the cardboard file and started reading, muttering the words as he read them in an irritatingly incoherent speed-reading mumble, with occasional breaks for a sentence or name that he considered interesting or important, at which point he'd slow down and speak louder. 'Founded by Amici Lucis. Fancy Latin name for the Friends of Light.' He cocked one eyebrow. 'I'm sure they were in Game of Thrones.'

Catrin side-eyed him. 'For someone who claims not to be a fan, you're full of G.O.T. references, I've noticed.'

'I'm a man with eclectic tastes. My preference being chocolate eclectics.'

'And anyway,' Catrin ignored Gil's poor attempt at a patisserie joke, 'they were the Brothers of Light, I'm pretty certain.'

That drew Gil's attention. 'You and Craig fans, are you?'

'We watched it all.'

'Ending?'

'Let's not go there.'

'Personally, I thought it was pretty good. And yes, okay, I've seen bloodier battles on Saturday afternoons in West Wales rugby derbies, but it had spectacle, poignancy, and grandeur.'

Catrin waited for the pointed barb that usually accompanied these opening salvos, but none came.

Instead, Gil carried on, 'I mean, it's sword and sorcery fantasy. And, if you ask people about what they would have liked to see in the ending, everyone wanted things tied up in neat bows. But life isn't like that. Take this place we're going to. What does it say?' He let his eyes drop to the page Catrin had downloaded and printed off. '"Bryn Encil. Hill Retreat. A wonderful name for a wonderful place. A remote sanctuary where the lost elements of healing can begin. Where the material world, the source of so much misery, sickness, and evil, can be shut out, allowing the purity of mind to shine through and bring the completeness of healing so many of us seek."' Gil let his eyes slide up in a sideways glance at Catrin. 'That's sword and sorcery all over again, if you ask me.'

'Almost. As far as I understand, it's a kind of quasi-spiritual sect that,' she took her hands off the steering wheel for a microsecond to make bunny ears, '"treats" troubled individuals who have given up, or want to avoid, traditional medical methods. It's about trying to convince people it's all in their minds.'

'I wish I could convince this lumbago of mine that it's all in the mind.'

'I didn't know you had back pain.'

'Oh yes. Had it for years. In fact, it's that bad, I went back to the GP last week and asked for a second opinion. He said, okay, you're morbidly overweight, too.'

Catrin shook her head slowly.

Gil continued, 'I bet you the Friends of Light charge a bomb for people to go there.'

'People get desperate,' Catrin said. 'When they do, they turn to the weirdness.'

'There, see, I told you this had Da Vinci Code elements to it. If I see any albino monks, I'm running for the hills.'

'I'd like to see that.'

Gil put down the file and threw her a glare. 'You haven't been talking to my GP, have you?'

Bryn Encil had to be approached from the north. Catrin took the same fire road that Warlow and Rhys had taken on their way to George Marsden's property but didn't turn off until they got to the isolated chapel of Soar Y Mynydd.

Gil gazed at the whitewashed low building in awe. 'Must have been a dedicated congregation to walk here on a wet Sunday in December when there weren't any cars,' Gil observed.

'Pony and trap?'

'I went before we left, thanks.'

Catrin, determined not to smile, succeeded. But with difficulty. 'Do you take anything at all seriously? How does your wife put up with it?'

'The Lady Anwen is a woman of refined good taste, I'll have you know. But she is also partially deaf. That helps. And I take some things very seriously. Food is one. The state of the national rugby and football teams is never a laughing matter. And then there is Peppa Pig.'

'Peppa Pig?'

'Having had to watch every episode at least four times, Peppa would be my specialist subject on Mastermind. I have a great deal in common with Daddy Pig since we're both challenged in the girth department. In fact, I'm thinking of identifying as oink.'

'See, you're doing it again.'

Gil studied his younger colleague and dropped his voice. 'Alright, you want serious? We're stumbling blindly into one of the most isolated pockets of West Wales where one elderly man has been brutally murdered already with no idea who the killer is. The place we're going to has been deliberately chosen because, I suspect, they do not welcome outsiders. So, who knows what we'll find around the next corner. We have weird symbols drawn on a door at the victim's property. The only witnesses are probably carrion-feeding red kites and a couple of crows. For all we know, the killer could be watching us now. If I was honest, there are things about this case that already disturb me deeply.'

Apart from the bounce and rattle of the car's suspension, a sudden silence filled the vehicle. Gil sat back and folded his arms.

'I think I prefer you trying to be funny,' Catrin said eventually.

'I rest my case, your honour. Now, did I tell you the one about the two rabbits and the carrot?'

CHAPTER TWELVE

As WARLOW HOPED, the post-mortem, under Sengupta's efficient control, went quickly. Rhys, as was now the norm, took everything in and asked a barrage of questions. Warlow zoned in on the essentials. George Marsden died from stab wounds to the chest and shoulder. Eleven in all, two of which had struck the heart and caused massive internal bleeding.

Warlow stood back, enjoying the exchanges.

'I've read that if you pierce the heart, it can bleed into the surrounding sac and the fluid tension stops it from expanding,' Rhys said.

'True.' Sengupta looked up from the open chest cavity into Rhys's face. 'But pericardial tamponade occurs only in blunt trauma or, rarely, in an infarct where the weakened wall of an atrium or ventricle blows out. But in a stabbing, the pericardium, the sac around the heart, is punctured, too. Blood would escape into the thoracic cavity. It's precisely what happened here.'

'Got you.' Rhys nodded, his eyes crinkling above his mask.

She had the heart out on a tray and a small silver

instrument had been placed through the injuries in two places as indicators.

'Here, the knife was thrust in several times, pierced pericardium and heart muscle twice, on separate occasions, and then withdrawn both times. So, the heart was struck twice. Once in the right atrium,' she demonstrated on the organ, 'and once in the left ventricle. Given the size of the weapon, and that removing it for further stabbing would have left holes to bleed through, death was an inevitability. Atrial injuries, from whatever cause, rarely make it to a hospital A and E. I would estimate loss of consciousness within sixty seconds. Death within five minutes, perhaps less. The rule is, if you're stabbed in the chest, do not remove the weapon if you can. Remember the natural history presenter who was stabbed by that Manta ray?'

'Australian bloke, uh, Irwin?'

'That's him. First thing he did was take the barb out. Not that he'd be relaxed about leaving it in. But doing that speeds up death. In Mr Marsden's case, the knife was in, but it wasn't in the heart by then. It was in lung tissue.'

The knife that had been protruding from the chest had already been bagged up on a side table. Warlow walked over to study it through the plastic wrapping. But Sengupta pointed to a board at the back of the room. 'We've already photographed it. They may even be in your inbox already. But the lab wants this to check for any DNA evidence. Or whether it had been used before.'

Warlow stepped over to the board. The knife had a black oxide coating and a black plastic handle. It looked cheap but effective and Warlow imagined it as one of a set. They'd photographed it with a measuring tape for reference. Seven inches long, an inch wide where blade met handle. He recalled Catrin's video footage of it sitting embedded up to the hilt on George Marsden's chest. Now, with the blade on display, the manufacturer's name and logo were clearly displayed. Procise. Warlow made a mental note and then thought better of it and wrote in his notebook.

Sengupta continued talking to Rhys, 'There are bruises on the forearms, but no lacerations. I suspect these may be defence injuries. It also implies that the attacker was quick in his, or her, actions.'

So, he fought. Good for you, George. Good for you.

There wasn't much else that Sengupta could help them with. Stomach contents showed a meal had been consumed a few hours before death. She also estimated the time of death, from temp readings taken at the scene and the amount of rigor mortis, to be between three and eight hours before discovery by the Amazon driver.

Not long, then. Not long at all.

On the way back in the car, Warlow quizzed Rhys. He didn't know the answers to his questions, but he didn't need to. He had all the confidence in the world that Rhys would. Whereas Gil's specialist subject might be Peppa Pig, Rhys's would be his burgeoning interest in forensic pathology.

'So, how do they estimate time according to body temperature, Rhys?'

'Roughly. It's 1.5 degrees loss per hour, sir.'

'What happens if someone dies in a freezer?'

'Like that woman we found in Pembrokeshire, sir?'

'Exactly like that woman we found in Pembrokeshire.'

'The one that had her arms and legs broken so that she fitted? The one you said was unlikely to have fallen in chasing that last Solero?'

Warlow smiled. 'Extra points for remembering the boss's jokes, Rhys.'

'How could I forget, sir? You put me off exotic ice cream made with sustainably farmed fruits for at least a month.'

'That bad, eh? But back to the question. How do they go about estimating time of death in those cases? With bodies in fridges and freezers?'

'You have to take into account the temperature of the surrounding medium and take a more accurate core temp on the victim, sir. Liver, probably.'

Warlow nodded. This was impressive stuff. 'Anything else?'

Rhys didn't even have to think. 'Degree of stiffness, sir. Rigor mortis. Then there's lividity, liver mortis. And stomach content, as Dr Sengupta indicated.'

Warlow waited. He knew there was more to come. Rhys was a fountain of knowledge when it came to the dead. It had become clear to the entire team that, were he not a detective constable, he would have been perfectly at home as an undertaker.

'And where death might have occurred sometime before, there's a degree of putrefaction of the body, or corneal cloudiness, or vitreous potassium levels, and insect activity.'

'Your favourite, Rhys. The creepy crawlies.' The DC had been a terrier in their last case, where maggot activity on one of the bodies had played a crucial role in sorting out a timeline.

'Sergeant Jones says I should have been called Fritz, same as Frankenstein's assistant.'

'He had no assistant in the original book.'

Rhys nodded. 'I told him that, sir. I don't think he heard me.'

Warlow nodded. 'Funny that, isn't it? Selective hearing is a terrible affliction, and DS Jones has it in spades. Now, there's a Sainsbury's at McArthur Glen. We'll stop for a comfort break, and you can buy something to stuff your face with and get me a Jimmy's coconut milk iced coffee which is less than half the price of you-know-who-bucks version. And then you can look up Procise knives on Google. See who supplies them, other than the Zon, who supplies everything.'

'Want anything to eat, sir?'

'No. I'm still post-mortem-rexic.'

'I promise no cheese and onion crisps, sir.'

Warlow gave a non-committal shrug. 'You're a grown-up, Rhys. You get them if you want to. But you'll be walking home if you do.'

Rhys did his toothless smile impression of the hapless one in the Laurel and Hardy double act. 'Message understood, sir.'

———

CATRIN PARKED on a rise two hundred yards above Bryn Encil. Both she and Gil had let out involuntary noises on arriving at that point. She, a gasp, Gil, a drawn out, 'Wow,' on seeing the property laid out before them. Catrin wasn't sure what she'd been expecting, but a low, stone, single-storey longhouse with a pitched roof and a round tower at one end surrounded by manicured grounds had not been it.

'There's money behind all this,' Gil whispered.

'Plenty,' Catrin agreed. 'What does it say about who runs the place?'

Gil slipped his glasses down from where he'd perched them on his head and re-opened the folder. '"Rudy and Sigrid Bidulph look forward to welcoming those who wish to embrace the Friendship of the Light and find solace in this wonderful place of solitude and beauty. Their previous work in Nepal and India in exploring the spiritual origins of the Friends and exploring less travelled areas where similar spiritual communities exist have led them to a deep understanding of the sicknesses that afflict us all. Though not qualified as practitioners within the narrow confines of today's society, they bring with them a breadth of understanding, patience, and hope.'''

'What exactly does that mean?' Catrin asked.

'Yoga, I expect. Hot, tantric, or the pose of your choice, thong permitting. But why don't we go and find out,' Gil suggested.

Catrin put the car in gear and rumbled down the road. Once through an open steel gate at the end of the stoned track, the way flattened out and they rolled over golden gravel, out of place in this area of natural grey granite and sandstone. But it lent the place an oddly exotic feeling. The road continued between a couple of renovated outbuildings which may well have been chalets, into a courtyard where two benched picnic tables were arranged in the curve of the building, each with a neat centre flower arrangement in terracotta pots. Catrin parked next to a couple of Land Rovers. One a racing-green Defender, the other a sleek pale-blue Range Rover.

Once they came to a halt, a studded oak door in the middle of the longhouse opened, and a man and a woman emerged. The man, average height, trimmed beard and parted hair, the woman, slender and pale and slightly taller than the man wearing loose-fitting sweatshirt and trousers over expensive trainers. They crunched across the drive as Catrin and Gil got out of their car, all smiles.

Rudi and Sigrid Bidulph wasted no time in introducing themselves with handshakes.

'Thank you for seeing us,' Catrin began after she'd introduced herself and Gil.

'It's the very least we could do under the circumstances,' Sigrid said, her voice tilting up and down and trapping the 'r' of 'circumstances' in a Scandinavian burr. 'Poor George.'

'You've heard the news, then?'

'We may be in the wilderness, but news travels fast. The postman told us.'

'You knew him, then?' Catrin asked. 'Mr Marsden?'

'We did. He's been here a long time.' Rudi Bidulph had no lilt. His was an accent from the Southwest of England. 'When we moved here, we made it our business to introduce ourselves, though the Retreat was here before we came.'

'How long ago is that?' Gil asked.

'Nigh on ten years,' Rudi replied.

'Come on in,' Sigrid said. 'I'm sure you could do with some tea.'

Across the yard, two men appeared. One much younger than the other, dressed for the outdoors, pushing firewood stacked high in two wheelbarrows. They took no notice of the visitors and headed for the outbuildings. Discretion, it seemed, played a big part in the way Bryn Encil worked.

Inside was as tasteful as the exterior. Exposed beams, calming colours, plain furnishings.

'Would you like a tour while we get the tea organised?' Rudi asked.

'Why not?' Gil glanced at Catrin, who nodded a reply.

From the reception area, Rudi Bidulph led them towards the far end, through a big room set with two long tables.

'This is our refectory.'

'How many people are there here?' Catrin asked.

'Sigrid and me, three paid staff members who provide hotel services and our maintenance worker Thomas and groundskeeper Jonah.'

'The men we saw earlier?'

'Indeed. And, of course, our guests. We only have a few at any given time. Presently, only one. An unfortunate soul who has struggled with addiction and depression. We are helping her find the way back.'

'How?' Catrin asked. They were in the room labelled The Rotunda by a sign above the door. Like everywhere else, the walls were not smooth, but lime rendered as they would have been originally, painted white and almost two-feet thick. Comfortable chairs were arranged near windows looking out into the countryside.

'By engaging with the self. This might involve contemplation. Long walks up in the hills or in the garden that Jonah maintains so well. We do not believe that one deity has the answers in the Friends of Light.' Rudi smiled at the two officers. He had an open face, short hair, and a conviction that he was absolutely right about whatever he was talking about.

'So, no prayers here, but no conventional therapy either?' Gil asked.

'Most of our guests come seeking answers that traditional resources could not supply.' It struck both officers that Rudi didn't have to think about these exchanges. They tripped off the tongue like well-practised verses. 'Many conditions that have been labelled illnesses or diseases are often illusions that require nothing more than an awakening of the realisation that we should not allow ourselves to be subject to the corrosion of material things. All it takes is a change of perception.'

Catrin could see Gil's lids coming down to half-mast. 'So, I could think myself cured of a cold?'

Outside, the noise of a quad bike starting up and fading away as it left came to them.

Rudi smiled again. One glance at Gil told Catrin that he'd enjoy nothing more than wiping that grin away. 'That may be an oversimplification,' Rudi said, calm and collected.

'Your guest, we'll need to talk to her. And to your workers.'

'We prefer to call them friends,' Rudi said, no sign of the smile slipping. 'And as for our guest, talking to her might prove to be a problem, as she has opted for silence while she is with us. However, I think you can eliminate her from your enquiries.'

'Oh, what makes you so sure?' Gil asked.

'She is a wheelchair user after sepsis from a contaminated hypodermic resulted in bilateral amputation of her lower limbs.'

Sigrid appeared in the doorway, her long, blonde hair framing her pale face. 'We have tea if you'd like it.'

'Why not?' Gil said, turning towards her. She and Rudi led the way, leaving Gil and Catrin to follow.

'I don't see any albino monks, do you?' Catrin whispered.

'No, but it's early days. Look out for flying monkeys too. We are definitely not in Kansas anymore.'

CHAPTER THIRTEEN

THE TEA WAS PALE, weak, and vaguely perfumed. There may have been something in Gil's face that gave away his surprise when he tasted it that prompted Sigrid Bidulph to explain.

'It's Earl Grey. We find the bergamot very soothing. We have a range of herbal teas as well if you prefer?' She flashed a perfect smile.

'No black builder's, though?' Gil asked with a fixed smile.

'Too much caffeine,' Sigrid said in earnest apology, which both officers realised was her default state. Indeed, her default state full stop.

Catrin put her at a well-preserved fifty-ish. Pale and fair, great cheekbones, and the kind of ironing board frame, under the loose-fitting sweatshirt, that looked like it might rattle if she turned too quickly. If she ate, it was probably cucumber in an air sandwich. The DS opened her notebook and clicked on a pen. 'Did either of you visit George Marsden in the last few days?'

Rudi answered, 'We didn't.' He waved a hand between Sigrid and himself. 'Neither did our guest, for obvious reasons. Our hotel services staff did not know George Marsden.'

'Did he supply you with eggs?'

'He did. Once a week, towards the end of the week.'

'Did he deliver?' Gil asked.

'No, Jonah drove over there when he picked up our weekly groceries from Llandovery.'

'Today is Tuesday. So, did Jonah pick up eggs on Friday?'

'He did.'

Catrin wrote in her notebook.

'We'll need a list of names of your employees, and we need to speak with Jonah,' Gil said. He gave the tea one last sip before replacing the cup back onto its saucer and sitting back. He pressed the thumb end of a closed fist to his sternum. 'Looks like the bergamot doesn't agree with me,' he winced and arched his back. 'Any chance?' he added.

'Of what?' Sigrid asked.

'Speaking to Jonah?'

'Of course.' Rudi got up and left the room.

Sigrid regarded the two officers with her cool smile. 'You'll have to excuse us. We do not get many visitors out here. Except for our guests.'

'You say your current guest is a wheelchair user,' Catrin said. 'How did she get here?'

'We pick up all guests from the train station in Cardiff or Shrewsbury,' Sigrid explained.

'Not a short journey, that,' Gil observed.

'No. We have a Mercedes for that. Thomas makes the, how do you say it, run?'

'Your handyman?'

'Yes. He's been with us for three years. He keeps the place running.'

'And Jonah?'

'A year or so.'

'How do you recruit people?' Catrin asked.

She got a smile in response. 'Often, the people who come here to continue the Friends' work are on a spiritual journey of their own. For whatever reason.'

Later, Gil would comment on that smile in typical Gil fashion. Supercilious might come closest as a descriptor. Though Gil would mutter in response to Catrin's suggestion, 'super bloody irritating, more like.'

But they both agreed that it was a nice nebulous answer if ever there was one. An answer with all the validity of secret writing. The kind where messages written in lemon juice only appeared over the flame of a closely held candle. The kind of misdirection exploited most often by children's authors. Only here, the words, once exposed to the heat of scrutiny, had all the substance and tangibility of drifting smoke. All that was missing were the mirrors. Catrin cast her gaze around the room. It got caught on a framed tapestry hanging on the wall above the mantel of an enormous fireplace. On a green background, an embroidered image of a golden crown sitting over a stylised mountain with a sun and rays above it.

'What is that?' Catrin asked.

'A throwback to our origins. It was used as a symbol for the Friends of Light. We have since modernised it, but that is the original embroidery when our founder established the movement at the turn of the last century.'

The door opened and Rudi walked in, followed by the older of the two men that Catrin and Gil had noticed crossing the yard as they'd pulled in.

'Thomas,' Rudi said, 'these are the detectives looking into George Marsden's death.'

Thomas Seaton nodded. He was not a tall man. Younger than Gil and dressed in navy overalls with a woollen hat on his head, which he removed to reveal an untidy mess of grey hair. But his beard was darker and only flecked with a few silvery strands. He wore large bifocals that made his eyes look larger than they were.

'Unfortunately, we've just missed Jonah. He's gone into the valley to cut more wood,' Rudi explained.

'How long will he be?' Gil asked.

Seaton shook his head and replied in a broad Scot's accent. 'There's no telling. He'll be gone a wee while. We're stocking up logs for winter.'

'Have a seat, Thomas,' Sigrid offered.

Thomas shook his head. 'I'm too dirty. We've been sorting out the septic tank earlier.'

Catrin wrinkled her nose. Come to think of it, a ripe aroma had accompanied Thomas Seaton's arrival.

'We'll keep this brief,' she said. 'George Marsden. Did you know him?'

'I've met George, aye. Before Jonah arrived, it was me who did the goods run into Llandovery.' He pronounced the town with just the one L, as non-native speakers sometimes did, to avoid the difficult, unvoiced, lateral fricative. 'Lovely old chap.' Seaton clamped his lips together.

'And on Sunday, what do you normally do around here?'

'This is a seven day a week job. I walk. Sometimes I fish. But if there is anything that needs doing, I don't count the days.'

'And Jonah?'

Seaton gave Rudi a quick glance. It was he who answered, 'Sometimes Jonah will go into Llandovery on a Saturday or a Sunday. He fishes, too. But he spends a lot of time on his phone. So, he finds different ways to make use of his days off.'

'This Sunday?'

'He wasn't here,' Seaton said. 'I think he went to town.'

'And you?'

'Here all weekend.'

'In the building?'

Seaton's smile was apologetic. 'As I say, we're busy harvesting and stacking logs.'

Catrin took the names of the hotel staff, two of whom were from Croatia, the third from the Midlands. All of them could vouch for each other on the weekend. Catrin asked to see the kitchen where they prepped the food, too, and Sigrid was very obliging.

Shortly after that, she and Gil took their leave with a promise from Rudi and Sigrid that as soon as Jonah got back, he would contact them.

As they drove away, a very unusual silence from Gil prompted Catrin to pre-empt any comment. 'I know what you're thinking.'

'What, that I'm never going to drink Earl Grey tea again?'

'No, about the Friends of Light.'

Gil nodded. 'It's a retreat alright. But I've read about people like this before. Wasn't there a scandal a few years back when someone brought a kid to one of their places and she died?'

'I can't remember it.'

'I do. I remember things about kids because they depend on responsible adults to take care of them. In the case I remember, the anti-vaxer, anti-medicine, anti-bloody everything, waste-of-space parents wanted a spiritual, mindfulness, self-healing approach for their daughter's rash. Only the rash turned out to be meningitis. And if they'd taken the girl to a doctor or an A and E, she'd still be here. The parents are still in jail, I hope, with the key thrown into a deep and dark hole. The old Friends of Light took a battering in the press for that.'

'But they survived,' Catrin said.

'Yes, they did. More's the pity.'

'You didn't like them?'

'Bloody secret societies. Smug and spooky as hell.'

'I agree,' Catrin said.

'Let's get back to HQ. Carmarthen is hardly the centre of the known universe, but it's a damned sight more down to earth than this shower.'

———

'As far as I can see, sir, Procise knives are sold in lots of places, including Argos.' Rhys had been googling on his phone for the last ten miles.

'Right,' Warlow replied, unable to hide his disappointment. 'Ubiquitous, then.'

'No, sir. They're made in China.' Rhys kept his eyes in front but failed to keep his face straight for more than a few seconds.

'That sounds like a Gil joke.'

'It is, sir.'

'Heard from the other two?'

Rhys checked his phone. 'Ah, yes. Looks like they're back in signal range. They spoke to the owners of Bryn Encil, sir. They're on the way back to HQ. And DS Richards says they had a complete set of knives in the kitchen there with not one missing.'

Warlow nodded and cracked a smile. He'd been at the point of asking Rhys to remind Catrin about the knife but needn't have bothered. He glanced down at the floor. In the footwell of the passenger seat, a flotsam of wrappers and cans lay at Rhys's feet. Warlow sent the DC a pointed look.

'I'll sort it out, sir. I've got a plastic bag on the back seat, but I can't reach it.'

'Are you this messy at home?'

'Gina says I am, sir. And I need to work on it.' Rhys's

expression hardened, and he seemed to come to some great decision. 'Any advice on how to tell my mother I'm actually moving out in two weeks, sir?'

Warlow frowned before a smile of realisation took its place. 'Aha. The qualm at last. Indeed, the qualm before the storm, eh? Have you tried, hey Mam, I'm moving out, *at last,* in two weeks' time. She'll probably do a cartwheel. Several, I suspect.'

Rhys nodded, his mouth forming a strained smile.

Warlow read the runes. 'Your mother likes Gina, doesn't she?'

'She loves Gina, sir. Everyone does.'

'So, what's the problem?'

Rhys shrugged. 'There isn't one, not really. Except, since Covid, I'm the one that's done most of the shopping for my parents. Taken them places. Sorted out doctor's appointments for my dad.'

'Good. Highly commendable, I'm sure. But they're capable and they have a car. They'll be glad to see the back of you.'

'My mother keeps saying I ought to get on with things.'

'Sounds to me like you're the problem here, not your parents.'

Rhys's expression had morphed into a sickly smile. 'How did you feel when your boys moved out, sir?'

Great question. Warlow's deceased wife, Jeez Denise, had been bereft for a short while. But only as long as it took to unscrew the top off a bottle of Grey Goose, which was her answer to all of life's problems, large or small. He, busy as usual, had been too tied up in work to take a great deal of notice. And it had been a staged leaving; first university with the long holidays in between, then the boys had secured jobs in faraway places and girlfriends were always more interesting than a chat with their busy old man and their alcoholic mother. Rhys was asking the wrong man for advice here. But that didn't mean he couldn't come up with some.

'I saved a lot of money on petrol for the car. Astonishing how the boys never quite worked out how to open that petrol cap.'

Rhys's little snort was polite and Warlow knew his quip was an empty gesture. So, he tried again. 'But overall, I felt a sense of accomplishment. Being a parent isn't easy. You want the best for your kids. Seeing them take steps of their own into the world, even when they're old enough to be called adults, brings with it a sense of achievement. Personally, I think your mother and father will be proud of you. Your own place and with Gina? That's a lottery win if ever there was one.'

Rhys was staring at him, listening to his words, the little uneven position of his eyebrows a sure signal that he was processing everything. An increase in blink rate was another giveaway that Warlow's perspective on all this was one that Rhys hadn't properly considered. Eventually, he nodded. 'Thanks, sir. You're probably right.'

'No probably in it, Rhys. I know I'm right. Your mother will bake you a cake and you'll still go round there for Sunday lunch and Christmas and Easter and join your dad in front of the telly for the Six Nations, if you're not working. That's the way the world goes around.'

More nods from the DC. 'When we've settled, sir, Gina wants you and the rest of the team to come around for supper.'

'Does she now?'

'That's what she said, sir.'

Warlow could see that this new concept of entertaining held a certain wonder for him. A final great leap into the unknown world of being a grown-up.

'So long as she cooks, I'll be there,' Warlow said.

'I'll tell her that, sir.'

'Make sure that you do. And make sure you pick up all that rubbish from around your feet or I'll tell your mother what a messy, bloody pup you are. Now, we're half an hour from HQ, so why don't you think about how you are going to present the post-mortem findings without making DS Richards throw up.'

CHAPTER FOURTEEN

WARLOW PARKED the Jeep at Dyfed Powys Police HQ and waited while Rhys cleaned up his detritus, his bony backside atop his long legs poking out from the open passenger-side door.

'Let's hope there are no seagulls about, Rhys. You could do yourself a nasty injury.'

The DC's head popped up. 'All done, sir. I thought there was a Mars bar wrapper somewhere, but I couldn't find it. That's because I'd stuffed it into my pocket.' He tapped his jacket.

Warlow tutted. 'Bloody hell, Gina has her work cut out with you.'

Rhys grinned.

On the way to the main entrance, Warlow's phone rang. He waved Rhys in. 'I'll be there in a minute. Get the kettle on and make sure Sergeant Jones gets the biscuits out.'

'I thought he wasn't doing that now, sir.'

'If he isn't, he's taking our kitty money under false pretences.'

Warlow turned away and accepted the call. 'Jess. How are you?'

'Hi, Evan. It's going well. Really well. The scenario they've given us has lots of similarities to the Rhaeadr Falls case, believe it or not. No bodies, signs of violence. Most of the others haven't got a clue how to proceed.'

'But you do?'

'I do.'

'That's good to hear.'

'How about you? How's that thing up near the dam?'

'Early days. Just come back from the post-mortem with Rhys, so I'm feeling a bit queasy.'

'That bad?'

'The PM was fine. Watching Rhys eat his way through enough snacks to fill a Red Cross parcel is what's turned my stomach.'

Jess laughed. 'I spoke to Molly earlier. She's enjoying her staycation at yours.'

'Haven't seen much of her. She's self-sufficient.'

'She's a coppers' daughter. Goes with the territory.'

'So I've noticed.'

A slight pause followed. Warlow let it grow until Jess spoke again. 'Did she tell you about this kid in school who's hassling her?'

'Is this Zac something or other?'

'Yeah. It is. I first heard about him last year, but Bryn was on the scene at the college. And you've met Bryn. He was enough to keep the coyotes at bay.'

Warlow had met Molly's boyfriend, Bryn, who was now university bound, being one year older. Local stock, farmer's son, rugby player. Not someone you'd mess about with unless you had to.

'But he's not there now,' Warlow said.

'No. Obviously, Molly's seventeen, and the college,

besides being a learning facility, is also a cattle market with all the bidding done online, as you know.'

'I don't. All that passed me by. My lot are just that bit older. They escaped swiping right or left or up or down; unless they were cleaning windows.'

'Lucky them,' Jess said. Warlow detected the strain under her words.

'Are you worried about this Zac?'

'Yes, and no. Molly doesn't tell me much about college, but she's mentioned this boy twice and in a negative way. Which isn't like her.'

'She called him an irritating horsefly,' Warlow said. 'Would you like me to have a chat with her? DCI to DI's daughter?'

Jess snorted. 'I wish. But how does she seem to you?'

'She seems like Molly. But I'll see what I can find out.'

'Thanks. This is me, the anxious mother, by the way. Normally, I'd sit her down with a cup of coffee and probe. She'd tell me not to make a fuss but, if it was important, she'd tell me in her own way.'

'Got you.'

'Right, I'll let you go. I expect you're off to a four-course lunch?'

'More one course. Our first catch-up. So, tea and the Human Tissue For Transplant box with a bit of luck.'

'Enjoy,' Jess rang off.

By the time he got to the Incident Room, everything was set up. A mug of hot tea sat steaming on a desk next to an empty chair. Gil had indeed opened the Human Tissue For Transplant box, a biscuit repository so labelled to avoid curious eyes and hands. However, since almost everyone in the place now knew what it contained, it seemed a little self-defeating. Until Gil had revealed to the team that, just occasionally, he would leave some defrosting pig's liver in there to put off any chancers.

Today, however, the contents of the box were on display on a plate, with bourbons, digestives, custard creams, and Hobnobs and, treat of treats, a packet of Tunnock's caramel wafers. They were special occasion fodder. In response to Warlow's raised eyebrows, Gil explained.

'Sainsbury's special offer, apparently.' He nodded towards Rhys.

'Couldn't resist, sir. As a thank you for taking me to the PM.'

Warlow considered commenting on that, since most young officers would consider a visit to the mortuary to watch someone being dissected in the most brutal way was, at the very best, an unwelcome chore, if not sometimes considered a punishment. But this was Rhys. And they were caramel wafers. Now and again, it was better to keep your powder dry.

'Good shout,' he said and went rogue with a wrapped wafer as well as a custard cream before sitting down to face the Gallery and the Job Centre. A board, he was delighted to see, already populated with crime scene photos and notes.

'Not your usual poison,' Gil observed, glancing at the biscuits.

'Sometimes you need to shake things up a little, sergeant,' Warlow replied. 'Keep things fresh. Right, let's get this show on the road. Who's first?'

Gil stepped over to the Gallery. 'Crime scene photos are up, supplemented by Catrin's art-house shots of her video visit. The timeline has the Amazon driver arriving late on Sunday afternoon at 5.20pm. Catrin and Rhys got there at just after six. Given the HOP's estimation of time of death, George Marsden was attacked between 9am and 2pm on that Sunday. From our visit to the Friends of Light, we've established that their man collected eggs from George on Friday.'

'Who's the man?' Warlow asked.

'Jonah Crosby. We've yet to speak with him as he was out chopping trees down when we were out there. We're waiting for his call.'

'Okay. What's your take on this place, Bryn Encil?'

'Spooky central,' Gil replied.

'Is that what's in your report?' Warlow sent the sergeant a disdainful stare.

'The Friends of Light, sir,' Catrin explained, 'is a charitable organisation who have more than one property in the UK and several in Europe. They promise a centre for spiritual reconstitution. For people recovering from serious illnesses. A kind of rehabilitation devoid of, and away from, traditional medical resources.'

'Spooky central, like I said,' Gil muttered.

'There are staff and guests,' Catrin continued. 'But Jonah Crosby was the only one who had any contact with George. That's why we need to talk to him. He may or may not have an alibi for last Sunday. He was definitely not at the Retreat.'

Warlow nodded.

Catrin took an A4 sheet from her desk and added it to the Gallery. 'This tapestry on the wall of the Retreat shows the same design as what was drawn in chalk on the back of George Marsden's front door.'

'Significance?'

Catrin shrugged. 'Don't know, sir. Not yet. But it ties them together somehow.'

'Agreed,' Warlow said. He turned to Rhys. 'Your turn.'

The DC got up, long limbs springing out of the chair. 'Shall I do the post-mortem stuff first, sir?'

'Why not?'

Smiling, like a kid asked to perform at a party, Rhys

outlined what Sengupta had told them about the cause of death, the two penetrating heart injuries, the bruises on the arms. 'We know the make of the knife. We know it's sold in many places. From what I've found out, it's only sold as part of a set, not as an individual piece. It's called a utility knife within that Procise set.'

Suddenly, an image on the Gallery was circled by a red light.

'What the hell is that?' Gil asked in horror.

A sheepish Rhys grinned. 'Laser pointer, sarge. My mother gave it to me. She got given some at a conference. She said it might come in handy.'

'Well, don't laser point that bloody thing in my eyes, that's all,' Gil warned.

'Oh, no. It's perfectly safe. Class 1 laser. It can't cause any damage.' Rhys pointed the little red dot at Gil's cup of tea and a custard cream nestling on a piece of tissue paper next to it.

'Boys and their toys,' Catrin muttered.

'So, somewhere there's a set with that knife missing,' Gil said.

Rhys circled the image again with the red dot.

'And we've checked it hasn't come from the victim's kitchen?' Warlow asked. 'I had a look and didn't see anything.'

'There's nothing in the search inventory, sir,' Catrin said.

Warlow stood up. His turn.

'As far as the other two properties are concerned, we drew a blank in both instances. That means we still have to check them out. The Airbnb was unoccupied, though with some signs of occupation.'

'I've left a message with the owner, sir. She hasn't got back to me yet. I'll chase it up again,' Catrin said.

'It's an isolated property.' Warlow pointed to the glossy

images from the website that Catrin had posted. 'They all are. The sooner we eliminate whoever is renting, the better. Then there's Foynw.'

Catrin, who'd stayed sitting when Warlow had stood up, got up now. 'The Thorleys,' she said and walked to the Gallery and pointed to an image on the board. A grainy black-and-white photograph from the Bristol Post showing three people holding a gigantic cheque for £3.76 million under the headline, 'Hartcliffe Lottery Winners says they won't change.'

'Hmm,' grunted Warlow. 'More's the pity.'

'You may remember this from three years ago. But then again, it might have slipped under your radar. But they hit the tabloid limelight again after buying somewhere on the Thames and upsetting several influential neighbours by racing quad bikes around their garden in the early hours of the morning. They made bloody nuisances of themselves and eventually moved on and bought the parcel of land known as Foynw two years ago.'

'How big?'

'Thirty acres.'

'PNC?'

Gil had the answers. 'The father, William, had a history of petty crimes, theft, public order convictions and driving under the influence, prior to the lottery win. The son, who had been fourteen at the time of said win, already had convictions for public order offences, including criminal damage, joyriding and burglary. Their attempts at setting him on the straight and narrow at two expensive private schools backfired badly.'

'What about the mother?'

'Angela Thorley was cautioned for suspected benefit fraud six years ago. There was no conviction.'

Warlow studied the photograph. The lottery offered life-changing opportunities for the lucky winners. But sometimes, all it did was allow aggravating little sods to be more aggravating, with louder noises and more garish toys. It sounded very much like what had happened to the Thorleys. He vaguely remembered the headlines when they'd upset the Thames Valley apple cart. The long lens newspaper images of a bare-chested William Thorley, his son, and their cronies tearing up a once picturesque garden and turning it into a muddy racetrack for motorbikes and ATVs. It made him wonder what they were capable of if someone, even an octogenarian, challenged them. He also understood but didn't condone Angela Thorley's reluctant attitude towards cooperating.

'What about the laptop we found on George Marsden's property?'

'Povey hasn't come back to us yet,' Gil said.

Warlow sipped his tea and studied the Gallery and the Job Centre again. There were a great number of threads here that needed pulling. Some they would offload to the Uniforms they'd co-opted. Some might only need pulling when they had more information. But one or two could do with a little yank from him or the team right now. He turned to address them.

'Rhys, that friend of yours with the drones that takes videos of out of the way places, what's his name again?'

'You mean Steffan, sir?'

'He's the bloke that took those photos of the crashed plane on the Beacons, yes?'

'He helped find it, sir.'

Warlow grunted. 'Hmm. And you said you can fly one of those things?'

'Steff's got three, sir. He lets me use the smallest one. The cheapest one. Good to learn on, he says.'

'Think he'll let you borrow it?'

'I'm sure he will, sir.' Rhys wore a half smile and a wary look. 'I thought you didn't like drones, sir. In fact, I remember you saying they were the worst invention since—'

'Good. Give him a ring,' Warlow cut across the DC. 'I doubt we'll get much, if any, cooperation from the Thorleys. So, while Gil here stays put and chases up a few loose ends, I think we'd be better off going back up into the wilds and poking the hornet's nest.'

'Who's we, sir?' Catrin asked.

'You, me, and Rhys, plus a couple of Uniforms as backup. I have a feeling we might need some on this one.'

CHAPTER FIFTEEN

WHILE RHYS CONTACTED his friend with the drones and Catrin got herself organised, Gil ambled over to Warlow's desk and bent at the hip, leaning his big frame down with his back to the room. From the sheaf of papers in his hand, he slid out a single sheet and placed it face down on the desk.

'I spoke to Dai Vetch about the mysterious Zac.'

'And?'

'Not so mysterious. Through Vetch, I then spoke to one of the INTACT PCSOs down in Pembrokeshire. Zac Menzies is no stranger to them.'

Warlow turned the sheet over. It had a list of contacts and a breakdown of the various incidents where the Menzies family had been involved in County Line activities. The INTACT initiative was another multi-agency partnership set up to counter organised crime infiltration into rural areas. Clampdowns usually led to arrests. But Zac had never been arrested, though an older brother and his father had been.

'Sounds like a real charmer.'

Gil nodded. 'My guess is that he's playing it straight

and probably trying to recruit, or coerce, students at the college. They are aware of him down there.'

'Then why the hell haven't they excluded the little sod?'

'Lack of evidence, maybe?' Gil hesitated. 'None of my business, but isn't he at the same college as Molly Allanby?'

Warlow's glance was a telling one. 'You didn't get that detective badge for nothing, eh?'

Gil, for once, stayed serious. 'If there is anything I can do, just say the word.'

Warlow nodded. He read the brief notes one more time, folded up the sheet and slid it into his jacket pocket. He might give one of the INTACT PCSOs a ring.

Across the room, Rhys got off the phone, looking very pleased with himself.

'Drone sorted, sir. Steff lives in White Mill. He says we can pick it up anytime. We could do it on the way.'

'Shall I drive, sir?' Catrin asked.

'Good idea.'

Rhys, mouth open and on the point of objecting, saw the warning in Warlow's eyes. 'You're going to be our drone pilot,' the DCI said. 'You can fiddle with the controls and such as we drive up. Make sure you're up to speed. I, meanwhile, will sit in the passenger seat and try to ignore the sound of you chewing in the back.'

'Are we stopping for food, sir?' Rhys asked, brightening.

'No, we are not. But I know you will have secreted something about your person to masticate.'

Rhys's hand slid towards his jacket pocket in a dead giveaway. 'Just a Snickers or two, sir.'

'What a surprise. Ready Sergeant Richards?'

Catrin shouted back a 'Yes, sir.' Her fingers gave the keyboard of her computer a last couple of clicks and she dragged her eyes away from the screen to regard the DCI.

'Good. Let's get this show on the road.'

'Tidy,' Gil said.

With that, the posse left the building.

———

They'd been gone only ten minutes when the Incident Room door swung open to reveal the rangy figure of Superintendent Sion Buchannan. He stepped in and peered around, nose wrinkling. 'Have I missed him?'

'On the way back up to Llyn Brianne, sir,' Gil explained.

Buchannan's shoulder sagged; disappointment etched on his face. 'Bloody stupid name, isn't it? Brianne. Sounds like a pop singer. All because of some twit of a mapmaker misspelling Bryniau, the plural for Bryn. If he'd gone to bloody Specsavers, the place would be called Llyn Bryniau, the Lake of the Hills. Much more poetic.'

'*Mynufferni*, there's a lot to be said for proofreading, sir.'

Buchannan lowered his head. 'How's it going?'

'Slowly, sir. DCI Warlow is targeting the Thorleys, they own an adjacent property and they're not being very helpful. I suspect he has a plan.'

'Good. Evan generally does.'

'Anything I can do, sir?' Gil put down the papers he was holding.

'Good question. I've just come off the phone with someone in Cybercrime. Apparently, a laptop taken from the property of the deceased is causing a bit of a stir.'

'That would be George Marsden's, sir. Have they found anything interesting?'

Buchannan nodded. 'It's what they haven't found that's making heads spin. In that they have been able to access it, but some files remain locked because they're encrypted, and the encryption is of a very sophisticated variety found only in high-level security circles.'

Gil smiled. 'I had a sneaking suspicion old George could be a spy.'

'Really?'

'He worked in Berlin after the war and during the time of the Wall before coming back to London.'

'Right, well, we've had to alert some bods up in London who tell us that whatever is encrypted stays encrypted. We can use everything else, of course. Bit of a fly in the ointment, though.'

Gil nodded.

Buchannan's puzzled expression didn't budge. 'Is there any chance that this has anything at all to do with what happened to him, you think?'

'Are you asking if I think it's the Russians, sir?'

The question caused Buchannan to muster a smile. 'Perhaps I am. I'd put nothing at all past those little sods.'

'From what we've seen of their assassination attempts of late, it's more likely they'd have covered the door handle with neurotoxin than stabbed him eleven times in the chest.'

'Agreed. But it is a bit of a wrinkle, isn't it?'

'It is that, sir. But one I'm sure DCI Warlow will iron out.'

Buchannan stood at the Gallery, his head six feet some-thing off the floor like Rhys's, tilting forward to study the images. 'Any relatives?'

'Still looking, sir. We were hoping the laptop might lead us somewhere.'

Buchannan swivelled his long neck to regard the sergeant. 'I'll get them to send you what they have pronto. Give Evan my best.' And with that, he left.

But he was as good as his word. Fifteen minutes later, Gil's email chirped with a file, including George Marsden's email correspondence. Confirmation of Amazon orders and deliveries featured heavily. But there were one or two private email addresses, and one, in particular, that appeared more frequently of late. George had been corresponding with a woman called Celia Robinson and they'd been discussing something that George had been writing. Gil took the plunge and composed Celia Robinson an email of his own, read it twice, and sent it off to await events.

———

THEY PARKED outside the steel gates guarding Foynw House. Warlow got out and pressed the intercom button. Once again. A little beep presaged a voice. This time, male.

'Yeah?'

'Mr Thorley? I'm DCI Warlow, Dyfed Powys police. Would it be possible to have a word?'

'You've already spoken to the missus, right?' Warlow heard the broad Bristolian accent come through.

'Indeed. But we'd like a word with you and your son.'

'Nothing to do with us, mate.'

'A man has been killed, Mr Thorley.'

'Like I said, nothing to do with us.'

'Your wife told us that there's a path that leads directly to Nyth Y Gwcw.'

'Cuckoo's Nest is what I know it as. I can't be doing with the bloody Welshy stuff, mind.'

Warlow filed that one away for future reference.

'Cuckoo's Nest, then.'

'So?'

'We'd like to look at that path. The easier access is from this side.'

'Bullshit. You just want to snoop.'

'It would only take a few minutes, Mr Thorley.'

'Come back with a warrant.'

The intercom clicked off.

'That went well, sir,' Catrin said.

'No surprises, I'd say.' Warlow came back to the car and stood by the entrance to the property. From the gate, the house and the nearest paddocks were on view, but beyond that, the land dipped and some outbuildings and fields were not visible until it rose again to reach the forest edge.

'Right, Rhys, you're up.'

It took a good few minutes for Rhys to set up the drone. He added an enthusiastic voice-over to his actions.

'This is a DJI mini. Steff has three. Different generations. More flight time and better cameras and all that. But this one is brilliant, too.'

Folded up, the drone sat easily in Rhys's palm. Only five and a half inches long and perhaps three wide and pale grey. He unfolded its four arms and slid his mobile into the remote-control device.

'Expensive?' Warlow asked.

Rhys shrugged. 'Couple of hundred quid.'

'Not bad, then.'

'The third generation is almost a thousand.'

'Bargain,' Warlow said, and threw Catrin, who stood leaning against the Audi with her arms folded as she watched Rhys, a side-eyed glance.

Rhys kept talking, 'This one has a half an hour flight time before the batteries need recharging. It has auto take off. Auto landing. Auto GPS, live camera…'

'Does it make coffee as well?'

That elicited a disparaging glance from Rhys. 'Not this model, sarge, no.'

'It's a bit windy, Rhys. Aren't you worried it'll get blown away?' Catrin asked, stroking a strand of hair from her eyes only for the breeze to whip it back.

'It won't.'

'I hope one of these is on your list for Santa.'

Rhys didn't look up from what he was doing with the remote control this time. 'Might be,' he muttered.

'Right. Well, let's see the bloody thing fly, then,' Warlow said.

The drone buzzed into life and rose smoothly into the air.

'It's not as loud as I thought it would be,' Catrin said.

Thirty metres above them, the drone hovered steadily, untroubled by the breeze. Or automatically compensating for it somehow. 'Now what, sir?'

'I want you to fly over this property towards the forest. See if we can pick up this path.'

'Really?'

'Yes. Can it do that?'

'It can, sir, but—'

'What?'

Rhys squirmed. 'Shouldn't we ask permission? From the occupants, I mean.'

Warlow dipped his chin. 'Oh, so even though you fly these things with your pal, Steff, you don't know the law?'

'Uh…'

'The law, DC Harries, states that you should, at ground level, remain one hundred and fifty metres away from residential property. In the air, you can fly over any property at a height of sixty metres or more. You do not need permission for that.'

'What about the camera, though?' Catrin asked.

'Ah, now, that's where it gets tricky.' Warlow's response implied that he'd been waiting for them to ask. 'We're interested in the path on the other side of the property. But, as you rightly point out, sergeant, we'll be flying over said property. It would be completely unethical, not to mention illegal, for us to use any images without the owner's permission.' He grinned at the junior officers.

'Why do I feel that I'm missing something here, sir?' Catrin peered at Warlow askance.

'I'd like to see the path that links these two properties. The Thorleys have denied us permission. I am now exercising my prerogative in utilising the technology at my disposal.'

'Is it going to annoy them, sir?' Rhys asked.

Warlow's smile didn't shift. 'Remember what I said about poking a stick into a hornet's nest?'

'No?'

'No? How about a practical demonstration instead, then?' Once again, Warlow used the index and middle fingers of his right hand to point skywards. 'DC Harries, make it so.'

CHAPTER SIXTEEN

RHYS STOOD, feet firmly planted on the ground, staring at his mobile phone attached to the drone's remote control, tongue slightly protruding from the corner of his mouth, the thumb and forefinger of each hand controlling the controller's joysticks.

Warlow and Catrin kept their eyes on the drone. Its buzz when it hovered was very low key, but when Rhys sent it up, the tone increased towards angry wasp level. Four green lights flashed constantly at the corner posts of the legs supporting the propellors.

'Do you want to come and look at the screen over my shoulder, sir?' Rhys suggested.

Warlow threw Catrin a glance. Rhys was much taller than both of them. But Rhys had thought it through. 'I'll sit on that rock and you and sarge should be able to see what I see.'

It worked well. Warlow and Catrin stood behind Rhys and stared at his phone screen, now a part of the control system, revealing the drone camera's astonishing picture. The image shrank as the drone ascended, displaying the surrounding area, the three officers and the Audi parked outside the boundary of Foynw, as well as the response vehicle that Warlow had asked as backup.

'What now, sir?' Rhys asked.

'Follow the fence line and then head towards where the forest begins.'

The drone's technology eliminated shake, and the image displayed on Rhys's phone appeared remarkably clear and steady as the ground drifted by.

'How high are you now?' Catrin asked.

'Seventy metres,' Rhys replied.

Foynw was revealed in all its glory, including its outbuildings, the horses in the paddocks and what looked like some kind of scrambling or ATV track at the bottom of a dip. At the north-eastern end, the more rugged moorland melded with the fenced-off areas.

'Head for that top corner and get lower if you can,' Warlow said.

Rhys complied. The drone descended until it hovered over the edge of the forest. Rhys manoeuvred back and forth until Warlow said, 'There.'

It wasn't so much a road, but the trees had been thinned out and a narrow track led into and through the forest. Rhys followed it above the treetops for a couple of hundred yards.

'Shame you can't follow this all the way to Marsden's property,' Warlow said.

'The drone doesn't have that sort of range, sir.'

'No. Still, we can see that there is a path of sorts. One big enough for a quad bike to travel along, too.'

Rhys flew back up above the dark forest. With height, the thin snaking line of the track gradually got lost in amongst the foliage.

'Talking of quad bikes,' Catrin said and pointed to the bottom of the phone's screen. A single quad bike had appeared and came to a stop. Two human shapes dismounted, unrecognisable from this distance, but from their animated gestures, obviously irate about the drone.

'Who are they?' Rhys said.

'I'd hazard a guess that they are the male Thorleys, senior and junior.' Warlow sounded oddly sanguine.

'That doesn't look like a happy dance, sir,' Catrin observed.

Arms were being waved. V signs thrown.

'Rhys, get lower and follow the edge of the forest line again. Let's make sure there is no other path.'

Rhys did as asked. The drone's movement brought a stop to the Thorleys' gesturing until it got to the edge of the plantation and then reversed its flight path.

'Can't see another entry, sir,' Rhys said.

'Agreed.'

'Shall I bring it home, sir?'

Warlow looked pensive. 'Did you note those big flexible ducting pipes coming out of the side of their outbuildings?'

'Can't say I noticed, sir,' Rhys said, his thumbs hovering over the joysticks.

'I counted three,' Catrin said.

Warlow nodded. 'I wonder what they're up to in there.'

'Making yoghurt?' Rhys suggested.

'That's not at the top of my list, Rhys, but it is a thought.'

Catrin leaned a little closer to Rhys's shoulder. The drone remained stationary above the forest. 'What are they doing?' she asked.

Warlow watched as the bigger of the two men took something from the back of the quad bike. Something wrapped in black plastic. The image shifted as the drone, still over the trees, crept nearer the gesticulating figures.

'That,' Warlow said, squinting in concentration, 'is a shotgun. Rhys, get away from there.'

They saw the shot before they heard it, of course. And

a second later, the image shifted and whirled sickeningly on the screen as the drone jerked upwards and then plummeted to the ground. The camera stayed on as it fell through the trees to come to rest with an image of a fern, at an extremely odd angle, a few inches away.

'I've been shot, sir,' Rhys wailed.

'You have,' Warlow muttered. He got up and strode across to the gatepost and pressed the call button again.

This time, Angela Thorley answered and launched right into it.

'A drone. Are you serious?'

'A drone which your husband or son has just shot down.'

'What do you expect if you fly over our property? Snooping on us.'

'We were snooping on the path into the forest. And that isn't illegal. But what is illegal is destroying private property. And I suspect, owning a shotgun without a licence.'

No reply.

'Now, you have two choices. Either I get an armed response unit out here with automatic weapons, or you open the gate and let us in. Is it just the one gun?'

'We found it here. In one of the buildings—'

'I don't care if the Easter bunny delivered it. I want it on the ground outside the gate with no person within fifteen yards of it.'

'I don't—'

'Not a discussion, madam. You have five minutes before I call in the heavies. Do you really want a siege here? Imagine what the press will do with that.'

'You flew a drone over our house,' a petulant Angela Thorley said, but there was little venom left in her protests.

'I flew a drone because you would not let us get access. You now have four minutes and fifty seconds.'

Warlow walked back to Catrin and Rhys, a tinny tirade of noise from the intercom following him. He ignored it, and a few seconds later, things went dead. Rhys looked very sorry for himself. 'What am I going to tell Steff?'

'He'll make a fortune from the YouTube video. Tell him he'll have first dibs once we've finished with it as evidence.'

Catrin sent Warlow a wary glance. 'You knew something like this would happen, didn't you?'

'I did *not* know they had a gun.'

'No, but poking the hornet's nest?'

Warlow shrugged. 'Better they shoot at a drone than at us.'

He walked over to the Uniforms in the response vehicle and told them what had happened. Where guns were involved, they'd need to run a risk assessment. Especially if the weapon wasn't given up. Then he came back to Catrin and Rhys.

'I suggest a tactical withdrawal to somewhere where we can watch the gate for the next ten minutes.'

They didn't argue. Catrin drove them fifty yards up the road and parked behind the marked car on a slight rise. The Uniforms were already out. One of them had binoculars trained on the gates. Warlow got out and waited. They heard the quad bike before they saw it. Even without binoculars, Warlow made out a shape standing at the gates, opening them and placing something on the ground before getting back on the bike and driving away.

Warlow and both Uniforms walked back down the road to the gate. The shotgun was double-barrelled, the dark metal dull, the stock chipped. Overall, it looked well used. The Uniform took some photographs and, with gloved hands, wrapped it in some plastic sheeting, and took it away.

Warlow had one bar of signal on his phone. He texted Catrin.

Stay put. Wait for my word.

She texted back.

OK

Warlow walked through the still-open gate towards the converted barn with the second Uniform. The door opened without him needing to knock. The burly man that stood in the doorway wore a waxed jacket and a wild look in his eye. Warlow didn't bother with introductions.

'Was it you or your son who fired the shot?'

'Me.'

Warlow had his doubts about that, but it didn't matter. Not in the grand scheme of things. 'I was going to offer to discuss what we needed to discuss up here, in your nice, converted barn, but that gunshot changed everything.'

'Piss off. No one got hurt.'

'Except the drone. Which you took out. So, that's destruction of property for a start. And I doubt that you or your son have a shotgun license, do you?'

Thorley's lips moved, but no words came out.

'I didn't think so,' Warlow said.

'I had no idea it even worked.'

'Really? So, what was the plan? Wave it at the drone and shout bang?'

'I was pissed off.' Thorley's sour face flushed.

But it was an appropriate answer under the circumstances. Yet, Warlow noted the brief hesitation. The momentary delay before he came up with the argument.

It wasn't you, though, was it, Mr Thorley? You're simply being a good dad.

'Right. But you still pointed it and pulled the trigger.'

'I wanted to scare you off.'

'You scared the drone, alright. With two barrels' worth.'

'I'll buy you a fucking drone. And it wasn't my gun. It was here in one of the sheds under some tarpaulins. We found it. And we didn't even know it was loaded.'

'Is that your defence?'

'You had no right to—'

Rights. Why was it that people were always so keen on their bloody rights even when they'd committed a crime? Victimhood had become a disease as rampant as Covid. Warlow was having none of it. 'A man has been killed not three miles from here. So we have the right to investigate what we consider relevant. This little debacle could have been easily avoided. All I wanted to do was ask you some questions in a civilised manner.'

'Right. Okay. Ask away.'

Warlow shook his head. 'Too late for that. I want you down to HQ in Carmarthen. You and your son.'

Thorley shook his head. Through gritted teeth, his eyes flaring, he said, 'Not a fucking chance.'

'Then I bring in the heavy mob. They'll tear this place apart. There'll be more headlines. A mob of tabloid paparazzi camped out here for weeks, too. So, here is the deal. You and your son come down to Carmarthen with us now after you let my DC find his drone. There, you'll offer a voluntary interview, and I will talk to my boss about the firearm charges. That or the hyenas outside your gates for days.'

'The gun was here already; I swear to God.'

Warlow's patience was wearing thin. 'This is my only offer. Of course, your free exercise your rights and I'll get a warrant. You will get armed response, News at Ten and a shitfest. So, we'll go from there, shall we?'

Thorley didn't move. Firearms offences carried custodial sentences. Anything from seven years to life. But Thorley would get a good defence, and much as Warlow hated to admit it, he might well have found the gun hidden away in an old place like this. A good barrister would argue that he hadn't purchased or acquired it. Forensics would tell if it had been used a lot. Or even fired at all until the drone shot. But Warlow was more interested in George Marsden at this moment than anything else.

'Well?' Warlow asked when Thorley didn't answer.

'A voluntary interview?' Thorley asked.

Warlow nodded. Thorley turned away and spoke to the two people in the hall behind him. A family discussion. It didn't take long. Two minutes later, he turned back.

'Your DC can get his drone.'

Warlow sent Rhys and Catrin a text. A few minutes later, they and the second Uniform appeared. When they did, he spoke to Thorley again.

'Right, we'll give you ten minutes to get yourselves prepared while we try to find the drone. These officers,' he nodded at the Uniforms, 'will give you any help you need.'

Warlow walked away around the end of the house towards the paddocks. 'Right, Rhys. Let's find the Millennium Falcon.'

Rhys frowned. 'That's not Star Trek, sir, that's—'

'Star Wars. Yes, Rhys, I know. But give me a little slack here.'

'You don't have to come, sir. Me and sarge—' His words cut off when he saw the glare Warlow shot him. They were still within earshot of the Thorleys, but to give the PC his due, the penny dropped quickly, and he recovered well. 'Could do with the help, though.'

'My pleasure, Rhys. My pleasure.' Warlow led the way towards the nearest outbuildings in the general direction the drone had gone down.

CHAPTER SEVENTEEN

THEY HURRIED along a well-used track between the buildings, heading for the farthest edge of the property where the forest began. Warlow moved quickly.

'Why are we in such a hurry, sir?' Catrin asked, quick-marching to keep up with the DCI.

'Because I want to be on the other side of these buildings before someone in that house realises they've given us carte blanche.'

A little smile appeared on Rhys's lips.

'What?' Catrin demanded, with a sharp wariness that suggested she would regret asking.

'It's just that Sergeant Jones says that carte blanche is nowhere near as nice as carte D'or. The posh ice cream.'

'Dessert humour?' Catrin said. 'Is that all you can think about?'

'I thought it was funny,' Rhys muttered.

'It is,' Warlow said as they reached the corner of the last building before the track dipped down towards a muddy quad bike figure-of-eight track. 'But not half as funny as seeing all these ducting pipes coming out of these buildings.'

They stopped, well out of sight of the barn now, and turned back to peer at the two outbuildings they'd walked between. Black corrugated iron jobs with curved roofs and those white expandable duct pipes coming through blacked-out and taped-up windows.

'Rhys, can you get up there and have a sniff of what's coming out of one of those pipes?'

Rhys studied the problem. He chose the pipe at the far end of the building. The bracket holding the concertina tubing had broken, and it hung drunkenly nine feet up. 'I might reach that one, sir. If I can get up on the window ledge.'

Catrin and Warlow stood back and watched Rhys do his impression of a mountain goat.

'Catrin, keep an eye out for approaching… anything,' Warlow muttered out of the side of his mouth, his eyes never leaving the gangly DC doing an impression of a stick insect ascending the building.

Catrin crept back along the track, while Rhys clambered up, grabbed the ducting, and yanked it down to where he was perched on a window ledge. A level where he could get his nose into it.

'Well?'

'Not ice cream, sir.'

'No, I doubted it would be.'

'Definitely not.' Rhys's expression crumpled into disgust.

'What, then?'

'Musty. The slightly damp smell you get in old houses.'

'Wet rot?'

'Exactly that, sir.'

'Right, get down. We'll file that away. Let's get this drone of yours.'

It took them another twenty minutes of walking and finding a way through the trees. And although the drone wasn't flying, its position via the GPS tracking showed up on the screen on Rhys's iPhone/remote control conglomeration. Rhys homed in on that and found it on its side, looking forlorn but still flashing. Two of the propellor units had been damaged enough to render the drone un-flyable. Rhys regarded it woefully. 'Steff is going to kill me.'

'Thorley offered to pay. We all heard him. I will hold him to that,' Warlow said.

'You think he will, sir?'

'I hope Mr Thorley will be very cooperative once we get him in the interview room. Now, stop cradling that thing like an injured bird and let's get back to work.'

———

GIL GOT the call back from Celia Robinson just after 3pm.

'Thanks for getting in touch,' Gil said.

'Your email said it was to do with George?' Celia Robinson sounded young. He'd assumed, with a name like Celia, she'd be middle-aged. But then, you could never tell with names anymore. The old was becoming the new again. She also did not sound local. Plummy was the word that sprang to Gil's mind. Which was about as old-fashioned as you could get.

'It is. Can I ask how you know George, Ms Robinson?'

'I'm an editor with Lambton Publishing. I've been doing some work with George on his memoir.'

'Memoir?'

'Yes, a historical account of his personal life.'

'Forgive me for saying this, but isn't it a bit late for him to do that sort of thing?'

'You might think so. But George is a very young eighty-plus. Besides, some things he wanted to put in there were subject to the Public Record Act. In other words, he's had to wait until certain documents were released into the public domain. Used to be thirty years, now it's twenty. George is a stickler. Always wants to double-check the things he remembers.'

'When did you communicate with him last?'

'When? Last Tuesday but…' Celia's tone changed, and her voice rose a little higher. 'Why are you asking me that?'

'I've got some bad news, Ms Robinson.'

'Call me Celia, please. What kind of bad news?'

'The worst. I'm afraid George Marsden was found dead on Sunday.'

A choking rasp came down the line. 'Dead?' whispered Celia.

'I'm sorry to have to tell you this over the phone. I hate doing it this way. But you aren't local, I take it?'

'I'm in Guildford. I've never made it down to George's part of the world. Though I was planning a trip next spring to… Oh, God. Poor George. He was so keen to get all of this finished.'

'I have to ask you this. Did George ever mention to you that he was being watched or followed?'

'No. Why? What happened to him?'

Gil saw no way around telling this woman the truth. 'I'm afraid George was murdered, Ms Robinson.'

'Oh, no, no, no, poor George,' she muttered the last two words as a half sob.

'As I say, I am sorry to have to give you this news on the phone, but your email address was the one that he seemed to have contacted the most.'

Lots of sniffs came from Celia before she spoke again. 'You'll find my number on his phone records, too. We chatted. He was a charmer.'

'Was it interesting, his book?'

'Amazingly so. He's had such an incredible life. Sacrificed a great deal for his country. One of the truly unsung heroes.'

'Was there anyone who might not want what he had to say read? Was his book going to embarrass anyone?'

'Spies, you mean?'

'Or the security services, or some individual perhaps?'

'No, no. This was a book from the past. A very interesting past. But nothing that could be construed in any way as sensitive these days. George's sphere of knowledge was the Cold War.'

'Smiley's People?'

'Not quite, but not far off.' She sniffed again, loudly. 'He was never trying to be Le Carré. George's stuff was more commercial, if anything.'

Gil frowned. 'George's stuff?'

'His fiction. He wrote as Bernard Ripley. Amazingly enough, his US sales were better than the UK market.'

'Spy novels?'

'Political thrillers, we prefer to call them.'

'*Mynufferni.*'

'Sorry?'

'No, my apologies. Slip of the old Welsh tongue there. I had no idea.'

'Oh yes. He sold a couple as film rights, though my thinking was that they'd have been better as a series.'

'So, George Marsden sat in his farmhouse in the middle of nowhere and wrote?'

'Exactly. We have some authors who'd give their left arm for the opportunity to be as secluded as he was. His civil service pension was more than enough to get by on. He wrote because he loved doing it. It was me that suggested the memoir.' She sniffed. 'Sorry. This is such awful news.'

'Did George talk to you about any next of kin?'

'There is a brother somewhere. But he was not well. He moved back from Australia and is in a nursing home. Alzheimer's, but the details I have are sketchy. Since

George lost Beryl, he'd been concentrating on his memoir. It was his homage to her. A record of their life together. He'd made it his reason for getting up in the morning.'

'Was there much left to do?'

'Hardly.'

Gil's next sentence took both parties by surprise. 'Then why don't you try to publish it for him?'

Silence followed. 'It isn't my book.'

'Just an idea. Be nice to leave a legacy, wouldn't it?'

'We're a tiny company.'

'Worth thinking about, though.'

'You know what? It jolly well is, Sergeant Jones. Will you contact me about the funeral arrangements?'

'Someone will,' Gil said. 'I'm sorry for your loss, Celia.'

———

THEY TRAVELLED BACK to Carmarthen in convoy. Catrin driving the Audi in front, the Thorleys following in their Porsche Cayenne and the response vehicle with the Uniforms behind them. Though it was only forty miles, it took well over an hour.

Warlow got a uniformed sergeant to put the male Thorleys in separate rooms. For now, he didn't see the need to talk to Angela Thorley, though that might change.

Depending on what he learned from the men.

He let Gil and Rhys talk to the father. William Thorley's surly demeanour had accompanied him all the way to the interview room. Warlow felt it might be a nice touch to let Rhys, still aggrieved by the attack on his friend Steffan's drone, glower across the table at the man. Thorley didn't know Rhys, and the young officer's physical presence, to the uninitiated, lent a definite air of puissance to the proceedings. He wouldn't need to say anything. Just one look at his pursed lips said it all.

In the meantime, Warlow and Catrin would have a chat with Thorley the younger, seventeen-year-old Nathan who, on first inspection, had inherited his mother's lighter frame, but his father's miserable expression.

Just before they went their separate ways, over a quick cuppa in the Incident Room, Gil filled them in on his discussions, first with Buchannan, and then with the editor, Celia Robinson.

'Blimey,' Rhys said. 'A spy? So much goes on out in the sticks, doesn't it?'

'She seemed quite upset, the editor. Said George was a nice old chap,' Gil said.

Warlow shrugged. 'That's a definite theme. He's a man with no enemies.'

'Plus, we don't think the killer was after the laptop or the files, whatever they are,' Catrin said. 'I mean, there was no sign of any attempt at searching the property.'

'Agreed.' Warlow nodded. 'Let's not go down that rabbit hole unless we have to.'

'There's an old joke about the Russian police,' Gil said, a digestive poised mid-dunk above his mug.

'Really?' Catrin rolled her eyes.

'It might put you in a good mood…' Gil paused for effect before adding, 'but then again, that would be asking quite a lot of a couple of lines of Soviet-era comedy, even in a person blessed with a sense of humour.'

'What is that supposed to mean?' Catrin bristled.

'Let's hear it, sarge,' Rhys urged Gil.

'Okay. Why do the Russian police always travel in threes?'

'I don't know. Why do the Russian police always travel in threes?' Rhys played the straight man.

Gil obliged. 'They need one who can read, one who can write, and one to keep an eye on the other two dangerous intellectuals.'

Rhys's smile died on his face.

'Soviet-era joke,' Gil explained. 'You had to be there.'

'Do they have tumbleweeds in Russia?' Catrin muttered.

'I don't know, but they do have the gulags,' Rhys replied.

'I had those once,' Gil said. 'Cleared up nicely with some ointment and a cushion.'

This time, Catrin almost spat out a mouthful of tea and ended up in a watery-eyed, coughing fit.

'Giddy up,' Gil said, watching Catrin splutter. 'Always nice to see someone falling off their high horse. I have to say I am disappointed in you, though, Sergeant Richards. There you are, deriding my attempt at political satire, but then throwing up your PG Tips at a bodily function joke.'

Warlow drained his mug. 'Let's get this show on the road before it all descends into further chaos and DS Richards has a stroke.'

CHAPTER EIGHTEEN

NATHAN THORLEY HAD the sort of adolescent features that looked as if they hadn't quite settled into their ultimate positions on his face. His nose was a little too large and hormonally driven hair growth was attempting to join his eyebrows across the middle. His beard, however, remained a wispy version of the dark, short-boxed version, including moustache, his father wore. No doubt it would fill in, but for now all the straggly thing did was make him look ratty.

He sat with the hood of his grey hoodie up over his head, playing incessantly with the drawstring of that same hood.

'So, Nathan,' Catrin said. 'Tell us about your quad bike.'

Nathan didn't move his head but let his eyes drift up, full of derision, to study Catrin. 'How do you mean?'

'I saw that someone had made a quad track on your property. We know from previous noise abatement orders that riding quads is something you like to do.'

'Has someone complained about the effin' noise again? Out there?'

'Noise is not the issue.'

'What, then?'

Warlow leaned in. 'You use your quad a lot, Nathan? For getting about?'

Nathan's brows crept even closer together. 'That's what they're made for.'

'Indeed. So, you ride through the forest to George Marsden's property sometimes?'

'Who?'

'George Marsden. Cuckoo's Nest?'

'The egg bloke, you mean? Yeah, I can be out and back in like, twenty minutes.'

'When was the last time you were out and back, Nathan?'

'Friday. Why?'

'Because your mother said she picked the eggs up on Saturday.'

'Oh, yeah. She's right.' The lie came naturally to him. As if he'd had a lot of practice.

'And was George okay when you saw him last Friday?'

'Maybe I didn't. If Mum says...' Something in Warlow's expression made Nathan Thorley reconsider his options. 'Yeah, fine. He seemed to be, anyway. I mean, we don't exactly discuss the state of the world. I give him money, he gives me eggs. Why?'

'How many eggs?'

'Six. Look, why is any of this important?'

Catrin ignored the question. 'So, you went to Cuckoo's Nest at what time?'

'Morning. It was morning because we had burgers for lunch.'

'Do you like George, Nathan?'

'He's alright. He's that bloke that sells eggs.'

Warlow and Catrin exchanged glances. 'He was a lot more than that.'

Nathan's lids hardened. 'Mum told me he'd croaked. But what's that got to do with me?'

No flies on old Nathan.

'That's why we needed to speak to you and your dad, Nathan.'

He sat up straight. 'Mum said that you'd called because of some BS about a serious incident. She said you used that to check on us. Nosing.'

'The pathologist thinks he died sometime on Sunday,' Catrin drove home the point.

'I didn't go anywhere on Sunday. I was at home. Practicing.'

'For what?'

'Racing. I might race. On the quads.'

'Is that a thing?'

'Yeah.' Nathan sounded defiant. 'There's a league and stuff. I done some under-sixteen races. But you got to be eighteen to do adult racing. I'm eighteen in five months.'

'You have a plan,' Warlow said, not unkindly.

Nathan nodded. 'And that plan does not include doing anything to George Marsden.'

'Does it include using a shotgun to shoot down a drone?'

Nathan flinched, his mouth working behind closed lips. 'That weren't me,' he said, somewhat reluctantly in Warlow's opinion.

'Pardon?'

'That weren't me. I didn't use the gun. I found it, but… it weren't me.'

A lie if ever there was one. The second one in as many minutes, Warlow surmised. Nathan's mother had lied about getting the eggs to protect him and now, Warlow would put money on the fact that somewhere on that journey down in the Cayenne, his father had told him to deny using the gun. The DCI did not condone the conspiracy, but he understood it. Parents needed to be parents. Even dysfunctional nouveau riche lottery winners like the Thorleys.

Catrin shifted in her seat. 'And when you go off into the forest on your quad, you don't meet anyone else?'

Nathan's expression twisted into a crooked smile. 'Like who?'

'Someone who might sell you drugs. You used to like drugs, eh, Nathan?'

The smile faltered. 'I don't... I don't do that, not anymore.'

'Glad to hear it,' Catrin replied, her eyes never leaving Nathan's defiant face.

Warlow nodded. 'Right, then. Fine. How about you make a statement about the last time you saw George on... Friday, right?'

Nathan nodded.

'And chuck in a paragraph about what happened to the drone. We'll even give you a pen and some paper. Capitals if you like. We won't expect joined-up writing.'

'I can write,' Nathan said.

'Delighted to hear it.'

———

THEY'D MADE William Thorley a cup of tea and Gil had also come up with a couple of second-tier biscuits. Not that there was anything wrong with a plain old dunker, except that they'd run out of the redoubtable Marie. These were a definite poor relation, and it had become all too easy to lose a half or a quarter in the process of biscuit dipping. No one wanted a soggy, semi-dissolved biscuit floating in their tea. It made for burnt fingers and altogether too much cursing.

But these discount offerings were good enough for William Thorley.

'Alright if I call you William, William?' Gil began the interview with one of his standard opening gambits.

'Fine,' Thorley replied.

'Tidy. Now, this might sound a little odd, but you aren't part Russian, are you? No Russian relatives?'

'No. And it is a bloody odd question.'

'They're my specialty.' Gil made a show of writing something down, muttering as he did so, 'No Russian connections.'

Rhys, meanwhile, sitting back with arms folded, kept up an aggrieved glower that Thorley did his best to ignore. But it brought out another apology.

'I'm sorry about your drone. I meant it when I said I'd pay for a new one, mind.'

Rhys didn't move, but he nodded another acknowledgement.

'Whose idea was it to shoot at the drone, William?'

'I already told you; I didn't know it could bloody shoot. It hadn't worked before when we tried it. Nathan said he'd have a go at cleaning it. For all we knew, it might have been a fake gun all along.'

'You need a licence for a shotgun, William,' Gil said.

'Yeah, well, that's the bloody point, isn't it? It hadn't fired anything despite us trying. We had it on the back box of the quad because Nathan had been having a go at cleaning the damned thing…' William moved his head forward. 'Like I just said.'

'But it was loaded, correct?'

'Nathan must have…' He shook his head. 'Like I say, just send me the bill for the drone.'

Rhys kept up the glare.

'So, how are you enjoying life out in the, uh, country, William?' Gil asked, though the way he pronounced country implied middle of nowhere.

'It's something we had to do. Move away, I mean. Place is as good as any.'

'You mean as remote as any, don't you?' Rhys said.

Thorley took a couple of swallows of his tea. The cup looked tiny in his big hands; the fingers stained with ingrained dirt or oil. 'People get jealous. Some people didn't like us winning the lottery—'

'How much was it again?' Gil cut across.

'3.8 million.'

Gil whistled.

'Yeah.' Thorley smiled sourly. 'The money is great, but there's a price to pay.'

'You can't change who you are, right, William?' Gil was all smiles.

Thorley nodded. 'I thought it might change us. For the better, like. And especially for Nath. He hasn't had it easy in school. ADHD and all that stuff. He was never going to go to university. But you know what kids are like. Me and the missus did our best to keep him on the rails, but it's not always easy. The money got us out of Hartcliffe. That's one thing it did.'

Gil understood. It didn't need spelling out. The area was known for all the wrong reasons. Just a few months before, Avon and Somerset police made national head-lines when they obtained a court order to close one of the tower blocks in the South Bristol suburb because it had become too risky for residents. This after years of complaints from young families constantly exposed to used needles, blood-soaked tissues, faeces and urine, gang violence, and abusive behaviour. Hartcliffe appeared on no one's list of destination places to spend a night.

Thorley continued, 'Nathan was getting into trouble there. What kid wouldn't? But then we found out that too much money, too young, isn't always the best either.

Though we moved away, some of Nathan's mates found out where we were. They liked a good party.'

Gil listened. Here was Thorley, the father, talking. 'So, you brought him out here, to the middle of nowhere?'

'I thought quad bikes would be a distraction from… other things. And they are. He's a strong rider. He can handle a bike alright.'

'Just not within shouting distance of the Thames, right? I mean, who wants their Pimm's spoilt by the roar of an engine?' Gil made a sympathetic face.

'It was a mistake to move there, I'll admit. But they were all twats, our neighbours. All of them.'

Gil nodded and put his pen down. A prearranged signal for Rhys to come in.

'Can we talk about George Marsden?'

'The egg man?'

'The man you buy eggs from, yes.'

'It's usually Nathan or Angela that does that.'

'When was the last time you saw him?'

Thorley shook his head. 'Couple of months ago. We were out on the quads and ended up over that way, so we called in, me and Nathan. For the eggs.'

'So, you did know him?'

'Of course. Not many people live out that way.'

'What can you tell me about him?' Gil asked.

'That he kept chickens.' Thorley seemed to run out of patience then. 'Look, your boss said that he'd died. Is that what this is about?'

Rhys sat forward. Time for cards on the table. 'It is. George Marsden was murdered.'

Thorley gave nothing away, but his mouth became hard. He kept looking at Rhys. As if he was waiting for the next line in the joke. The one that came with a punch line to ease all the tension. But it didn't come. Realisation began with a little shake of his head, which developed into a full-blown denial. 'No, no, no. This isn't happening. Definitely not happening. You bastards.'

'What isn't happening, William?' Gil asked.

'This.' He slapped his hands on the table. 'Okay, we've had some problems in the past. I'm aware of what our rep is. But this.' His head shakes became more vehement as his expression hardened. 'No way. I'm not being set up for this by you muppets. No bloody way.'

'We're not setting anyone up,' Rhys said. 'All we're doing is—'

'Trying to trick me into saying something. Right. No more. End of voluntary interview. Everything else goes through our solicitor.'

'Okay,' Gil said. 'Even the firearms issue?'

'You bastards,' Thorley sneered.

'It wasn't us who shot down a drone.' Rhys had his finger up.

Thorley stared at it, nostrils flaring. His next words came out in a whisper, 'I gave my word that I'd pay for that. I will. But that's all you're getting.'

Gil paused, waiting, but Thorley's lips had clamped shut. 'In that case, thank you for your help.'

'Where's Nathan?'

'In a different interview room. Once the DCI has finished—'

Thorley stood up and lifted his chin. 'Nathan. Nathan,' he bellowed. 'Say nothing else, son. Tell the bastards fuck all.'

CHAPTER NINETEEN

WARLOW SAT in the SIO room, aka cupboard, scrolling through the Amazon sales pages of one Bernard Ripley. He'd counted twelve books in a series as well as three standalones. All based around the fictional Cold War adventures of an MI6 Mandarin known as Hopwood.

This stuff wasn't Warlow's cup of tea. He preferred the sheer escapism of something otherworldly. He wasn't even averse to a little fantasy now and again. He'd read the Hobbit and Lord of the Rings when he was in his early teens and still remembered names and scenes. These days, though, he was as happy indulging himself in fiction where the concept of evil was explored. He currently had one of John Connolly's Charlie Parker novels on his bedside. He liked the style as much as the locations: mostly the USA, but with occasional forays into the UK. But more than anything, something about the concept of wrongdoing being linked to an undertow of evil appealed to him. Not that he expected to find demons in his own work, other than the ones that came to him in the early hours as a product of his own imagination. And, even then, they were firmly grounded in the horrors he'd faced as part of the job. But there was no doubt that the things he'd heard and seen sometimes strayed towards that concept of a darkness that was inexplicable in any other terms.

Warlow did believe that evil existed. But only in men's hearts.

Bernard Ripley's accounts of the adventures of Simon Hopwood were not his normal escapist fictional fayre. But the Amazon sales pages still held a fascination. He'd been pointed here by Gil, who'd received a second email from Celia Robinson, Chief Commissioning Editor of Lambton.

George Marsden might have been planning his memoirs but, for the previous twenty years, he'd been published as Bernard Ripley. So far, Warlow had seen nothing on these web pages to help them in their investigation, but it was fascinating. Ripley's books were popular, with plenty of four-and-five-star ratings, too. But it was all background noise.

Which was exactly what had ended Nathan Thorley's interview. They'd touched on what might have been growing in the outhouses at Foynw. Apparently, William Thorley's big idea for Nathan's future was setting up a mushroom-farming business.

No magic mushrooms; at least not by design. The Thorleys had opted for the low-tech approach and aimed strictly towards the gourmet market with hydroponic tents in the outbuildings. Hence the fungal smell that Rhys had picked up on.

They'd been getting Nathan to open up about all that when they'd heard the shout from William Thorley echo through the building. Since his interview room had only been two doors down, the sound had travelled straight into Nathan's ears.

As a result, he'd clammed up.

And even though they could have pressed charges for

the shotgun episode, Warlow had decided to let them go. It hadn't been a gun that had killed George Marsden.

'Do you want me to begin a warrant application for Foynw, sir?' Catrin had asked.

They'd have no trouble getting one, not where a shotgun had been used. But Warlow wanted the Thorleys to stew a little.

'Not yet,' he'd said to her. 'We'll keep that on the back burner for now.'

He shut the web pages down and wandered back out into the Incident Room just as the door opened and a uniformed female police officer walked in. She strolled surreptitiously over to Rhys's desk where the DC was busy studying his screen, stood behind him without saying a word, wet her little finger by placing it in her mouth for a second and then put that same wet finger into Rhys's ear.

The DC's reaction was priceless. He flailed backwards, reared up from the chair and turned in one movement ready to explode. That was when he saw who the woman was. The woman he was about to move in with. Gina Mellings.

'Gina. What are you doing here?' He spoke in a half whisper. But Rhys's inside voice technique left a lot to be desired and what emerged was a whisper loud enough to be heard in the car park at Llyn Brianne.

'Apart from giving you a wet willie, you mean?'

'That's not funny, Gina. I'm at work here.'

'That's debatable,' Warlow said.

Rhys turned to his boss, his face reddening. 'Sorry, sir.'

'Don't apologise. She had my full permission. It was worth it to see you reacting as if you'd been bitten by a bloody snake.'

'Couldn't resist it,' Gina said. 'I have two brothers, sir, and I've had to put up with a wet finger in my ear for years. The swines still do it when I'm distracted.'

Rhys, realising that this wasn't the mother of all embarrassing moments he thought it might be, recovered quickly, wiped his ear and smiled at his partner. 'Okay, then it's nice to see you, Gina.'

'And you,' she replied with the kind of smile that could stop three lanes on the M4.

From an adjacent desk, Gil's voice drifted up. 'Did I drift off and come to in the middle of an episode of Police Interceptors, the afterglow?'

Gina sent him a grimace. 'Sorry, sarge. I only need a quick word with him.'

'Take all the time you need.' Gil turned back to his paperwork. 'My ears could do with a rest from the constant chomping noises.' He nodded at the small hill of empty snack packets on Rhys's desk.

'Outside?' Gina said to Rhys.

'No bother.'

But as the two of them walked to the door, Warlow called to Gina. 'Since you're here PCSO Mellings, could I have a quick word in the office?'

She followed him to the SIO room, exchanging wide-eyed looks with Rhys whose expression dripped with schadenfreude.

'No need to shut the door, Gina,' Warlow said when they got to the room. 'This is a bit off-piste. It's about the INTACT team in Pembrokeshire. They've seconded a couple of PCSOs to it to do community reach out. I wondered if you knew them.'

'I do, sir,' Gina replied. 'I know them both.'

Warlow had gambled on this. Dyfed Powys was a small force spread thinly. But almost everyone knew someone who knew someone. 'If I needed some off-the-record intel, who would you recommend I talk to?'

Gina didn't hesitate. 'I'd speak to Rhiannon Collins, sir. She's one of the good ones.'

'Great. Now, off you go and don't discombobulate him too much.'

'I won't sir. It's just about the move. I think I've sourced a van.'

'Ah yes, the great escape.'

'I can't wait. I mean, living at home has its merits, but there are five of us. My mum still waits up when I've gone out for the night.'

'That's what mums do. If you need a hand with the move, just shout.'

'We will, sir, thank you.'

———

'WHAT DID THE WOLF WANT?' Rhys asked as soon as Gina joined him outside. The day was shaping up nicely. No rain yet, and the sun was doing its best to nip out between the clouds when no one was looking. When it did, it stirred memories of a summer so warm and dry that drought had threatened even the wet environs of Eastern Carmarthen. And that only happened when the rest of the country had fried to a crisp. The sun appeared now, lit up Gina's face and made it glow. Not that she needed any help with being the centre of his world.

'Said he'd help us with the move if we needed any.'

'Really?'

'That's what I wanted to see you about.'

Panic galloped over Rhys's features. 'You've changed your mind.'

An exasperated Gina shook her head. 'No, of course not. I think I've sourced a van, though. A big one. One of my dad's mates said we could borrow it for the day.'

'Great,' Rhys said.

Gina frowned, detecting the little hesitation that

implied less than a hundred percent enthusiasm. 'What's wrong? I thought you'd be pleased.'

'I am,' Rhys said. 'A van will be good. It'll mean we can get everything done in one journey, right?'

Gina considered him. He'd perched himself on a wall so that his head was at the same height as hers while she stood in front of him. Not close enough to draw stares, but close enough for anyone watching to know that they were together. 'You *have* told your parents that it's a week Saturday, right?'

Rhys opened his mouth to speak, but all that came out was a strangled exhalation of air. 'I was going to last night and then something came on the box that they're both into, so I didn't want to disturb them.'

'My God, Rhys. They're not going to throw themselves on the floor and wail.'

'I know, I know. It's choosing the right moment, that's all.'

'Your mother and me have had lots of discussions about this. She's given us bedclothes, towels, even an electric blanket. She's on board with it. What's there to be frightened of?'

Rhys dropped his head. 'Nothing, there's nothing to be frightened of.'

'What is it, then?'

'I don't know. I don't want them to be upset, that's all.'

'They've already put your room up for rent, you *did* know that?'

Rhys's head snapped up. 'What?'

Gina couldn't keep a straight face. 'As if.'

Rhys shook his head, but a smile replaced the serious expression of before.

'Just imagine waking up together every morning.' Gina leaned in. 'You in nothing but your shorts. Me in nothing but my winceyette pyjamas.'

'I bloody hate those things.'

'I only wear them in the winter. The rest of the time, I… don't. Imagine me turning over towards you. I reach over and… take the cup of tea you've just made for me.'

Rhys feigned umbrage. 'Is that a part of the deal? That's just like being at work.'

Gina dropped her chin.

'Well, maybe not exactly like being at work,' he conceded.

'There we are, then. I mean, if that's not enough of an incentive…' Gina's brows rode up.

'I'll speak to them tonight.'

She reached across and squeezed his hand. 'Are you going back up to the dam today?'

Rhys puffed out his cheeks. 'I expect we will. We're no further forward than we were this time yesterday. Except I'm one drone lighter and Steff is going to kill me.'

Gina waited politely for the explanation.

But Rhys simply shook his head. 'Long story. I'll tell you over a Prosecco and a pint.'

'Still, it gives you a chance to drive that snazzy Audi.'

Rhys brightened at that. 'There is always that.'

CHAPTER TWENTY

WARLOW FILED AWAY the information Gina had given him about the INTACT team. He'd chat with Molly about Zac. But for now, his thoughts were back with George Marsden. The death of an elderly and reclusive author was bad enough. As so often in cases like this, especially ones where there was no relative to champion the deceased's cause, Warlow's sense of duty somehow felt more acute. And yet, something else, something so intangible he could hardly even credit it as a feeling, worried away at him like the sting of a nettle. It niggled, but he could not recall at which point in the investigation he'd brushed up against the cause of the pain.

They were missing something. That's all he was aware of.

Rhys came back into the Incident Room with a tray resplendent with four steaming cups, penance for taking personal time. By now, the afternoon was racing by, and before they knew it, it'd be evening. Warlow strolled out to get his mug, needing a fresh perspective now that they'd lost the initiative with the Thorleys.

Catrin had already posted up the relevant information

regarding Foynw, but there remained big gaps around everything else. Warlow pointed at the image of Bryn Encil.

'Heard back from this lot yet, Gil?'

'Not yet. It's possible their boy isn't back from playing woodsman.'

Warlow glanced at his watch. Five had come and gone with not so much as a whimper. 'Catrin? What about the Airbnb?'

'Still no joy, sir. I've left three messages for the owner. They're based in Swansea. I can try again, though.'

'I daresay they'll get back to us. Probably at work.'

'I found one thing that might be relevant, sir. Foynw. It wasn't always called that.'

'You do surprise me,' Gil said.

'Its original name was Pencraf.'

Gil pondered this for a moment before commenting. 'Craf is an old word for wild garlic. Many of these old names come from significant geography or habitats.'

Warlow frowned. The name rang some sort of bell. Catrin read his expression. 'I know, I couldn't quite place it either, sir. But then I remembered those chalk marks on the back of George Marsden's door.'

'Remind me,' Warlow said, walking across to the images on the Gallery board. Catrin joined him and pointed to a couple of obscure scene of crime images provided by Povey's team. 'There was the one showing the logo of the Friends of Light, the crown over the mountain, and then this other one. That one was much more faded, but Povey thinks it read Craf and the number 6.'

'More Dan Brown stuff?' Gil said from his seat.

But then Warlow saw it for what it truly was and smiled. 'George Marsden was a practical man. An intelligent man. He'd know Foynw as it had been. Pencraf. What we're seeing here is nothing more than his order book.'

'How do you mean, sir?' Rhys, mug in hand, stood behind the DCI.

Warlow half turned and looked up at Rhys. 'Ever heard "I am the Walrus", Rhys?'

'Is that a bit like "I am Spartacus"?'

Warlow saw Gil shake his head and volunteer an explanation. 'No, nothing like I am Spartacus. It's a Beatles song.'

'There's a line in it about being an "egg man",' Warlow added. 'Like George Marsden was.'

'I don't follow, sir.'

Catrin put him out of his misery. 'George Marsden sold eggs. He only had a few customers. One was the Friends of Light. One was the Thorleys.'

Warlow nodded. What had been an enigmatic bit of Dan Brown BS was suddenly a very simple bit of book-keeping. 'George used the old logo of theirs to remind him of how many they needed. Two dozen.'

'Twenty-four,' Catrin said with a thin smile. 'And Craf was probably a shortened version of Pencraf. The number six would have been the Thorley's order. George may have preferred to reference the true old name of the property.'

Warlow nodded again. 'I doubt whether George Marsden had warmed to the name Foynw.'

'So, that's another dead end, sir.' Catrin sounded disappointed.

'Think of it more as another box ticked, sergeant. Now, I suggest we leave everything until the morning. I promised Molly I'd make it back this evening. We're all tired. Let's get an early start tomorrow.'

———

CATRIN, not unusually, was the last of the team to leave the Incident Room. The civilian indexers had long gone. Craig was off at seven, so she'd get home, get some pasta on, and they could share a bottle of wine. She'd gone five miles along the forty-eight when her phone rang.

'Hello, is this Sergeant Richards?' A woman's voice and not one she recognised.

'It is. Who am I speaking to?'

'Oh, hi, my name is Rebecca Lineham. You left a couple of messages for me to get in touch?'

'You're the owner of the Airbnb near Llyn Brianne?'

'Cysgod y Mynydd, near the reservoir, yes.'

'Hang on, I'm just pulling off this road.' Catrin decided not to risk ringing her back. It had been tough enough to get hold of her and now that she was on the line, she didn't want to let her go. Instead, the DS took the turnoff to the National Botanic Gardens and a minor road exit to a lay-by just a hundred yards off a roundabout, where she parked up.

'Sorry about that, Rebecca.'

'That's okay. I was wondering if you were calling about the occupants. I was hoping you were, actually. I don't think I can stand another phone call from the parents. I mean, it's my property and all that, but I'm not responsible for the people who stay there. If they want to not answer their phones, that's up to them. And as I was trying to explain, the reception can be patchy up there and—'

'Whoa, Rebecca. Hang on just a minute.' The woman was a runaway horse that needed reining in. 'Let's start with the basics. You own the Airbnb, right?'

'I do, but—'

'Can you tell me if there is anyone occupying it right now?'

'Yes. Two girls. A Lucy Pargeter and a Nola O'Brien.'

'And how long have they been up there?'

'Change-over day is a Saturday. So, what, four days now?'

Catrin had her notebook out and the phone running through the car's speaker system. She wrote down the names. 'Right. What's this about their relatives?'

An exasperated sounding Rebecca sighed. 'Since yesterday, I've had four calls from this Lucy Pargeter's mother asking me if I knew where she was because she wasn't answering her phone. I mean, I live nowhere near the place. I tried to explain, but apparently, this girl always rings her mother because her dad's not too well and—'

'You say girl, how old?'

'Well, this is it. She's not a kid. She's twenty-nine. We don't take anyone under twenty-five, it's not worth the hassle. I have friends with properties trashed by people on hen do's. And you can forget stag parties.'

Catrin zeroed in on the details again. 'You know for certain that they are there, these girls?'

'Definitely. I ask everyone to email me once they've arrived to make sure all is well. I got that email on Saturday evening.'

'But you heard nothing from them since?'

'I wouldn't expect to. Not unless something was wrong with the property. No water, or the heating system playing up, you know? People don't go to the valley to go mad on social media. They go there to walk. For peace and quiet.'

'And how is it you have a property out there?'

Rebecca laughed. 'Long story short, it was my ex's idea. An investment, he'd said. He'd seen it online. A complete ruin. It had been nothing more than a shepherd's hut. He splashed some cash, and I got it in the divorce settlement. Not exactly a money spinner, but its upkeep is cheap. I get someone from Llandovery to change the sheets and run a Dyson around it.'

'Okay. Do you have a number for these girls?'

'For one of them, yes. Lucy Pargeter.'

'And what about her mother?'

'I do. Tell you the truth, when I see it now, I refuse to answer.'

'May I have it, please?'

Catrin committed everything Rebecca told her in her notebook. When she'd done that, a rare few seconds of silence followed. It didn't last long. Not after Rebecca's mind started whirring.

'Hang on, why is it you wanted to speak to me in the first place?' Rebecca asked.

'There's been a serious incident up near your property.'

'At my place?'

'No. Some of our officers visited your property and found nothing untoward.'

'Good, I'm glad. Serious incident, though? An accident?'

'Not an accident, no.'

More silence. Catrin could almost hear the synapses firing on the other end of the line. 'You don't think these girls had anything to do with it, do you?'

'I doubt that very much.'

'But they're alright, are they?'

'We haven't spoken to them yet.'

'You don't think anything's happened to them?'

'Again, I doubt that. As you say, reception is patchy. They may have been out walking or in a tent somewhere when our officers called.'

'That's what I told the mother.'

'Still, it might be necessary for us to gain entry. Would you mind us contacting the person who cleans and changes the beds? I presume he or she has a key?'

'She does. I can text you her details.'

'That would be great.'

'I hope nothing's happened. I'm booked up throughout October.'

'Let's keep our fingers crossed, then, Rebecca, eh?' She rang off and looked at her watch. Craig was going to be home before her. So much for pasta. She texted him and suggested he pick up a takeaway from the Lucky Wok. Then she dialled the first of the two numbers Rebecca Lineham had given her. It rang four times before it was answered.

'Hello, Mrs Pargeter, my name is Detective Sergeant Catrin Richards, Dyfed Powys Police. Do you have a moment to talk to me?'

———

BY THE TIME Warlow got back to Nevern, Molly had picked Cadi up and taken her into the fields for a run. That meant that instead of ten minutes of presenting him with a variety of soft toys shoved into his hand, the greeting ritual lasted only five minutes before the Lab sauntered off to her bed and stretched out, content and, Warlow suspected, plum frisbee'd out.

'This dog will be the fittest she's ever been by the time you leave,' Warlow observed.

'Who says I'm ever leaving?' Molly grinned at him. 'I like it here. No one to nag at me. No one to make sure I go to bed at a reasonable time. Your Wi-Fi is terrible, but that's about my only complaint.'

'So, should we discuss rent, then?'

'Ha, ha, you should consider stand-up.'

Warlow let out a grunted breath. 'I doubt I'm woke enough. What happened to being funny? What happened to jokes? Now you have to score Twitter-worthy points or you don't count.'

Molly, who'd been laying the table, stopped what she was doing to stare. 'Right, remind me never to mention comedy again.'

Warlow grinned. 'See, now, that was smart. That was funny. And you didn't even need to mention the fact that I'm a reactionary old fart.'

'Gammon?'

'I prefer honey-smoked ham. And talking of food, what you got cooking?' Warlow sniffed the air. 'It smells good, whatever it is.'

'Mum made me bring this huge frozen lasagne. She said if you were going to be back before eight, I should heat it up. Besides, you forgot to take the pasta bake thing out of the freezer.'

Warlow grimaced. 'I did.' But then he sniffed the air again. 'Just as well, I say.'

'I made a salad to go with it.'

'Is it one of your special ones with added protein in the form of live caterpillars, like last time?'

Again, Molly stopped what she was doing to consider the man who was insulting her. 'I could just let you make some toast.'

'No, you're alright. I quite liked the taste of caterpillar juice.'

'That was a one off. I was a bit hung over after a party.' She continued laying cutlery. She didn't look up when she next spoke. 'I was going to ask you about your pills. I mean, there are loads of them in the bathroom cabinet.'

'Oh, sorry. Do I need to make room?'

'No. I was looking for some toothpaste and I came across a small chemist shop.'

'Your mother has told you about me, hasn't she?' Warlow asked.

'She's told me a lot about you, most of it I can't repeat.'

'About my health?'

'What, that you're like the Witcher? That some evil

sorceress has cursed you so that you have to drink bat's milk every night or you'll turn to stone?'

Warlow ran with the analogy. 'More or less. Except that the sorceress was a junkie who hid contaminated pins in her hair. The "curse" is HIV. The little bottles you see all contain bat's milk of various compositions with very long scientific names.'

'So, the tablets keep the HIV at bay?'

'They do.'

'Will you ever be cured?'

'Hmm. Good question. I have no symptoms of anything, so you could say I'm already cured.'

'Except that the virus is in you, like a malevolent spirit?'

'Netflix has a lot to answer for, doesn't it?'

'But seriously, though?'

'Seriously, my doctors tell me I'm 99% normal so long as I keep taking the retrovirals.'

Molly said nothing. Warlow hoped his words had pacified her. But there was more to come. 'I suppose that explains your hermit existence. I mean, Mum has locked herself away because she never wants to see another man's pants ever again, and I quote. Understandable after what Dad did. But you… it's a deeper thing, right?'

Warlow didn't answer because he had no words. But Molly took it as an admonishing silence. She grimaced and muttered, 'Shut up, Molly. Sorry. Too soon, right?'

'No, you may be right. I haven't thought about it too much.' Warlow heard the lie in his words. He had thought about it, but preferred, given the choice, not to. Best he change the subject. 'How is your serial texter?'

'Zac? Still texting. Weirdly, in his last text, he was asking about Bryn. How he was getting on in London. Weird.'

'Oh?'

'Yeah. I know. Maybe my method of ignoring him is getting results. See, I told you I could handle all this. Will you be wanting wine?'

'I may have a glass.'

'Not a pint glass, like Mum, though?'

'You know you're being recorded, right?' Warlow cocked an eye. 'She will hear these slurs.'

'The truth and nothing but the truth. Right, can you get the plates?'

Warlow wanted to tell her she was a credit to her mother but contented himself with knowing it.

CHAPTER TWENTY-ONE

WARLOW TOOK Catrin's call on his way in to work the next morning and listened while she told him all about what she'd learnt the previous evening. He agreed with her they should revisit the Airbnb and said he'd meet her and Rhys up there. It meant adding another hour to his commute, but he got there a little after nine to find a car parked outside the little hut. He pulled his Jeep in behind and got out.

Both the Audi's doors opened at the same time and Catrin and Rhys exited, the DC from the driver's side. If he'd driven, it meant that Catrin had been working on the way up. The only way she'd ever concede driving duties to her younger colleague usually. Catrin was her own woman.

'Morning, sir,' they said in unison.

'You practised that duet on the way up, did you?' Warlow asked.

'Nah. Great minds, sir,' Rhys said.

'Where?' Warlow did a quick three-sixty.

'Ha, ha, sir. Good one.' Rhys grinned.

'Any trouble getting the key?' Warlow turned to Catrin.

'No. The cleaner said she came up here on Saturday morning and the women had not arrived by midday.'

'But you say the owner had confirmation later that night?'

Catrin nodded.

Warlow turned again to look at the hut. Yesterday's sunshine had long gone, and an off-white blanket of cloud covered the sky. A thin wind cut through the gap between two buttons on his shirt and found skin. 'Right, let's see what we have here. Gloves and overshoes, just in case.'

Catrin stuck the key in the double doors. They slid open smoothly. Inside was tasteful, as the glimpse Warlow had stolen through the chink in the curtains previously promised. A sweater on the bed, bags on the floor. Catrin moved across to the only other room.

'Tiny bathroom, sir. Empty. Looks like they hadn't even unpacked.'

'Nothing's changed from when Rhys and I called here two days ago. Wherever it is they've gone to, they haven't been back here.'

'They must have driven, then, sir,' Rhys said.

'Good point. Where is their car?'

'Sir,' Catrin called to them. She stood next to the kitchen work surface and pointing to a couple of bags. One a small backpack, only six or so inches across, the other a handbag in red leather. Again, not large.

'They've gone without their accoutrements,' Warlow said in a low voice.

'Should I, sir?' Catrin asked.

'You should,' Warlow responded.

Catrin opened the red bag. Inside nestled a purse. Inside that, a collection of credit cards, some paper money and coins and a driver's licence. 'Nola O'Brien, sir.' Catrin turned the bag over. Tucked into a side pocket was a phone. She took it out and held it up. She pressed the power button. It lit up, showing an image of a woman sitting on a chair near a stunning view of a lake. Then the DS turned her attention to the little rucksack. Inside that was a smaller purse with cards and a driver's licence issued to Lucy Pargeter. But no phone.

'Why would Nola O'Brien go out without her phone?' Rhys asked.

There were answers, of course. Some people didn't want the hassle and were glad to get away from the damned thing for a while. Admittedly a rare breed, but they existed. Warlow sometimes did that when he went out with Cadi. But the accompanying guilt made him resist the urge in case one of his boys wanted to get hold of him.

Or, of course, work.

Then again, some people used their phones as cameras. What if Nola was a photographer? One who preferred a proper camera with interchangeable lenses. Enough scenery around every corner up here to shake a stick at. But then Lucy Pargeter's phone was not in her bag. She'd taken hers and the door had been locked. These two women had walked out of this room and locked the door. Finding a phone here meant bugger all.

Rhys walked across to the sofa towards a small pedal bin. He put a foot on the release; the lid lifted, and he peered inside. 'Sir, you should see this.'

Warlow joined him and got down on his haunches. The bin's plastic liner could be easily removed. It held nothing solid, but something red stained the otherwise empty clear plastic liner in streaks of scarlet.

'Blood?' Rhys asked.

Warlow shrugged, but his face stayed grim.

'Maybe one of them had a nosebleed, sir?'

'Perhaps.' Warlow stood up and turned to Catrin. 'Did the mother give you her daughter's phone number?'

'She did, sir. I rang it twice last night. No reply.'

'Try it again now, in case it's in here somewhere.'

Catrin did. They all stood and listened. But no sound came from within the cabin. Rhys, however, stepped towards the door and stood, a pained look of concentration on his face.

'What?' Warlow demanded.

'I can hear something, sir.' Rhys walked outside towards the two vehicles, and, his head cocked, started moving around them and staring into the open stretch of rough moorland just beyond the low and crumbling wall that marked the border of the property. He stepped over and walked forward, stopped, reached down, and then stood up, holding another phone in his gloved hand but pointing animatedly with his index finger to the ground.

'Shit,' Warlow whispered.

'And sir, there's a scrunched-up tissue here. About two feet away. It looks like it's been soaked in blood.'

'Sir.' Catrin's voice from behind him in the hut wasn't loud. But the urgency embedded within it made him snap his head around. She stood at the kitchen counter again, next to a gleaming silver toaster and a kettle and a kitchen roll on its end that had half obscured the things she was pointing at now. A knife block capable of holding five knives.

But that now held only four.

'Alison Povey is going to love us,' was all the DCI said as he reached for his own mobile.

―――――

GIL HAD TEA, and a plated-up display of *biscuits* awaiting the other three when they got back a little after 11am. Warlow had made the judgement call to get well out of Povey's way and leave the crime scene team to do their voodoo. The scene was cramped as it was. Having three impatient detectives staring over everyone's shoulder would not help. He'd made that mistake before. Povey was methodical in her approach. She would not be hurried. And if she found something, Warlow had no doubt he'd be the first to know.

'So, do we classify these two as missing persons yet?' Gil asked when coats had been shed and mugs handed out.

'We do,' Warlow replied. 'There may be a perfectly reasonable explanation for all of this, but I am buggered if I can think of one for now.'

'Want me to call the PolSA?'

Warlow pondered that one for a second as wisps of steam from the mug coiled up in front of him. If these women were missing out in the open, they ought to call in a search team. But as yet, he didn't suspect enough to brief any PolSA. He needed more information.

'I want everything there is to know about these two. Rhys, you take on Nola O'Brien. Catrin, since you already have contacts for Lucy Pargeter, get hold of the mother again. Find out what their plans were. Were they going to hike? Read books? What? Gil, get a background check on the Airbnb owner.' He glanced at his watch. 'It's 11.05 now. Let's regroup at 11.30.'

No one objected. Tea was slurped and biscuits munched as Gil, Catrin, and Rhys slid into their chairs and got to work.

Warlow had a bad feeling about all of this. And yet, he had a worse feeling when he tried to fit the jigsaw piece that was George Marsden's murder into the picture. Were the two things even related?

He let out a quiet, rueful snort meant only for his own hearing. The team was well aware of how much he hated the "C" word. Coincidence had little or no place in a murder investigation. Not in Warlow's book.

He wandered back to the SIO room and jiggled the

mouse connected to his computer. Nothing new in their team inbox. But then the phone rang and Warlow snatched it up.

'My God, Evan, do me a favour and take a holiday for a few days. You're working us to the bone, here.'

Warlow felt a smile curve up at the corner of his mouth. Povey's words were scathing, but he also heard the total lack of conviction within them. She was a workaholic. It took one to know one. 'Find anything, Alison?'

'Only that the crumpled tissue Rhys found was soaked in blood before it all dried off. That's a simple test. But the interesting thing from your point of view is that the bin liner also tested positive on presumptive testing for blood.'

And there it was. They'd been looking for a sign of violence, and Povey had just delivered it. Several scenarios flashed through Warlow's mind. Of course, someone might have sneezed and got a spontaneous nosebleed. But you had to take these things in context.

And, where women missing in one of the remotest areas of the country was concerned, you had to ask a fresh set of questions. For instance, had one of them been attacked in that room?

'There is also a wiped area on the floor about two feet in diameter. Remember, it's a laminate floor, so zero absorption. But we found a large negative fluorescence in a swirl, and presumptive tests also confirm that it's blood.'

'So, someone bled, and it was wiped up by the kitchen roll?'

'Yes.'

'Someone threw the tissue in the bin, but then removed it?'

'That would be my take.'

'Removed it and discarded it, close to a phone.'

He was talking to himself now. Imagining a scenario

where this might plausibly have happened by accident. He couldn't think of one.

'Thanks, Alison. As always.'

'Pleasure.'

Warlow sat back. 11.15.

The next fifteen minutes dragged by. He called up the Airbnb's website. Cysgod Y Mynydd in all its glory. He studied the photographs again and read the spiel. They sold it as "Completely secluded. Literally get away from it all", and "Isolated peace and quiet".

It might be all of those things.

But it might also be an ideal spot for a predator to strike.

At 11.29, he walked back out into the Incident Room and addressed the team.

'For God's sake, tell me we have something to work with here.'

CHAPTER TWENTY-TWO

RHYS WAS on his feet at the Job Centre, sticking a post-it note up on the board.

Warlow picked him out. 'Since you're the one standing, off you go.'

'Nola O'Brien, sir. Hers was the red handbag. From that, we've been able to trace her address in Manchester where she works as a researcher for the BBC. I spoke to her sister, who was listed as a next of kin on a donor card in her purse. Karen O'Brien lives in Belfast. I've tried contacting the flatmate at the Manchester address and left a couple of messages, but she hasn't come back to me so far. From what her sister says, it sounds as if Nola and her friend Lucy Pargeter had booked this stay a while ago.'

'Are they walkers?'

Rhys responded with a forced smile that told Warlow he would not like what he was about to hear. 'Not really, sir. The reason they chose Cysgod y Mynydd is that it was the closest to a place called Carn Ddu.'

'As in a black cairn? A pile of stones?'

'Exactly that, sir.'

'Dare I ask why?'

Rhys elaborated, 'The sister said that Lucy Pargeter and Nola were at university in Durham together. They've stayed close friends. Both of them are big fans of a podcast. It's called the Stone Tape Files. It has something to do with paranormal investigation. Apparently, last year, the podcast claimed that this Carn Ddu – as you say, translated as the black cairn – is the site of some kind of ritual activity at the summer and winter solstice, sir. Plus, rumours of strange sightings up there. Nola and Lucy wanted to visit it.'

Warlow squeezed his eyes shut. He couldn't bloody believe it. First the Friends of the sodding Light and now the para sodding normal. This was all they needed.

'I can confirm that, sir,' Catrin added. 'I spoke to Lucy Pargeter's flatmate. Pargeter has a room in a shared house in Brixton. She works for a recruitment agency in London. The flatmate confirms that Lucy drove to Manchester and was planning to spend a four-day break in a Stranger Things cabin, as she called it.'

'Do we have a timeline?'

Catrin continued, 'Lucy left London on Friday, aiming to drive to Manchester. They were then going to drive down to the cabin from there using Nola's bigger car.'

'Which is?'

'A black Nissan Juke. I've already circulated the number plate, and I'm getting the Uniforms to instigate an ANPR search. See if we can flag it up somewhere.'

'Do we have a location for Carn Ddu?'

Rhys pointed to the map. 'It's about four miles from the Airbnb. Halfway between it and Bryn Encil, the Retreat. No road in there, sir. Just a hard slog up and down the moors.'

'Did the owner of the Airbnb know anything about this?'

Gil was swivelling back and forth in his chair but

stopped to reply to this question. 'I've spoken to her, too. She admits that some of the feedback she's had online has hinted at this Carn Ddu. And she referenced the podcast, but she hasn't heard it herself. She only knows that after it was broadcast in January, interest in the place picked up.'

'Has anyone listened to it?' Warlow asked. 'This Stone Tapes Files thingy?'

'Not a big podcast fan myself,' Gil said.

'I have, sir. It's a bit of a mockumentary,' Catrin said. 'There's a woman who plays a journalist linked up with a paranormal investigator who goes around debunking claims that there are really ghouls and ghosts around. But occasionally they come across what they call a real find. That's when the dramatic music comes in. Carn Ddu was one of them. The podcast is all tied up with conspiracy theories and ancient cults. Not my cup of tea, sir.'

'But it was for these two women?' Warlow asked.

'Apparently so.'

'Nothing else in their backgrounds? No jealous ex who might have followed them there?'

Catrin answered first. 'Lucy Pargeter is in a relationship, sir. I've spoken to her partner, and he's in London and has been all along.'

'What about the Irish girl?'

'No, sir,' Rhys said. 'She is single. According to the sister, the girls both listen to the podcast and then dissect it and, because it is UK based, list the locations. They've been to an old Abbey in Gloucestershire. An abandoned mansion in Derbyshire. All sorts.'

Warlow walked over to the Job Centre and studied the posted-up notes, blue for Catrin, yellow for Rhys. 'The press is going to be all over this like flies at a festival bin.'

Gil grinned. 'That reminds me of an old joke. What has four wheels and flies?'

They all looked at him.

'A bin lorry. Or, if you're from across the pond, a garbage truck.'

'Nice imagery, sarge,' Rhys said.

Warlow shook his head. But he didn't object. He never did because injecting these little gobbets of lightness even into moments of harrowing seriousness got them through the day. Gil was an inveterate joker. Sometimes the things he said were cringeworthy, but they eased the tension. That was the important thing.

'There is something else, sir.' Catrin stood up with a sheaf of papers in her hand. 'The podcast encourages feedback. They have up to five hundred people commenting online after each episode. Some people phone in, most leave comments. I read through them—'

'All of them?' Rhys asked.

'Yes,' Catrin answered, enunciating the affirmative as slowly and as patronisingly as she could while defiantly regarding Rhys. 'And there is this one entry. I've blown it up for you to see.' She stuck a single A4 sheet up. Warlow took a step closer. Thick black lines above and below the text showed where Catrin had redacted the irrelevant responses to ensure they read only what they needed to.

> Great pdcst tnite. I bin up to black cairn. It's
> spooky AF. Will watch for black figers. I am
> close by. It's in nowhere. Like me.

Gil had stood to read it too. 'Christ, has this been written by a five-year-old?'

'It's not so much the text. What's important is the signature beneath it.'

'F.O. Yournotwelcomeboy,' Rhys said.

'Charming,' Gil muttered.

'More than charming,' Warlow said. 'I feel a need for that warrant.'

'You do?' Gil asked.

'F. O. Yournotwelcomeboy.' Catrin put them out of their misery. 'F.O.Y.N.W. boy.'

'Nathan Thorley,' Rhys voiced the group thought.

Warlow turned from the board. 'Gil, get a warrant for their place. Unlicensed firearms should do the trick. Catrin and Rhys, as the whippersnappers of the team, I want you to get up to this Carn Ddu before the press or even the PolSA gets wind. You up for it?'

'Absolutely, sir,' Rhys said.

Catrin nodded.

Gil saw his chance. 'Don't worry, Catrin. You can borrow my crucifix and I'll give Rhys a wooden stake and a hammer. Best to be prepared.'

The cold stare she sent him would have severely worried a brass monkey.

————

Sigrid Bidulph stood in the rotunda, staring out at the surrounding countryside. She was used to emptiness, having grown up in Northern Sweden. But she'd always felt that out here, in this patch of wilderness, she was never alone. The apprehension that something lurked, that the hollows and the small copses harboured a watching entity, meant she never went anywhere out of sight of the property. This was a miserable land. Not like her home, where winters were winters and summer saw the light stay in the sky for twenty hours of the day. Here, the summers only meant less rain than the winters. And the winters, though mild, brought with them a dampness that somehow seeped into her bones and chilled her to the core.

Sometimes when she got too stir crazy and took a walk, Jonah or Thomas might appear from around the edge of the building and a wave of relief would wash over her. It didn't matter if either of them saw her. In fact, knowing they were out there, tending to the gardens, finding firewood to sustain them in the cold winters, gave her a sense of relief.

But today, there was no relief. Only foreboding.

Lunchtime had come and gone and there had been no sign of Jonah returning. A creak of a door behind her made her start and turn around. Rudi, dressed as usual in a collarless shirt, khaki slacks, and a pair of black Nikes on his feet, stood in the doorway regarding her.

'Still no sign?'

'No.'

'What time are we expecting Thomas back?'

'He left at six and got to London at ten-fifteen. He texted me at ten to say he was on the way back at eleven.'

They'd made the difficult judgement call immediately following the police's visit. The whole ethos of what they were trying to achieve here, and the reason they could charge so much money, was all to do with exclusivity. The guests – Rudi preferred that term as opposed to client or patient – needed to feel safe. To feel that there was no way the outside world could intrude. But with the police calling and the inevitable press interest that would follow once news of a murder got out, Rudi and Sigrid had cut their losses. It had been a bitter pill to swallow. But a necessary one. They asked the guest to leave and had driven her home, using the murder as their reasoning.

'As soon as he's back, we'll get him to search for Jonah.'

'Should we tell the police about Jonah's background?'

'Why? Discretion must be our watchword.'

Sigrid smiled. Rudi couldn't help himself. Even with her, someone aware of all his tricks, it was impossible for him not to stay in character. Like any good actor, he adopted a method and did so again now. 'If we have cast off our previous lives, it is only fair that we give those who come to us an opportunity to cast off theirs.'

'But Jonah—'

Rudi stopped her with a raised finger. 'What Jonah may have done in the past is something he chose not to share with us.'

'Not us, but the central office knew. If they found out, the police surely will.'

'We need to give Jonah the benefit of his choices. He lives a different truth now. So long as he embraces the light and doesn't let the darkness engulf him, he will be helped. And we will be vindicated. Everyone comes here to escape something, Sigi. Even you.' He paused before adding, 'We don't have to wait. You and I can go and search for him.'

'I'm not going out into those hills, or those trees, or between those rocks.'

'There's no bogeyman out there, Sigi.'

'No? But there is something.'

Rudi's smile irritated her and triggered another response.

'You can mock me, but I don't care. Something is here. Something has woken up.'

'Now you're being dramatic.' He reached out to her and held her hand. 'We might need to ride out the storm for a month or two. But this will pass. Central office knows we're profitable. In the end, that's all that matters, isn't it?'

'Is it? What if Jonah killed that man? What if he never changed at all when he came here?'

Rudi balked. 'You have no proof of that—'

'Not yet. But what if he did it? Shouldn't we tell the police about him now? About what he did before he came here?'

Rudi shook his head. 'We made promises, Sigi. To everyone who joins us here. What they've done in their past is forgotten.'

'Someone has died, Rudi.' Sigrid's words came out mashed in with a small sob.

'Let's give him the benefit of the doubt until Thomas comes back and has a proper look. If we don't find him by tonight, I'll ring that Chief Inspector. But I'm telling you, Jonah's found someone in one of the pubs and he's taken off to meet him or her. He's young. We can forgive him that, surely?'

Sigi searched Rudi's eyes for the lie, but she saw none. He was so good at this. Calming people, filling them with confidence, convincing them that real soul-searching and self-belief were the only true paths to health. He was so good at it, sometimes even she believed him.

But not today. Deep down, she knew he was wrong. Yet, his argument was compelling. She'd text Thomas and ask him to call in Llandovery to check out a few of the pubs before he got back. And if the boy wasn't there, they'd send Thomas out on the other quad to search for him.

And if that came up blank, she'd phone the police herself.

CHAPTER TWENTY-THREE

CATRIN MADE Rhys drive the Audi while she linked her phone up to the car's speaker system via Bluetooth.

'You got a new playlist, sarge?' Rhys asked.

'No. I'm going to play you some of the Stone Tape Files podcast. So, you can get a handle on this stuff.'

They'd come along the bypass on the A40 and Rhys eased the Audi back to a steady forty as they passed through White Mill and its petrol station, casting his eyes around with exaggerated nervousness.

'What's up with you?' Catrin asked.

'Be just my luck if Steff saw me now. I haven't told him about his drone yet.' He winced at the memory.

'He's hardly likely to recognise you in this, is he? It's unmarked. The idea is that no one knows it's a police car. He'd be looking out for that clapped-out blue Astra of yours, wouldn't he?'

Rhys winced a second time. 'Harsh.'

'The truth hurts.'

'Just because I don't drive a souped-up BMW like Craig.'

Catrin scrolled through her phone apps as she talked.

'Says he fancies a Jag. He's always got his nose in What-Car.' She pressed something on the Audi's dash screen and a bubbly female voice began introducing the podcast and segued seamlessly into advertising trekking underwear.

'I've never understood these weird ads,' Rhys said. 'Pretending these sports knickers are the best thing since sliced bread. I mean, come on.'

'They sponsor the podcast. They have to make money somehow. It's either ads or Patreon.'

'Who?'

'A way for fans to pay the creators for their work. Like a subscription.'

Rhys scrunched up one eye.

'Don't mock until you have a listen. I've found the bit of the podcast dealing with Carn Ddu. Episode fifteen.' She turned up the volume.

I'm Georgia Kinsay from Consett Media. This season on the Stone Tapes Files, we've joined up with Dr John Lester, director of the Lester Institute. The Stone Tapes refers to an old TV film from the seventies which put forward the stone tape theory. A theory that suggests significant events, often of a horrific and violent or supernatural nature, may be held as memories or recordings by the surrounding physical environment. John Lester has dedicated his life to investigating these phenomena. This season, we continue to explore Dr Lester's work.

Suitable atmospheric introductory music followed.

'Sounds pretty spooky,' Rhys said, grinning.

Georgia Kinsay's voice came back and Catrin shushed Rhys.

Welcome back. Last week, you remember the strange phone message left at the office by someone calling himself the Wayfinder and his weird mention of the black cairn.

Another voice, a recording, kicked in. Both Catrin and Rhys twigged the accent was Welsh, but that it sounded like someone affecting a dramatic, croaky Welsh accent. As Welsh speakers, they could always tell.

"This place is, like, ancient. No sheep or any other animals go near. And the cairn is, like, geometric. Not like the tumbled down ones you normally see. Square, like. The front, at ground level, it's half buried now but if you squint, there is a shape there. Like a door shape. It's just how the stones are arranged, but above that door shape in the stone, there's this figure, a dark smudge that looks like it has long arms and fingers. As if the moss had died in that shape. As if it's locked in the stones. You got to see it, like. And hear it. The wind was blowing and… I swear I could hear something moaning in there. And that night… that night when I woke up at around 3am, something was in my room. I swear to God. I'm no bloody pussy, man, but something had come in. A dark shadow against the window with these long bloody arms. I tell you, that place, that Carn Ddu… you should definitely see it."

So now, here I am with Dr Lester, on the way to a part of the world I don't know very well. And though it's in the UK, and only a few hours from our base in London, as we travel north from the motorway, the look and feel of the landscape is changing into something strange and almost alien. No people. Only a vast landscape with few dwellings. And those that are visible look isolated and small. Little fortresses against whatever lurks in the wild. As we trek up from the very last road which peters out into nothing, literally an end to things, I get the distinct impression that if anywhere has witnessed something unearthly, something ancient and powerful, it's here.

"Don't forget people considered these places of spiritual solitude hugely significant. Perhaps even totems of something truly ancient, a culture, or beings, present long before men arrived."

Thanks for that, John.

Next to me, dressed for the weather, John Lester walks quickly. He's keen to get there. I've been with him on many expeditions, but this time, something else triggers a smile. An excitement. A kind of knowing. Usually, he dismisses people's claims and tales, but not today. Not here. And I know how he feels because this place, this emptiness, is anything but empty. As if the land itself knows we're here.

"Reference to cairns such as these exist in a variety of places. The Vézère Valley in the Dordogne, Anatolia in Turkey."

"What claims?"

"That these places are pre-historic. Remnants of a culture that existed millions of years ago. A non-human culture. They have many names. Gods, demons, elder ones. Take your pick, Georgia."

I look across at John, waiting for him to laugh as he so often does when these words are bandied about. But today, there is no laugh. No smile. Today, I think he means what he says.

Catrin stopped the tape and looked across at Rhys. 'Well?'

'Bloody hell, that's… I don't know. It's wow scary. The way they've done it, as if they don't want to believe. Makes it more believable somehow. But they're actors, right?'

'They want you to believe it's all true, yes.'

'It's working. I want more.'

Catrin wrinkled her nose. 'It gets weird from then on. Everything is based on what went on in other episodes. Stuff about a strange cult in Russia, someone who can pull sound out of rocks, shadows that appear in every photograph of a place over a fifty-year period no one can explain. The point is, there are lots of fans out there. People ready to believe all this stuff.'

'Like the missing women?'

Catrin held out both her hands, palms up.

'But what the hell were they hoping to find?' Rhys continued, his voice half an octave higher than before.

'Something, nothing. Maybe some selfies to prove they'd been there. People do the same thing at Dobbie's grave in Freshwater West.'

'Dobbie the elf? Harry Potter Dobbie?'

'Exactly,' Catrin explained. 'But there is no Dobbie. No such things as elves. All that's there are a couple of stones left where they shot the scene for a film. But it's a powerful story that moved a generation of people. They want to be a part of it. No matter how small that part is. It's the nature of fandom.'

Rhys stifled a grimace. But not enough to prevent Catrin from noticing.

'What?'

Rhys shrugged. 'Gil said never to type fandom into Google. He says it's too easy to misspell it.'

'Misspell it as what?'

'Femdom. I didn't know it was such a big… thing.'

Catrin squeezed her eyes shut. 'Don't tell me you typed in femdom?'

Rhys nodded. Rapid, regretful little shakes. 'I was in the office. That was the longest twenty seconds of my life trying to get back off the page that loaded.'

The DS shook her head. 'Learn anything?'

'Only to type in fandom really, really carefully.'

Catrin smiled. A classic Gil/Rhys interaction. Her fellow sergeant loaded the bullets and sat back to watch the DC fire them, hoping one might explode in the chamber.

'Right, but no more Stone Tape Files. I've had enough of that twaddle.' She kept her gaze forward, ignoring the little sceptical glance that Rhys threw her. 'How about Radio Six?'

'Fine,' Rhys said. They'd got past The Salutation pub in Pontargothi now and he pushed his foot forward and nudged the Audi smoothly up to sixty. 'I'll get us there as soon as I can.'

'Just make sure we arrive in one piece. I'm going to see if I can get hold of Lucy Pargeter's work. Someone might have something useful.'

In the end, it proved a fruitless exercise. Lucy had booked a week off. No one was expecting to hear from her, but if they did, they'd be sure to let Catrin know.

Rhys drove on and headed up the valley. Both officers kept one eye on the weather. No rain yet. With a bit of luck, they'd get up to the cairn and back before the showers that were promised got to them.

An hour later, after a few tunes they both hummed along to, Rhys pulled the Audi into a lay-by. Catrin, map open on her lap next to her phone, leaned forward to peer through the windscreen and the rolling moorland and the dark hills beyond.

'According to this, it's through that saddle and around that bigger hill. A couple of miles, at least. I think I can see a sheep track up ahead going in just about the right direction.'

'I'll get our coats from the boot. We still have a signal, right?'

'One bar,' Catrin replied.

'That doesn't sound too good.' Rhys opened the door and let in a waft of cool air.

Catrin packed the map away into a clear plastic folder. She'd been on enough of these jaunts to come prepared for weather and lousy signals that meant Google Maps might become useless at any second.

She could think of better ways to spend the morning than yomping through tussocks on the way to find an ancient pile of stones and the secrets contained within.

Living or dead.

She shivered, sufficiently self-aware to realise that not all of that little shudder was to do with the sudden chill wind that filled the car.

CHAPTER TWENTY-FOUR

W<small>ARLOW</small> <small>KNEW</small> they'd get a warrant. The Thorleys' solicitor would know that, too. You got warrants from magistrates when you could show that a crime had been committed or that evidence of an offence would be found on the premises being searched. The Thorleys would not have a leg to stand on, having discharged an unlicensed firearm. There were reasonable grounds to believe that there might be another gun there. The Police and Criminal Evidence Act also allowed entry in order to arrest some-one, even without a warrant.

Not that Warlow wanted to arrest any of the Thorleys. But they didn't need to be aware of that. Now that he had two mispers and a definite link between the black cairn and Foynw boy, he didn't want to waste any more time.

Gil drove in his Volvo.

'I'm going to throw this out there. Feel free to shoot me down if you want.' Gil took the quieter back road through Capel Dewi along the valley floor.

'That's an offer I don't get every day.'

'We're going through Llandeilo. I'll ask the Lady

Anwen to fix us up some sarnies and I can pick them up on the way through. It's already lunchtime.'

'You and Rhys are bloody obsessed with your stomachs.'

'Leave *my* stomach out of it, if you please. I'm thinking of yours. I've seen you hangry.'

'I am never hangry,' Warlow said. 'Though I would murder a sandwich now.'

'Right, well, we'll be in Llandeilo in fifteen minutes. I can get her to fix up a flask and some lunch.'

'I was waiting for you to say picnic.'

'Wouldn't dream of it. We're not on holiday.'

'Tell Rhys that. Every journey is an adventure for him.'

'He'll learn.'

'Okay,' Warlow said. 'We'll stop for fifteen minutes.'

Gil did a double take. 'I wasn't expecting that response.'

Warlow had his phone out and was texting. 'Drop me off at that coffee place on the main street.'

'Really? What's this? An assignation?'

'Dee Sanderson. She's free for coffee.'

'Tidy,' Gil said with suitably raised eyebrows.

'Wash your mouth out, DS Jones. This is purely business.'

The little courtyard at Pitchfork and Provision was empty except for one couple and their dog, who sat in outside gear (except for the dog), dressed for walking. Warlow pushed open the door to the little café and waved at Dee who was waiting for him, a coffee already bought and on the table in front of his empty seat. The aroma of freshly baked sourdough bread hit him as he navigated a way between the occupied tables.

'Thanks for doing this, Dee,' Warlow said.

'Pleasure. Who could turn down a request for help from a Detective Chief Inspector?'

'A lot of people. The kind I often mix with, anyway.'

'I hope I am not a lot of people.'

Warlow smiled. 'You're not. A lot of people aren't lecturers in theology.'

'Ooh,' Dee said and sipped coffee from a cup. 'Now I am very intrigued.'

'The Friends of Light?'

Dee didn't answer immediately. She weighed up the question and tilted her head. 'Do you want the general answer or the philosophical one?'

'They have a retreat up in the Doethie Valley. I want some background.'

Dee nodded. 'Drink your coffee before it gets cold.' She nodded at his cup. 'You can listen and drink at the same time, I take it?'

'I'm a man of many talents.' He lifted his cup.

'They're an offshoot of Christian Science. Their numbers have dwindled, but one or two branches, FOL being one of those branches, have sprouted like fungus from that rotten root. The Friends of Light are one of the more successful ones. They've plugged into the holistic trend, offering stays in exclusive places, like the one in the Doethie Valley. They've stayed away from religion, though they are as proselytising as any religion you can think of. It's all about pure water to drink, supplements in the diet, strict absence of any pharmaceutical corruption. All allied to meditation as cleansing the body of disease. Accessing one's own truth. So, long walks in the hills, etc. And for that, they charge a bomb.'

'Sounds like a halfway house between a hospice and a rehab unit.'

'You would not be far wrong. But they've successfully applied for charitable status. Just like a religion.'

'Don't you have to believe in God, or a god?'

'You do not.'

Warlow considered this. He sipped more coffee. It was good, the crema just right.

'There's been a lot of debate about exactly that,' Dee added. 'Secular versus non-secular. Worship versus religion. They are considered separate entities. But as for the Friends of Light, what they advocate is a worship of the self allied to nature. To shine a light onto the truth of their existence.'

'Sounds like horse twaddle.'

She raised her eyebrows. 'Lucrative horse twaddle, don't forget. That's an essay title I often give to my students whenever we discuss these things.'

'How dangerous are they?'

Dee leaned forward over her cup, elbows on the table. 'They're happy to take money from people who may not be able to afford it. But then, that's the same for all snake-oil sales agents. The fact is that their exclusivity allows them to be choosy. They promise nothing. Only an opportunity for sick people to commune with themselves.'

'They told me their last guest was a double amputee.'

'Then he or she would not need the yoga and long walks sessions.'

Warlow puffed out his cheeks.

Dee looked amused by his discomfort. 'There is one thing about them that might be of interest. They have a policy of accepting everyone who wants to, to work for them. No matter what their background.'

'Illegal immigrants?'

'They have done that. And got into trouble for it. But these days they play the champions of the oppressed card. The twitterati love them for it. So, ex-convicts, people with troubled backgrounds. They espouse a doctrine of open to all.'

'Very… laudable. Is that the word I'm looking for?'

'Or cynical. Take your pick.'

She kept talking for another five minutes. Warlow finished his coffee, thanked Dee for the information, and walked down Rhosmaen Street in Llandeilo towards the primary schools and a Co-op. He'd arranged for Gil to pick him up at the garage.

'Worthwhile?' Gil asked when he pulled up.

'I'd say so,' Warlow replied. 'Confirmation that our Friends of Light are all bollocks. They hide under the shield of charity and reap the benefits of a gullible audience desperate to believe in anything but boring old, difficult, uncomfortable scientific fact. One of their founders was an Austrian. Did you know that?'

Gil shook his head, not fighting the little smile that came, anticipating what was to come.

'So, our Friends are the Austrians, if not the Swiss, of the spiritual, quasi-religious movements that have sprung up all over Europe. Always on the periphery, wanting to be neutral. And we all know what the Austrians are famous for.'

'Ooh, a riddle,' Gil replied. 'Skiing. White horses. There's a pub here named after them. Then there's the Danube and, let me think… oh yes, that other feller, uh, Hitler.'

'Exactly. At least the Swiss have bloody chocolate,' Warlow muttered.

Gil held up a cool bag. 'Let me calm that troubled soul of yours, Evan. I have here an excellent haul. We have tinned salmon sandwiches, egg mayo, and ham and tomato.'

Warlow took the passenger seat with a shake of his head. 'Who else are we feeding?'

'We might bump into Rhys, in which case only crumbs will remain.'

Never a truer word was spoken.

But, as Gil negotiated the roundabout and headed out

towards Llandovery, Warlow's thoughts returned to the Friends of Light. A light they were keen to extoll the virtues of, but which suddenly seemed murky and dim indeed.

———

TUSSOCKS.

A great word. Though Rhys came up with a few others that sounded very similar, especially in the last three letters, but which had very different meanings as he and Catrin made their way over the moorland. They climbed slowly but steadily until their car became a Dinky toy below them. They struggled through the saddle, keeping away from the very lowest point where the ground became too boggy with peat, before ascending more steeply to a rise where they both stopped to catch their breath.

And that catching was part exertion, but it was also a result of the sight that greeted them.

Carn Ddu stood above them but below another hill, this one steeper, its rocky face freshly scarred by a landslip of brown earth. The cairn itself stood only a dozen feet high and, from their vantage point, looked remarkably like the open maw of a mouth into the mountain behind. But their perspective shifted as they made the final ascent. Though not steep, the going remained tough as they stepped over and through the thick grass. Finally, fifty minutes after leaving the car, they arrived to stand staring at Carn Ddu.

As cairns went in this ancient landscape, this one appeared very well preserved.

'Someone must maintain it,' Rhys said.

'All the others I've seen look half collapsed.' Catrin looked around for signs of other stone piles, but there were none. 'Or are misshapen pyramid-shaped piles of stones. This one is… geometric?'

The soil had claimed some of the structure's foundations. Moss and grass had grown over the bottom stones that were also mottled with green and yellow lichen.

'I reckon it would have been even taller when it was built. Originally, I mean.'

'Hmm.' Catrin put her hands on her hips.

Rhys walked around to stand between the cairn and the hill behind. With the spilled scree at his back, he lifted a hand to shade his eyes from the brightness of the luminous sky.

'Wow,' the word escaped his lips.

'What?' Catrin demanded, walking around to join him.

Rhys pointed. 'See, there, the lighter stone making a kind of frame for a—'

'Don't say door,' Catrin warned him. 'This isn't the set of the Lord of the blasted Rings.'

'But it looks like a door. Kind of, doesn't it?' Rhys grinned, his voice breathless with enthusiasm.

But Catrin's eyes had drifted up above the lighter stone lines, towards a dark shape like a stain on the stone above. It stretched all the way to the top. Some trick of algae growth or water staining. Whatever the cause, it appeared to be a six-foot-tall stick figure with a strange oblong head and long arms with splayed fingers at the end. She, too, raised a hand to shield her eyes from the glare of the sky, and instantly, the figure disappeared.

'See it?' Rhys asked.

'Sort of. I can see something.'

'It's like a peat stain.'

'What the hell is it doing at the top of the cairn, then?'

'No idea. Unless someone painted it.'

'For the sake of a podcast?'

Rhys shrugged.

'Well, we found it. And that means those two women could find it. Forget the damned Stone Tapes podcast. Let's have a quick look around.'

'Totally,' Rhys said, and shifted his gaze to the ground. He noticed right away some tracks. 'A quad bike has been here.'

'Foynwboy?' Catrin threw out the suggestion.

'Could be. Let's split up. I'll do this side and west, you do the other two sides.'

'Good idea,' Catrin said. The wind had picked up as they'd climbed. A blustery thing that, though it wasn't cold, worried at her ears which, she knew, would feel the chill before any other part of her.

Slowly, both officers began combing the area around the base of the cairn, looking for any sign that someone had been there in the last couple of days.

'Think it's worth shouting out their names?' Rhys asked.

'What harm could it do?'

'Lucy? Nola?'

In the vast open space, Rhys's voice got ripped up by the wind and thrown into the heavens.

And though he repeated it twice more, there came no answer. Only the hiss of the tussocks as they shifted and rustled in the breeze.

CHAPTER TWENTY-FIVE

WARLOW PRESSED the button on the intercom outside Foynw. While he waited for a reply, he turned to Gil. 'I'm not going to call this place Foynw anymore. I'm going to refer to it by its original name. Pencraf.'

Gil nodded. 'Good idea.'

A click and a hiss from the little box on the post drew the DCI's attention. 'Hello?' This time, Nathan answered.

'It's DCI Warlow, Nathan. We need to talk to you.'

'Dad says I can't.'

'I know what he says. But something's happened, and we need your help.'

'What?'

'We have some missing walkers. We think they've gone up to Carn Ddu. You know the black cairn, don't you?'

Silence.

'Nathan?'

'I know about it, yeah.'

'Then you can help us—'

'Nathan, who the hell is that?' A different voice this time. Not as loud, but a hundred percent more urgent.

'It's the police, Dad. They want my help.'

'I bet they bloody do.' William Thorley's voice again, strident this time, approaching the intercom. 'You're not coming in without a warrant.'

'Fine. My officers are with the magistrates now. So, we could tear your place apart looking for another gun if that's what you'd like.'

'There is no other gun,' William Thorley's angry response came out through gritted teeth.

'So you say. But do I have to remind you about the drone?'

'I've sorted that—'

Warlow pressed on, 'I don't have a warrant on me. Not yet. And I don't want to tear your place apart, either, believe me. But this case is becoming increasingly complicated. A dead recluse and two missing walkers that Nathan might know the whereabouts of.'

'How? How the hell does he know?'

'Nathan?' Warlow asked through the intercom.

Voices off. Mutterings. William Thorley's voice raised in disbelief. Nathan's more petulant. Eventually, the elder Thorley's came back. 'Jesus Christ, you people.'

'It's a matter of urgency now, Mr Thorley. I can promise you one thing. If you let us in, if we can get on with what needs to be done, we'll be out of your hair quicker. If you insist on a warrant, I promise you that everything will be disrupted. We'll take computers, phones, the lot.'

'You can't—'

'Yes, I can. And yes, I will.'

Another silence. Warlow wasn't sure if the crackling coming across the speaker was static or William Thorley's knuckles cracking. But there were no further words from him. Only a click as the gates opened for the second time.

They could only guess at the kind of conversation that had taken place between the Thorleys in the short time it took for the gates to open and for Gil to drive the Volvo in and park. But something had changed. Angela Thorley stood in the doorway of the converted barn. This time with the door wide open behind her.

'You'd better come in,' she said as the two officers got out of the car. 'Will's put the kettle on.' She turned and walked inside.

Will? Kettle? Come in?

'Pinch me, will you?' Warlow said as an aside to Gil.

'Don't count those pullets yet. They may be waiting in there with two shotguns,' was Gil's cheery rejoinder.

But they were not. William Thorley stood near a dresser, arms folded, a sucking-a-lemon demeanour firmly painted on his face. He busied himself with making tea once Gil and Warlow had given their preferences. Angela Thorley sat next to Nathan, Gil and Warlow on the other side.

All very amiable.

'We appreciate this, Nathan,' Warlow said.

Nathan shrugged.

Gil slid over a sheet of paper. A copy of the one Catrin had posted up. 'F.O. Yourenotwelcomeboy,' Gil said. 'Is that you, Nathan?'

Both Angela and William Thorley frowned. Nathan turned to them and shrugged. 'It's a podcast.'

'So, it is you?' Gil persisted.

Nathan nodded. 'I seen one or two people up at the cairn since they talked about it.'

'When were you last up there?'

'Couple of weeks ago. S'not easy to get to. Pain in the arse to walk it.'

'But you go up there on the quad?'

Nathan nodded.

'You say it's a pain to walk it?' Gil asked. 'Is the way dangerous?'

'Depends. There's a few sinkholes, mind. Peat bogs and the like. Best you know where you're going.'

Gil exchanged a glance with Warlow.

'So, you haven't been up there this last week? Haven't seen two women on the trails?' Gil asked.

Nathan shook his head again. Slowly, in no hurry. And his eyes flicked only once from Gil to Warlow. If he was lying, the boy must have had some training.

'Any chance you could take me up there?' Warlow asked.

'What?' Nathan blinked several times.

'How long would it take us? From here? On your quad?'

Nathan shrugged. 'Twenty minutes.'

'I'd appreciate it.'

Another shrug. 'Fine by me.'

'Hang on a minute.' Nathan's father stepped forward. 'He's under no obligation—'

Gil rounded on him. 'None of you are under any obligation. You're right. But we'd appreciate the help. A lot of what we do depends on people helping.'

'Not much difference between helping and interfering in my book,' William Thorley muttered.

'Perhaps you ought to take that book back to the library and check out a new one.' Gil spoke evenly and his eyes never left Thorley's, who, this time, didn't answer.

'Nathan?' Warlow asked. He was playing into Nathan's hands here. Entering his world. But Warlow didn't see this as a dangerous strategy. If anything, judging from the ear bashing he would have been getting at home for shooting the drone, the boy needed a bit of an ego tweak.

Slowly, Nathan nodded and smiled. 'Okay. Let's do it. I'll get the quad sorted while you have your tea.'

Rhys and Catrin had covered the ground around the cairn. They'd gone about a hundred yards out and walked back in a grid pattern. Now they were both back in front of the stack. Neither of them had found anything other than the odd sheep.

'What about the hill behind?' Catrin eyed the mound with little enthusiasm.

'I'm sure I read something about some caves up here. Hideouts for the resistance.'

'Wait.' Catrin stopped walking. 'What resistance? Don't tell me the Germans invaded—'

'Not the Germans. The Normans. Guerrilla warfare up here, there was.'

'So, now we're going into caves?'

'We ought to have a peep, don't you think?'

With a heave of her shoulders, Catrin waved Rhys on and followed him towards the hill. The path they took wound left around its base. Rhys took his time examining the rocky outcrops and dips and hollows. When he eventually found a thin gap between the rocks, Catrin stood behind him, hands on hips, catching her breath.

'Is this it?'

'Could be. I mean, I don't have exact instructions here.'

'Hardly a cave, is it?'

Rhys shrugged and squeezed through the gap.

'Well?' Catrin asked when he'd disappeared from view.

'Come and have a look.'

Sighing, Catrin followed and stepped into a dark, chilly space. Rhys had his phone torch on. It was a cave. Room size, taller and wider at its mouth, where they stood, petering out into a narrow area of collapsed boulders a few feet away. Rhys made for the narrow end.

'I think there's a gap. Pretty narrow, but…'

'But what?' Catrin demanded. 'What would possess

two women to squeeze through a tiny hole into the middle of a mountain?'

'The lure of the unknown?' Rhys offered.

'Don't you start.'

'Lucy? Nola?' Rhys's voice echoed through the chamber.

'I hardly think that—'

'Shh.' Rhys froze. 'I heard something. Lucy, Nola?' He leaned forward and aimed the light into the narrow space before calling out once more. 'Lucy? Nola?'

Catrin heard it then. A scurrying noise. Coming from beyond that small hole at the funnel end of the cave. A definite sound of something hurrying across the ground.

'Rhys, get back.'

'There's someone there…'

Someone? Or Something.

'I don't like this, Rhys. I don't like this at all.'

Something moved in the darkness. Something pale in Rhys's beam. And then two yellow eyes reflected back the light.

'Shit,' said Rhys and tried to stand up just as something leapt up at him out of the hole.

He fell back, yelling, arms ups flailing against the… something.

Catrin could only stand in horror as it all unfolded. It took all of her willpower not to turn and run. The thing, whatever it was, scrabbled on the rocks and the floor. Rhys's phone had clattered away, face down, and the cave was pitch black.

But the scrabbling noise got louder. Whatever this was, it was running right at Catrin.

No, not at her, past her, towards the opening.

She stared into the blackness, wanting to see, but not wanting it to be something stick-like with long splayed fingers.

The bleat gave the game away.

Catrin looked down as a panicked sheep scuttled past, brushing her legs in its hurry to get out of the cave.

And at the moment, all Catrin could think of was how glad she was that Gil had not been here to witness that.

'Rhys, you okay?'

'A bloody sheep. What the hell was a sheep doing in there?'

'No idea but I wish it hadn't bothered.'

They both heard the engine drone at exactly the same time. Catrin switched on her own phone light and reached out to help Rhys up. He moaned.

'Are you alright?'

'Yeah,' he muttered disconsolately. 'I bet you the floor is littered with sheep poo. I expect it'll be all over my trousers.'

'Someone is coming.'

'I can hear that.'

They exited the cave and hurried back the way they'd come, around the hill and then down towards the cairn. They were thirty yards away when, from the east, a quad bike appeared over the horizon and made its way towards Carn Ddu.

By the time the two officers got there, both quad riders had dismounted.

'Where the hell have you two been?' asked Warlow.

'Long story, sir,' Catrin said.

'Really? Rhys looks like he's been rolling in something green and unpleasant and you look like you've just seen a ghost.'

'Goat, sir.'

'What?'

'Another Sergeant Jones's joke, sir.' Rhys put on a toothless smile. 'A man goes to the doctor's and says he can't tell the difference between a ghost and a goat. The doctor says you must be kidding.'

Warlow glanced at Catrin. 'Has he hit his head?'

'Amongst other things, sir, yes.'

'That explains it. Nathan here was kind enough to bring me up. It's a trek.'

'You aren't kidding, sir,' Rhys said.

Warlow's lids slitted.

'Oh, no, sir, I didn't mean that… not this time, sir,' Rhys backpeddled.

'Any sign of the women?' Warlow asked, bringing things back to what they were there for.

Catrin shook her head. Warlow examined the cairn. 'So, this is what all the fuss is about?'

'Can you really hear moaning from inside it?' Catrin asked Nathan.

He shook his head. 'Not from inside it. But sometimes the wind moans, anyway.'

'Right, well, you two get back,' Warlow instructed. 'Nathan here will run me back to Pencraf.'

'Where, sir?'

'The house Nathan now lives in. Its proper name. When you get to your car, head for Rhandirmwyn and wherever the PolSA's set up. We can meet there. Save us going all the way back to HQ for now.'

Warlow turned to Nathan. 'Is there anywhere else they might have gone to?'

'There's a cave—'

'Been there. Done that, got the sheep poo,' Rhys said.

'Then there isn't anything else up here,' Nathan said.

Warlow nodded. 'Okay. We'll leave the rest for the search team. Off you go.'

Rhys and Catrin began walking back down the way they'd come up.

Warlow turned to Nathan. 'Right, Drive, let me have a ten-minute wander and we'll head back.'

Nathan nodded, and Warlow saw that so long as he had the quad, he was happy. Maybe his father had seen that, too. As parents, you did what you could to help your kids. And it surely was difficult for a seventeen-year-old alone here in the hills. Possibly even frustrating enough to accost two young women out in the wilds... but he didn't think so. And Nathan had a hormonal escape route. While he and his father had gone out to prepare the quad, Warlow had learnt from Angela Thornley that they still had a flat in Bristol. And once every couple of months, Nathan went back with his mother for a long weekend. The deal was any sign of drug-taking meant no quad biking. So far, she'd said, as a bargaining chip, it had worked well.

Warlow turned to regard the two young officers getting smaller as they walked away and then turned to study the cairn.

So, this is what all the fuss is about, is it?

He took his phone out and began taking a few snaps.

CHAPTER TWENTY-SIX

Nola had been crying.

Though mewling might have been a better word to describe the noise in Lucy's opinion. Whatever injury she'd suffered, and Lucy suspected she'd lost consciousness when Humpty Dumpty hit her and she'd fallen, she'd made a partial recovery. Enough to struggle into a sitting position with her hands locked tight behind her and chained to a metal stanchion, just like Lucy had been.

Nola whimpered when she first came around. Whimpered and panicked. Growling in animalistic fear and horror through the tape.

It took a while before she'd responded to Lucy's muffled notifications. Eventually, Nola had turned her head to look over her shoulder.

Their eyes locked. And that was when the enormity of her situation hit home. When Nola's mewling began.

They'd tried communicating. At least Lucy had. But her words, or noises, through lips compressed and immovable under the tight tape, were meaningless.

And so, they'd given up and sat, slumped, waiting.

Yet, now they were not alone in that waiting. Not

completely. Something else had crept into their prison to sit with them. Torture them.

Thirst.

Lucy went over and over it in her head. They'd had a cup of tea ten minutes before Humpty turned up. The last time either of them had taken in any fluids. By her reckoning, they'd been locked up for three days. Sunday, Monday, Tuesday and today was Wednesday.

Needing to pee had been bad. Needing to drink was a thousand times worse.

Behind the tape, Lucy's mouth felt parched and her lips were already cracking.

Though she tried not to think about it, she kept wondering how long a person could survive with nothing to drink. Food, that didn't matter so much. But water was different. She should know. Hugo, her boyfriend, was obsessed with survivalist programmes on TV. *Man vs Wild, Alone, The Island*, he watched them all. More than once. He'd even curated a list of his best bits.

Hugo.

Lucy squeezed her eyes shut. She didn't want to think about Hugo. It hurt almost as much as the pee pain in her ureters and kidney had. Except Hugo pain was centred somewhere in her chest.

No. Thinking of him didn't help. But she couldn't not think of him. Of what he might be doing right now. Texting her to ask why she hadn't responded? Even though she'd told him that their 'Stranger Things cabin' probably didn't have Wi-Fi.

Yet, the actual time remained vague guesswork. She'd worked out only that it was Wednesday and still light and well into the day. Hugo would be planning his evening. Maybe messaging a friend to meet up for a drink…

Drink.

Oh, God, she was thirsty. So thirsty she would have

drunk a muddy pool dry. Thirsty enough to drink her own urine like the survivalists did.

'Mmmm!' Nola made a noise. A new, urgent noise.

'Mm?'

'Mmm! Mmm!'

Nola's mumbling brought Lucy back from her musings. And above the moaning… a noise?

An engine. Rolling tyres on leaves. The engine dying. Footsteps, followed by the rusty creak of a metal door and… there he was. Silhouetted against the light in the open door.

Him. She knew it was him. It had to be because he'd walked straight in with no hesitation, hadn't called out. Humpty Dumpty back again. Her eyes fell to his hands. One held a plastic bag, the other something small and silver. A Stanley knife.

He walked towards Lucy. She shook her head, made herself as small as she could, mewling too now, just like Nola. He knelt and brought the knife up to her face and pressed the blade flat against her flesh.

'Stop that noise.'

She did. In her head, the only noise heard now was her own snotty, rapid breathing through her nostrils. She followed his movements with her terrified eyes, her whole body trembling with fear. He reached into the bag and took out a litre bottle of water and unscrewed it. Then he grabbed her hair and yanked her head back. A shuddering image appeared. The dark outline of his features framed by a hoodie against the light in the open doorway. The knife moved quickly towards her mouth. She squealed and squeezed her eyes shut and felt the pressure on her lips as he cut a horizontal slit in the tape. And then she felt something else, something in her mouth. Smooth and small.

A straw.

He pulled her shoulders up and put the bottle between

her folded legs. Close enough for her to bow her head and get the straw in.

And drink.

Water. Cold and clear and fresh.

She heard his weight shift and saw his outline move away. But she didn't follow him. All she could do was drink greedily. When she eventually looked up, Nola was doing exactly the same. She'd have seen what he'd done and not struggled. Humpty stood up.

'Good girls. Drink up. Next time I come, we'll play some games. I promise.'

His voice. But not the one he'd used at the cabin. A different accent, perhaps?

Then he turned, and his footsteps faded. The door closed, and they were plunged into the gloom once more.

Lucy drank again. More slowly. She needed to make this last.

But with thirst driven away, and with Humpty's promise to come back and play some games, something else crawled in to take its place.

Sharp and bright, and fresh as a new wound, fear blossomed like a dark flower and pushed all thoughts of Hugo far from her mind.

With thirst no longer there to preoccupy her, there was nothing to do but wait for the sound of him returning. And the games he wanted to play.

Lucy wanted to scream. But there was no one to hear. Except Nola who flopped onto her side again. Quietly to herself, Lucy began to cry.

CHAPTER TWENTY-SEVEN

THE POLSA HAD SET up in a storage room at the back of the pub in Rhandirmwyn. The roots of the village went back a very long way. Romans had been here and dug lead out of the ground. But they had buggered off a long time ago. Now people came for the walking and the wilds. And to look at the Pwllpriddog Oak, a seven-hundred-year-old hollow tree reputed to be the hiding place of a king. Local legend held that the pub took its name from that same tree: The Royal Oak. Gil thought they were missing a trick, not capitalising on the tree side of things, especially with the Yanks.

'Dare I ask in what way?' Warlow shot him a glance tinged with anticipatory regret.

'I'd have renamed it the Royal Oak Hotel California. You know. You check in but you never leaf.' Gil delivered this with a completely straight face.

Warlow could only shake his head. 'Christ, I ought to get Rhys to arrest you for that as soon as we meet up.'

They found a spot to park the Volvo and joined the plethora of police vans and cars that lined the narrow roads. They'd accepted tea earlier from the now much more amenable Thorleys and demolished the Lady Anwen's sandwiches in the car in a lay-by before getting to the pub. Lunch, as expected by Gil, had been late. But hunger was no longer an issue.

The search team had been briefed by Catrin and Rhys, but Warlow felt the need to stick his head into the room and shake hands with the PolSA. Ken Morris had worked recently with Warlow on the Osian Howells kidnapping case. He was a no-nonsense, stocky sergeant with experience to spare. Warlow was genuinely glad to see him.

'You again, sir,' Morris said as they shook hands. 'Getting to be a habit.'

'Not by choice, I can assure you. Difficult terrain, this one.'

Morris nodded, his hunter's eyes behind the thick lenses of his glasses un-fazed. 'We've got a good few hours of daylight, so we're about to get cracking. We'll make Carn Ddu the centre point. Work out from there.'

Boxes and crates had been moved to one wall of the room and stacked, and a table set up in the middle with a map on an easel stand. Warlow nodded his approval. 'Right. I'll leave you to it.'

He found Rhys and Catrin ensconced in an alcove in one of the pub's back rooms. They'd snaffled a couple of tables and sat with their laptops open. Both had drinks in front of them. Rhys had a ripped open, and empty, packet of cheese and onion crisps at his elbow. Gil came around the corner from the bar with two glasses clinking with ice.

'Diet Coke, as requested.' He set the drinks down and Warlow and he pulled up chairs.

'The Wi-Fi is decent,' Catrin said.

'That's something.' Warlow sipped his drink.

'Any joy with the Thorleys, sir?' Rhys asked, looking up from his screen.

'Joy and the Thorleys somehow do not jibe in my

dictionary, Rhys. But Nathan proved to be remarkably cooperative. And the father just stayed out of the way with the threat of a warrant in the air.'

'Do you think he's involved with the missing women, sir?' Catrin asked. Blunt, but to the point.

'Nathan? I don't. The link is Carn Ddu, but that's all it is. I had a chat with him while we rode the quad. Or rather, I had a shout at him, because of the engine noise and wind. He's into conspiracy theories and the occult.'

'So were the missing women,' Gil pointed out.

'Let's just say he's not off the list, but he isn't on the top of mine, either.' Warlow nodded at Catrin's screen. 'Anything on the car?'

'The Nissan Juke seems to have disappeared off the face of the earth, sir. No trace on ANPR. But the bad news is that the press got wind of the death of George Marsden. Superintendent Buchanan is making a statement at 2.30pm.'

Gil glanced at his watch. 'Just about now, then.'

'That will mean the bastards will be here as soon as they can gear up their vans,' Warlow muttered.

'Like jackals on a wildebeest carcass,' Gil said.

He earned a grimace from Catrin.

'It would be good if we could find these women before they did. A murdered old man is tragic enough, but two missing women… it'll be a feeding frenzy. Throw in Carn Ddu and…' Warlow's words petered out, and he fell silent.

'Do you think the car is that important, then, sir?' Rhys asked.

Warlow shot him a glance.

Rhys blinked.

But it was a bloody good question, so the DCI peeled it apart for him. 'They must have got here in the car. And under any other circumstances, it's a good bet they might have ticked the cairn box and moved on.'

'But there's the phone and the bloody kitchen towel,' Gil said.

'Exactly.' Warlow nodded.

'What if one of them really had a nosebleed and panicked? I have a friend whose partner gets nosebleeds,' Rhys said. 'Sometimes it takes hours to stop. What if they dropped the phone in their rush to get to a hospital?'

Warlow considered this. As scenarios went, it had all kinds of flaws, but it had to be worth checking out. 'Okay. Nearest hospital is still Glangwili in Carmarthen. Rhys, give them a ring. See if either of the women pitched up there. I think it's about as likely as you leaving a crumb uneaten in that crisp packet, but let's eliminate it.'

Rhys got up, phone in hand. 'I'll do it outside, sir. Less noise.'

———

RHYS GOT through to A and E reception with no difficulty. He used his cop card and got put through to a charge nurse. From the background noise, the place sounded busy. He explained what he was after without giving too much away. Rhys knew a few nurses and had a soft spot for all of them, as he did with anyone who dealt with the public in all their glory on a daily basis. He'd had recourse to depend upon the NHS's help on more than one occasion, what with rugby injuries and on-the-job injuries which, since working with DCI Warlow, panned out at a ratio of fifty-fifty.

From talking with the DCI, whose son was an ENT surgeon, Rhys got the impression that the NHS was a very imperfect institution, but one that no one wanted to be without. Like everything, it could be better, he supposed. But within it, like the police force, he was pretty sure everyone did their absolute best. Rhys had some insight into realising this was a naïve assumption because he'd already come across a few rotten apples within his own profession. Yet, he wanted to believe that most people had an altruistic streak. Otherwise, what was the bloody point? As DCI Warlow was always pointing out, no one deserves to be stabbed or strangled or kidnapped, whether they wear a crown, or a scum-of-the-earth T-shirt with misplaced pride. Their job, as police, was to find out the truth and apply a little justice to an unjust world.

The charge nurse came back to the phone.

'No, sorry. No one by the name of Nola O'Brien or Lucy Pargeter has booked in over the last three days, was it?'

'Yes.'

'No. Can't help you. Sorry.'

Rhys said his thank yous and stood outside the pub watching the comings and goings of the search teams. A thin rain had begun, driven in by the westerlies. He didn't envy these Uniforms the trek up to Carn Ddu, inspecting every inch of ground in a line across the landscape. Not in this weather.

He stood in the lee of an overhang out of the rain. Through a window into the pub, he could see people tucking in to a late lunch. He'd made do with a couple of sandwiches and crisps. Tonight, his mother was making her Wednesday special: pasta night. Anything from prawn linguine to pork ragout with penne.

Rhys let out a sigh. He still hadn't broached the subject of his leaving date to move in with Gina.

Gina.

On impulse, he dialled a familiar number. Not another mobile. A good old-fashioned landline.

'Hello?' a woman's voice. Not young.

Mam, Fi y'w e. Rhys.'

'Hello, bach, popeth yn iawn?'

As always, Rhys spoke to his mother in Welsh, their initial exchanges nothing more than standard greetings, although it amused him that his mother still called him "*bach*", little one. An oxymoron if ever there was one, since he was a good fifteen inches taller than she was.

'Yes, all good. I'm in Rhandirmwyn. We've set up in the pub.'

'Alright for some. Remember, you're driving.'

'We don't drink on the job, Mam.'

'No, of course not, *Bach*. It's raining here.'

'And here.'

'You've got your coat, have you?'

Rhys smiled. Here he was, this big bad police officer, well big police officer, being reminded to wear his coat by his mother. 'Always two, Mam. There's the one we have for work and the one you always make me take.'

A silent beat. His mother waited for whatever it was he wanted to say. Rhys waited because even now, he didn't know how to bloody well say it.

Get a grip, man. Spit the damned thing out.

In the end, Mrs Harries broke the impasse. 'By the way, I've got everything bagged up and ready.'

'Bagged up and ready for what?'

'For the move. Gina rang me. She's organised is that girl. I don't know how you caught a hold of her, but I wouldn't let go if I were you.'

Panic gripped him. Had he forgotten some family commitment? 'What's happening a week Saturday?'

'Honestly, Rhys, sometimes I do despair. A week Saturday is when you and Gina move into your new place. It'll be a busy day, so she asked me to get your stuff ready and I'll make sandwiches and bring them over for you and your helpers.'

'Sandwiches? My stuff?'

'Yes, the things you need to take with you. Bedclothes

for the spare room there. A few knick-knacks that I don't want. Your pants, which I certainly don't want.'

Relief made him turn his face up to the sky and heave out a sigh with the phone held away from him so she wouldn't hear. But he brought it back to his ear quickly. 'Mam… that's…'

'What?'

'That's just brilliant. I was meaning to ask you all that.'

'But it slipped your mind. I know you're busy, *Bach*. Your dad will be here to help load up the van, but Gina says her brothers will help you offload. Your dad's back isn't special.'

'No. Not special.'

'Anyway, I wanted you to have peace of mind. Right, what is it you wanted to tell me?'

Rhys grinned. *Gina, you beauty.*

'Rhys?' Mrs Harries pressed him.

'Me, oh, nothing really. Only that I might be a bit late coming back tonight. So, best you plate up supper.'

'Chicken and broccoli pasta bake. It'll keep.'

'Brilliant. Okay, I better go.'

'Remember to wear that coat.'

Rhys ended the call and swallowed down the saliva that had flooded his mouth at the mention of the chicken and broccoli bake.

He was still grinning when Gil appeared in front of him. 'Ah, there you are.' He frowned. 'What's up with you? Why the big grin?'

'No joy with the hospital, but then I spoke to my mother.'

'And she told you what was for tea, right?'

Rhys's mouth fell open. 'How do you know?'

'Rhys, I can read you like a book. And not one of the hard ones full of streams of consciousness Irish poets, I'm talking more… DC comics. Not much writing, only pictures.'

'Thanks, sarge,' Rhys said, not sure if he'd just been insulted.

'Come on, over to my car.'

Rhys followed Gil to the Volvo. 'I almost forgot,' the sergeant said. He pressed a button and the tailgate swung up as they approached. He reached in and removed a nondescript manila cardboard box, about sixteen inches by eight.

'What's this?'

'Present from William Thorley.' Gil stepped back and motioned for Rhys to look. The box had been opened, and all Rhys had to do was peel back the leaves. Inside were two more boxes. Much smaller. White, illustrated with brightly coloured images.

'Wow,' Rhys said, a grin splitting his face.

'Drone?' Gil asked.

'Drone?' Rhys repeated the word as a rhetorical question and a scathing glare at his sergeant. He pulled out one box and held it carefully, like an offering to the gods. 'Not just a drone. This is a Mini 3 Pro. Top of the range. The controller has a built-in screen. No need for an iPhone. You're talking eight hundred quid plus. And he's thrown in the extra battery and spare propellor pack and a carry case.'

Gil started humming 'Jingle bells'.

'Steff is going to be so stoked.' Rhys grinned.

'Good. Well, now that Christmas morning is over, can we go back inside and do some police work?'

'Sounds like a plan, sarge. Sounds like a good plan.'

CHAPTER TWENTY-EIGHT

MOLLY THREW her hockey kit into the back of the Up and turned to look back towards the sports centre for Gwen. They both played. Both regular starters for the college teams. This year would be a tough act to follow since the mixed team won the National Championship at the tournament in Nottingham back in the spring.

Molly stayed fit in the summer, kayaking and hiking with Bryn. But hockey was her winter fix. She would never be the biggest player on the pitch, but she was nippy and lightning fast and still one of the fittest, despite not hitting the gym every other day like some of the girls. Their first game was next week and today they'd had try-outs and a skills session in the drizzle. A reminder of how crap the weather could be. But she'd enjoyed it and offered to give Gwen a lift home. When Molly'd left the changing room, Gwen had been almost ready.

So, what was the holdup?

The rain had eased and now would be a good time for Gwen to come. Had she forgotten? It would be just like her. They got on really well. Gwen was a try-anything hoot. But she could be so dizzy sometimes. Just like her to forget five minutes after being asked.

Molly trotted back the way she'd come, but as she rounded the edge of the building, she came to an abrupt halt.

Gwen was standing outside the entrance to the changing rooms talking to a boy. Molly's normal reaction would have been to shout a greeting, or, in this case, a reminder. But this time, she didn't. The two of them hadn't seen her. People were still leaving the building and the couple's attention kept being drawn to the doors opening and closing.

Quickly, Molly took a step back out of sight, turned on her heel and hurried back to the car, got into the driver's seat and texted her friend.

'*Where R U?*'

'*Coming, Soz. Frgt my file.*'

'*No worries.*'

Five minutes later, Gwen ran across the car park, her kit bag bouncing on one shoulder, backpack on the other, and a blue file folder clutched in one hand. At seventeen, Gwen was still one of those girls who looked too thin. But Molly knew how much she ate, chocolate especially. And thin was filling out nicely into slim with all the right junk. She threw everything into the boot, except the file, and slid into the passenger seat.

'I thought you'd forgotten,' Molly said.

'No way. How could I forget a trip in the catmobile?'

'Got your file, I see.'

'I did. Thank God. I have a Biol essay and all my notes are in there.'

'I saw you talking to Zac.'

Gwen beetled her brows and shrugged at the same time. 'Yeah, you should be thanking me for that.'

'How? He's a total pain.'

'Agreed. He was hanging about. Doing what Zac does.'

'Drugs, you mean?'

'Obviously. So, I told him you and Bryn were still a thing. And that he wasn't in with a chance and that he should stop bugging you.'

Molly searched Gwen's face for the lie, but all she read there was defiance. 'You actually said that?'

'Yeah. Well, it's true, isn't it? We both know he's been hassling you.'

Molly nodded and sighed. 'He has.'

'Well, now that he's been put straight with an arrow through his letch heart, maybe he won't?'

'Aw, thanks, Gwen.'

'*Sin sudar*, as Jakey says.' Jakey was one of Gwen's friends whose Spanish A level studies consisted mainly of trying to translate phrases he liked to use. *Mi burro se ha comido todos los plátanos* being one of his favourites. Molly found it a bit irritating that his greeting was always a statement about his donkey having eaten all the bananas. But *sin sudar* was cool. Everyone said no sweat.

'Now, are we going, or what?'

'We are.' Molly started the car.

Gwen's fingers flew over her phone's screen, texting as she spoke. 'Uh, when are you going up to London, by the way?'

'Bryn's course starts next week. There'll be freshers. I'm staying well away from that. I'm planning a trip in October. Why? Want to come?'

'Me, you, and Bryn?' Gwen's face twisted into faux disgust. 'No, thank you very much. But I may have a shopping list. Plus, there's a prezzie for my cuz. Her birthday is in November. Save me posting it, plus I do not trust postmen. I was thinking maybe you could take it up and give it to her?'

'Where's your cousin?'

'Goldsmiths. You'd like her. She's borderline mental.'

'I'll think about it.'

Gwen feigned shock and horror. 'What happened to gratitude for getting Zac off your back?'

Molly grinned.

Gwen scrolled on her screen and music suddenly filled the car; Dua Lipa and Young Thug doing their thing to Calvin Harris's *Potion*. Next to her, Molly saw Gwen start a sensuous, pouting, chair dance.

It wasn't just her cousin that was borderline mental, Molly thought, but she was grinning as she did.

———

WARLOW SAW a grin on Rhys's face as he walked back in and dared to hope.

'Tell me you're smiling because you have information on the girls?'

The DC's face froze. 'Sorry, sir. It's a blank at the hospital.'

'So, the Cheshire Cat impression was for the drone?' Catrin asked.

'It's a load off my mind, that's all.' Rhys shrugged.

Warlow turned to Catrin. 'What about the girls' phone records?'

'As you know, both phones were found at the scene and both were locked. We've contacted the service providers but there isn't much,' Catrin reminded him. 'A couple of texts when they arrived, and an email sent to the Airbnb owner. I've just had the report back from HQ. Everything goes blank on Sunday morning. All texts sent to them get no replies.'

Warlow shook his head. 'It all comes back to that, doesn't it? George Marsden gets killed that same Sunday morning. There has to be a link.'

'I suppose that means we can rule out the women as the murderers,' Rhys said.

That earned him a look from three pairs of eyes triggering a belated realisation from Rhys that he might have gaffed. 'That's sort of obvious, sorry.'

Warlow shook his head. 'Sometimes the obvious needs to be stated, Rhys.'

'But where does that leave us?' Gil swirled the ice in his drink.

'With fewer options.' Warlow was staring at a painting on the wall. A country scene. Sun rising over the mountains. Light, the sign of hope. 'Did I tell you I spoke to an expert in theology and philosophy about the Friends of Light?'

Catrin shook her head.

'They are the one group we haven't really delved into yet. My contact told me a couple of very interesting things. When people join the Friends, they're meant to shed their previous existences. I doubt whether anyone who works for them had a formal DBS check. That might go against their philosophy.'

'We still have had nothing back about Jonah Crosby,' Gil said.

'Then let's do our own digging. Catrin, you get on to that. Gil, give them a poke at Bryn Encil. Find out why we haven't heard anything back from Jonah Crosby. He's been identified as someone who had direct contact with George Marsden. Run a background—'

Warlow's words were suddenly drowned out by the blast of a loud horn followed by a shouted exchange.

'What's all that about?' Rhys stood up and craned his neck to look out of the window. Warlow didn't wait. With Gil and the others in tow, he strode to the entrance and stepped outside. Below them, on the roadway, an altercation was in progress. A tractor, its wheels coated in mud, was stationary in the lane, its progress halted by a white SUV that had pulled up opposite one of the police vehicles, rendering the way impassable. A man stood in the middle of the lane exchanging unpleasantries with the tractor driver, who looked down, somewhat bemused, by what he was hearing.

'What's going on?' Warlow turned to a uniformed officer about to walk down to the road.

'It's the press, sir. Thought they'd park up and use the facilities at the inn.'

Anyone with a modicum of common sense could see that parking where they had would block the road.

'Want me to shout at them?' Warlow asked.

'No need for that, sir. I've got a very loud voice of my own.'

The man in the road was telling the tractor driver, at high volume, to go around another way. The tractor driver's retorts were peppered with words not suitable for TV, even after the watershed. But the gist was that there was no other way around and that the SUV had better move unless it wanted a mud shower.

'The press?' Rhys said. 'They got here quick.'

'Too quick,' Gil replied, his lips pursed. 'No way they could have reacted to Buchanan's statement this quick.'

They hadn't seen Sion Buchannan's prepared and read out statement but it had gone out to the waiting press an hour ago.

'Someone has been blabbing.' Gil still had his drink in his hand. Suddenly, both drink and the hand holding it jerked forward as someone attempted to push through from behind the little posse of officers. But though his arm and drink responded to the shove, the man himself did not. He turned, face like thunder, to confront a younger, shaven-headed man attempting to barrel his way through the knot of onlookers. Behind him, a small woman, wearing an expression of high dudgeon, stood dressed in a designer tracksuit that looked as incongruous as a space suit in this part of rural Carmarthenshire.

'Excuse me,' said the shaven-headed man, holding one hand out like the prow of an ice-breaker and making no effort to accommodate the people in his way. Rather, his half apology was more an announcement of impending contact. But he had not factored trying to budge DS Gil Jones into his plans.

'No,' Gil said.

Shaven-head's belligerent expression took in the burly sergeant and, if anything, became a tad more belligerent. 'What did you say?'

'I said, no. I don't excuse you. Saying it and meaning it are two different things.'

Shaven-head's mouth twisted into a grin. 'Sorry, teach. Now, get out of my way.'

Gil clicked his tongue a few times. 'See, the way it works in polite company is that you say, "excuse me", wait, and then we move out of the way because we've bought into the interaction. It's meant to be a two-way tango.'

Rhys, whose tolerance for rudeness was not the best, stepped forward. But Warlow's hand on his arm stayed the DC's progress. The little shake of his head stopped Rhys in his tracks. The shake, combined with the slightest elevation of the DCI's eyebrows and the flicker of a smile, carried a message of the hang-on-this-should-be-good variety.

Rhys, suitably cowed, stood down and watched.

Watched and learned.

CHAPTER TWENTY-NINE

Sigrid Bidulph glanced at her watch for the tenth time in as many minutes. Rudi and Thomas had been gone for almost two hours. To be fair to the latter, he'd agreed to go out and search as soon as he'd arrived back from delivering their guest to her London home. He'd also drawn a blank when he'd called in to the Llandovery pubs on the way back. No one had seen Jonah since his customary Saturday night bladdering. He may, or may not, have gone home with one of the local girls then, but he had not appeared last night.

He had not been seen since the police had called.

Information that punctured Rudi's theory of him having escaped to the pub in response. That left them with the options of Jonah either hiding out in the woods or heading cross-country to the Sugar Loaf to get on the Heart of Wales train that would take him to Shrewsbury and all points east.

'But his stuff is still here,' Thomas had pointed out. 'He's hardly likely to bugger off with nothing.'

'Depends on how bad the police spooked him,' Rudi said.

'You're not seriously suggesting he had anything to do with what's happened?' Sigrid asked, her big eyes displaying genuine horror.

'Hang on.' Thomas looked confused. 'Why would the police being here spook Jonah especially?' His slow Hibernian drawl leant added inquisitiveness and drew a sigh from Sigrid. She sent Rudi a loaded glance. He nodded as if making a decision.

'Jonah... Jonah's had a troubled past, Thomas. You know, we insist that all baggage gets left at the gate once anyone arrives here. Mental baggage, I mean. Staff and guests alike.'

'So, did Jonah tell you about his troubled past, then?' Thomas asked.

'Did he tell you?'

'Not in so many words. But he hinted at it. At how this place was an escape for him.'

Rudi shut his eyes. He may not have been squirming, but it was a close call. 'He did not tell us. Not as such. Security, from outsiders I mean, isn't an issue here because we are so far from anywhere. But people are still people and we have had to vet our employees.'

'Vet them? Vet... us? What, like DBS checks and stuff?'

Sigrid shook her head. 'DBS checks require consent from the individual. So, we adopt a different, private approach.'

'What, like a private detective?'

Sigrid nodded. 'There are specialist firms out there. Central office insists.'

'So, you checked me?' Thomas asked.

'We did. And you checked out, Thomas. We are so grateful for you being here. You realise that.' Sigrid reached out a hand and touched the handyman's arm.

'What about Jonah, though?'

The reply from Rudi remained enigmatic and all the more meaningful for that. 'That's why it's important we find him, Thomas. We need to make sure he's safe. That everyone is safe.'

Now, two hours later and once again in the rotunda, Sigrid waited and watched. Something moved in the fading afternoon light. A fox crossed the gap between some trees under a gunmetal sky, oblivious of the drizzle that had now become persistent. Not a good day to be out searching for a boy with a disturbed past. Suddenly, half a dozen crows launched upwards from a tree in the nearby copse. Spooked, no doubt by something underneath.

The fox, perhaps. Or something else.

Sigrid squeezed her fist into her chest. Once there might have been a crucifix there. No longer. Now her fingers closed around a pendant in the shape of a crown over a hill.

The symbol of the Light.

She'd long ago given up praying. But if there was anyone listening, she sent a mental message to it, or her or him now.

Please, don't let it be Jonah. Please.

———

'I SAID GET out of my way.' Shaven-head inched a little closer.

'Happy to,' Gil said. But he didn't move. Around him, the knot of people had grown quiet.

'You are in this lady's space, fat man.'

Warlow leaned to the left to study the woman behind the shaven head. Perfectly made-up, she returned his gaze defiantly. Something clicked in the DCI's brain, then. He'd seen this woman before. She'd been a stalwart panellist on a daily chat show where most things were open to discussion. A "ladies who lunch" gossip-fest. And hadn't she done something controversial? A personal attack on some politician in that land of cancellation and no context, Twitter? Not for the first time, either. She'd lost the daytime gig and sunk into the obscurity of specialist on the digital TV channels. From what he could recall, she was a woman unable to keep her volatile temper under a professional lid. Warlow didn't know if Gil recognised her. He doubted it mattered either way.

'Two things I remember about space,' Gil said calmly. 'It's relative, according to Einstein, and once you're in it, no one can hear you scream, according to Jimmy Cameron.'

'A funny fat man. Aren't I the lucky one?' Shavenhead's grin was anything but amused.

Gil waved a thumb back towards the road. 'Is that your driver there causing an obstruction?'

'We needed to check on accommodation for Ms Milton.' He raised his chin towards the Uniforms dotted around. 'Unlike these keystone clowns, we're here to do some serious work.'

'Oh, well, why didn't you say that in the first place?' Gil grinned. 'Then of course all traffic has to be diverted while you and… the lady… use the bathroom, am I right?' He reached into a pocket and pulled out his warrant card. 'Detective Sergeant Gil Jones.' He held up a hand as if to stop any words from the two in front of him. 'No, please, the pleasure is all mine. But since your driver persists in holding up the traffic, might I suggest you join him as quick as your little legs can carry you. And, judging by the reluctance to move away shown by this shudder of clowns – which is the correct collective adjective if I am not mistaken – it may be quicker if you use the side entrance. Your driver has already suggested to the tractor driver that he go around. May I suggest the same to you? Because if that SUV stays where it is any longer than another three minutes, we will clamp it and get it towed away. Oh, and we'd arrest the driver for obstructing the police in their enquiries. Unfortunately, being a boorish idiot is not against the law, otherwise you'd be in handcuffs, too.'

Shaven-head's jaw clenched and unclenched.

Behind him, the woman said something barely audible. Warlow suspected the word 'clown' was repeated. But Shaven-head turned away without another word. As he followed the woman towards the side entrance, he held up his hand behind him with the middle finger extended.

'Charming,' Catrin said. 'Obviously, she needs a minder.'

'Bloody insulting, calling us clowns,' Rhys said.

'I should Coco.' Gil turned to him and grinned.

Catrin shook her head.

'The PR people back in HQ would have a fit if they'd seen that,' Gil said, still grinning.

'Are you sorry?' Warlow asked him.

'Not on your red nose, I am not.'

'Exactly. The PR people aren't here out in the wild trying to solve a murder and find two mispers. That reminds me. A little less conversation, a little more action, as the King once said.'

'Was that in his speech, sir? The one where he stuttered a lot?' Rhys asked.

Everyone turned slowly to gape at the DC. Catrin with her mouth open.

'Wrong king, Rhys. In fact, wrong in so many ways, I've already lost count. May be a record for you, though,' Gil said, clamping his lips together sadly.

'Cheers, sarge,' Rhys said, but there was no hiding the little shadow of doubt crinkling his eyes.

Warlow hung back. 'I'll be in shortly. Doesn't seem like

any of us will be getting home soon. I need to ring my dog sitter and my house guest.'

He did the dog sitter first. Bruce and Maggie Dawes were so well used to having Warlow ring them when he was embroiled in a case, eyelids were never batted. He, in return, made absolutely sure they were recompensed with vouchers for pub meals and never forgot either of their birthdays. The truth was, if he could ask Cadi if she minded, she'd probably stare at him with big brown eyes, curled up on the sofa next to her Golden Lab pal Bouncer, and likely say, 'And your point is?'

Molly, on the other hand, was a different kettle of herring.

'Yeah, yeah, I've heard it all before,' she said when he explained that he was unlikely to be home at anything like a reasonable time and so had okayed it with the Dawes for Cadi to stay with them overnight. That way, he was certain she'd get a walk.

'I could have done that,' Molly said, piqued.

'Yes, I realise that, but the weather is, for want of a better word, shite. And you're still at Gwen's, right?'

'How do you know?'

'You told me this morning.'

'Did I? For a minute there I thought you had a GPS tracer on my car.'

'That can be arranged. I'm well aware you can look after yourself, Molly, but the whole point of you staying at mine is that I'm there.'

'As a minder?'

Being the second time he'd heard that word in as many minutes, it threw him.

'Hello? Earth to Evan?'

'For want of a better word, yes. Any chance you can stay with Gwen this evening?'

'Her mum has already insisted I stay for dinner

because the bloke I was meant to be eating with has cried off.'

'Great. If there's a possibility of me getting back, I'll text you later. But things aren't looking rosy up here. We have a couple of missing walkers as well to contend with now.'

'No wonder me and Cadi get on so well,' Molly said with a delicate touch of the passive-aggressive. 'We're both used to being forgotten.'

'It's the job, Molly.'

'Doesn't mean I have to like it.'

'I'll make it up to you.'

'You realise that's tattooed on the under-surface of my skull, right?'

Warlow let out a throaty laugh. 'How is your pal Zac? Any more hassle?'

'Oh my God, you actually listened.'

'I always listen.'

'Like I said, it's all sorted. No need to worry your little police officer head about that. You or Mum.'

'Heard from her today?'

'She keeps texting me to see where I am. Now I'm going to tell her I'm having a sleepover at Gwen's.'

'I'll text her, too. Corroboration. The cornerstone of good police work.'

'The worst thing about all of this is that I won't get to give Cadi a goodnight cuddle.'

'You can make it up to her.'

'And I will. You, I'm not so sure about.'

'We'll talk tomorrow, okay?'

'What time will you be home tonight, then?'

'Who knows? I might have a sleepover, too.'

'Anyone I know?' Molly loaded the question with as much lasciviousness as a seventeen-year-old could muster.

'Sergeant Jones.'

'Oh, he's just a big teddy bear.'

'Yes, well, I won't be cuddling him. No chance.'

'And you owe me a supper.'

'Top of my list,' Warlow said.

'You are such a terrible liar.' She ended the call before he could respond.

CHAPTER THIRTY

In the Incident Corner, all was quiet. The kind of quiet inside a beaver's lodge when the entire colony was busy building and repairing the structure. It was now approaching 6pm. A part of Warlow knew he should let the team go and simply wait for the PolSA to come back to them with a report. That made for an uneasy evening of pacing. But from the look of them, none of the others seemed desperate to rush off.

It was Gil who was the first to come up with something significant.

'Rudi Bidulph. Aka a very inky equine.'

Rhys glanced up from his screen momentarily.

'He means a dark horse,' Catrin muttered.

'I knew that,' Rhys said, sounding like a miffed six-year-old and convincing no one in the process.

'Mr Bidulph used to run a much bigger Friends of Light concern down in the Southeast,' Gil explained. 'Somewhere on the Sussex Downs. I've dug up a report. One that smells distinctly of fish.'

Warlow, without his computer, had made himself useful by cadging some cups of tea from the pub landlord who'd made a kettle, milk, and tea bags available in the backroom. Gil's words made him sit forward. 'I'm listening.'

'The Friends of Light publish a bi-monthly magazine called Lucis. Nothing much in it. Bit of inspirational poetry and look-what-we-did articles. Charity work in far-flung corners of the empire, that sort of thing.'

'You can't say that sarge. It's colonialist.'

Gil paused and tossed Rhys one of his best side-eyed glares. 'Tidy. Then wait until they build a statue to me and feel free to rip it down and throw it into the canal. Until then, it's just language. Be triggered if you want to be but do it outside so no one has to see. There's a good lad.'

'Sorry, sarge,' Rhys said.

'Now, as I was saying. There's an announcement in this Lucis in 2017 that Bidulph was going to take on the running of Bryn Encil. But, through the wonders of Google, his name crops up in the mid-Sussex news section of the Sussex Argus. Not sure if it's a completely online newspaper, but in it there are hints of problems at the Friends of Light's Retreat in that neck of the forest. A place called Hawkforth Hall. Apparently, according to the Argus, a claim of unfair dismissal and sexual misconduct aimed at one Rudi Bidulph.'

'What happened?' Warlow asked.

'The details are sketchy. But there are two names mentioned in the article. Two women. However, I can't find any evidence of charges made on the PNC. So, I rang one of the women. Nice girl. A Madeline Howden. She said she couldn't talk to me about it. I explained we were making official enquiries, and she stopped me dead and said that she literally could not talk to me about what happened.'

'NDA?' Warlow asked.

Gil nodded. 'I'd put money on it.'

Warlow took one glance at Rhys's confusion and put him out of his misery. 'NDAs are Non-Disclosure Agreements. Legally binding ways of shutting people up about employment disputes.'

'Hush money,' Catrin murmured.

'Does that help us, then? If she won't talk, I mean?'

Out of the mouths of babes, thought Warlow. 'Good point, Rhys. It tells us nothing.'

'Except that Bidulph is shifty,' Gil said.

Catrin had remained oddly quiet during this discussion, her head buried deep in the screen, avidly reading with her brows knitted. Normally, she'd be on to something harassment-related like a Red Kite on a half-dead vole.

'I think I have something, too, sir,' she said into the brief lull that followed Gil's statement. And something in her tone of voice sent a tingle skittering along Warlow's coccyx. She looked up with eyes of flint. 'Something the Friends of Light should have told us days ago.'

———

THEY TOOK BOTH CARS, Rhys and Catrin in the Audi, Gil in his Volvo with Warlow. By car, it was ten minutes to the dam, but another twenty along the winding lanes to the Retreat. It was almost seven by the time they hit the rise and Warlow saw Bryn Encil for the first time.

'Impressive,' he muttered. 'Did we tell them we were coming?'

'Must have slipped my mind,' Gil answered.

'Good.'

With half an hour of light left in the day, the sun was sinking towards the horizon. A thin line of clear sky lay just beyond the ridge of clouds that had brought the drizzle. Low sunset rays picked out the high ground, spilling golden light onto the tops of the crags, throwing the buildings below into shadow. Warlow and Gil both took in the spectacle.

'I'm glad I didn't tell them. Some gullible people might think they'd put this show on for us.'

'Metaphysical fireworks?' Warlow stared out at the landscape. 'Not on my watch.'

The sound of the Audi approaching from behind broke the spell and Gil eased the Volvo down into Bryn Encil's courtyard. This time, no door opened, and no one came to greet them.

'Welcoming committee must be having supper,' Gil said.

All four officers got out and made for the oak-studded door.

'Pretty swish place for way out here,' Rhys observed. 'They've spent a bit of money.'

'A lot of money.' Catrin took in the huge lead planters with their manicured bay trees and trimmed box lining the courtyard. 'It's where it comes from that mystifies me.'

Rhys rang the bell. There were lights on in the building, but it took a while before anyone replied. Again, an intercom system clicked on and a woman answered.

'Hello?'

Gil recognised it at once as Sigrid Bidulph.

'Evening, madam. This is Detective Sergeant Jones again. We wondered if we could have a word about—'

Gil got no further. The intercom clicked off. Half a minute later, the door opened and Sigrid Bidulph, looking far less calm and composed than she had the last time she'd opened it, stood there. 'Rudi isn't here.' The words blurted out of her mouth.

'Are you expecting him back soon?' Catrin asked.

Sigrid's eyes flicked towards the wilderness beyond the courtyard. 'I don't know.'

'Doesn't matter,' Gil said. 'We have a couple of questions about Jonah Crosby. Perhaps you could answer them for us?'

Sigrid's hand strayed again to the pendant at her neck. She looked surprised and clearly shocked. 'You have news about Jonah?'

'Not exactly,' Gil said.

Warlow stepped forward. 'Ms Bidulph, I'm DCI Warlow. Can we come in?'

'This… isn't a good time,' her reply came out stilted.

'Why?'

'Because… Rudi isn't here. He's the director, you see.'

'Is Jonah here, Sigrid?' Catrin asked.

She shook her head. 'No. He didn't come back. That's where Rudi is now. Out looking—'

The noise of an approaching quad bike cut her off. The officers swung around as the bike's engine grew louder and the machine eased forward from between the two furthest outbuildings and came to a stop. The driver, dressed in a red fleece and scruffy jeans, took off his helmet. Rudi Bidulph's hair clung to his skull, and he ruffled it up with his fingers before he got off the machine.

'Any joy?' Sigrid asked, and there was no mistaking the desperation in it.

'No,' Rudi answered. He walked across and stood next to his partner on the threshold of Bryn Encil. Sigrid made the introductions, and Catrin responded by naming Rhys and Warlow.

'Looks like a show of strength,' Rudi said. But his attempt at levity came over as forced.

'We're looking for Jonah Crosby,' Warlow said.

'Aren't we all? He hasn't come back from his little expedition in the woods.'

'Since yesterday?' Gil asked.

Rudi nodded. 'Otherwise, he would have contacted you. I'd make sure of that.'

Catrin took a step forward. 'Jonah Crosby has a history of GBH and attempted rape. He's served time at a Young Offender's institution. Were you aware of that fact, Mr Bidulph?'

'I was. As I explained, we offer opportunities here for people. A chance to regain that which they have lost. Find an alternative path.'

'And you didn't think that telling us might have been helpful?' Gil asked.

'Unless Jonah volunteered it—'

'But he hasn't volunteered it, has he?' Catrin said. 'Instead, he's fled. Any idea why that might be, Mr Bidulph?'

'No. No idea.'

'Despite the fact that one person is dead and two others missing?'

'What two others?' Bidulph's composure shattered as he threw Sigrid an anxious glance. She responded with a shake of her head.

'Two missing walkers. Both young women,' Warlow told them.

'And Jonah Crosby was charged with abduction, though that charge was subsequently dropped when the victim refused to give evidence.' Catrin drew herself up.

'I... *we* knew nothing about missing walkers,' Sigrid said, clearly shocked.

'Well, you do now. So, we'd appreciate it if you let us in and tell us anything you can about Jonah. Where he's likely to go. If he knows anyone in the area—' Once again, the noise of an approaching quad bike put an end to the conversation. Once again, the bike appeared from the far end of the courtyard. This time, the approach was faster than Rudi's, the bike skidding to a halt as the driver, still with the engine running, half stumbled off the machine.

Six people stood waiting while the rider leant forward,

hands on his knees, as if he was catching his breath, or perhaps as if he was about to vomit.

'Thomas?' Rudi stepped forward.

The still helmeted driver looked up and finally unclipped his headgear and slid it off. Still dressed in overalls, but wearing a padded gilet, Thomas Seaton stood in front of his employers and the police, his face white, his breath ragged. It looked like he might have been crying.

'Thomas?' Sigrid's voice rose in alarm. 'Did you find Jonah?'

Thomas nodded. 'I did… I found him… He's only half a mile away. He's—' A groan followed and then a dry retch as Thomas turned away again.

Everyone waited.

Finally, Thomas turned back, wiping something that might have been bile from his mouth with the back of his hand. And his words, when he eventually found them, changed everything.

'I found Jonah. Oh, Christ… he's hanged himself. Jonah's dead.'

CHAPTER THIRTY-ONE

THEY FETCHED torches from the cars because Warlow didn't want to wait. Dusk was only minutes away; darkness would follow quickly. Warlow went with Thomas. Gil on the back of Rudi Bidulph's machine. For the second time in twenty-four hours, Warlow bounced and juddered along ropey tracks and down towards the trees. It was colder under the canopy. Warlow was bare-headed; there'd been no spare helmets for the officers. The sudden chill hit the DCI's face, and he sucked in air, inhaling an earthy smell of damp and rotting leaves mingled with the sharp aroma of petrol from the quad. Warlow would remember that pungent aroma for a long time.

The track took them down into a hollow and around a couple of turns before the ground rose again at a patch of cleared ground, lighter out of the trees. Logs had been stacked here and piles of sawdust littered the floor.

Thomas turned off the engine and Rudi arrived half a minute later.

'This is where we store what we've cut before transporting it back,' Thomas said after he'd slid off his helmet.

In the dimming light, he looked old. Warlow put him somewhere in his fifties. 'We have to walk from here.'

The path led down into another depression and an older wood. Skeins of moss hung off the boughs here. This was an ancient forest. Undisturbed for many years.

They walked on in silence. Four men, torches on in the approaching gloom, the beams bobbing against the dark trunks until at last Thomas slowed. He turned to face them. 'It's around the next bend.'

The other three nodded.

Jonah's corpse hung from the bough of a tall sessile oak. It didn't need to be that tall, of course. Just enough so that Jonah's feet were off the ground when the rope around his neck took the weight. As it was, a miserly couple of feet was all that separated the boy from solid ground. Warlow was glad of the darkness. It meant that the boy's dead face looked altered, but not horrifying, in the dusk. And the torchlight threw the features into a distorted relief. But he'd seen hangings before. He knew that properly illuminated, that face would look purple, the tongue swollen and protruding, the eyes swollen shut.

Hangings rendered the victim an ugly death.

'Shall I get a ladder?' Thomas asked.

'No,' Gil said. 'We touch nothing.'

'How did he…' Rudi's voice did not sound like his own.

Warlow glanced at the tree. 'I'd say he climbed up and let the bough take his weight.'

'He jumped, you mean?'

'Unlikely. If the bough broke, he would have survived. I assume he eased himself off the tree.'

Gil nodded. Not a quick death, then.

'I'll get something to cut him down,' Rudi said.

'No. Best we don't contaminate the site any more than it has been already.'

'Surely we can't leave him hanging—'

'Another hour will make no difference.' Gil's voice boomed with authority.

Warlow had his phone out, peering at the screen and frowning. 'No signal here.'

'No, it's a bit of a black spot,' Thomas explained.

Warlow turned to Bidulph. 'Can you get back to the house? Tell DS Richards we'll need the full complement. Pathologist, Scene of Crime, the lot. She'll know what to do.'

Rudi nodded and hurried away. Warlow turned to Thomas.

'Does he have any relatives?'

Thomas shrugged. 'He's estranged from his parents. But there's a sister in Brighton.'

'Can you remember what he said to you the last time you saw him?'

'I dropped him off about half a mile away. He said he was going to the north fence. That's in totally the other direction. That's why I haven't looked here until today.'

'Did he seem anxious, or worried?' Gil asked.

'He didn't say much. Jonah wasn't much of a talker. He was a deep one. The weather was going to close in, so we wanted to get things done. That's all I can remember. He didn't seem any different than usual.'

Gil nodded. 'We'll ask you to sit down and make a statement later. Sometimes, when you put a pen to paper, other things come to mind.'

Thomas had his back to the corpse and still looked as if he was about to throw up. The noise of Rudi Bidulph's quad bike firing up and accelerating away drifted down to them. 'Do you want to sit down?' Gil asked.

'Perhaps I should.'

Gil led the man away to a stump, out of the line of sight of the corpse. Warlow stayed where he was, taking in what he could in the dusk. On the surface, this looked very much like a suicide, but Povey would not be pleased if he and the others trampled over the ground any more than they had already. He let his eyes drift down and picked out an abandoned rucksack, a chainsaw, gloves, and a coat. It looked very much as if something had overcome Jonah as he worked. The police presence at Bryn Encil would have helped. Perhaps the prospect of no escape from this isolated spot had made him realise how limited his options were.

Warlow had no trouble in imagining how dark thoughts might intrude in this forgotten corner of the world. Whatever might have been the trigger for his earlier actions, perhaps with George Marsden, perhaps with the two women, the stark reality of his predicament would have come home to him here.

No car. No transport of any kind. No way out. Except one.

A shoe had dropped off the boy's foot and the exposed sock had come half off. An empty length of material hung down, elongating Jonah's right foot. Stretched out, perhaps, as that foot shook uncontrollably in the throes of strangulation.

It didn't bear thinking about.

That was when Warlow heard the voices.

———

'WHERE IS IT JONAH SLEEPS, SIGRID?'

They were in the rotunda, Rhys and Catrin on their feet, Sigrid sitting, folded in on herself in one of the chairs, one hand worrying at the pendant around her neck, the other clutching her elbow.

'Sorry?' Sigrid's eyes refocused on Catrin, brought back from wherever her mind had taken her a second before.

'Jonah. Does he have a room?'

Sigrid nodded. 'Thomas and he share an outbuilding. Thomas is at the top, Jonah below. They're self-contained units.'

'Can we see, please?'

Sigrid blinked at the question, hearing the words, but not absorbing them.

Rhys took a step forward and sat opposite her. 'Sigrid. I know this is difficult. But we're here to help. Mr Warlow will want us to do what we can while he is with Jonah. And we can help by seeing if there is anything we can find that might tell us what's been going on.'

Sigrid nodded and then stood and walked back towards the front entrance. She grabbed a coat and some keys and opened the door, crunched her way across the courtyard toward a stone building at the end with one door at ground level, and a stone stair leading up to a second door on the first floor.

Sigrid slid in the key and unlocked the ground-floor door, reached in, and flicked on a light. Then she stepped back and let the officers in.

'I'll wait in the rotunda.'

'Good idea,' Catrin said and smiled briefly.

Both officers donned gloves and overshoes. This was not meant to be a thorough analysis. Only a cursory poke around to ascertain if anything stood out.

One thing was clear immediately; Jonah wouldn't get a gold star for personal hygiene. The one room was a studio with an unmade bed and a sofa. The sheets could have done with a laundering. A small room at the back doubled as a kitchen/dining room, and beyond that was a tiny shower and toilet.

'Bijou,' Rhys said. A word he'd borrowed from Gil, no doubt.

Catrin turned her attention to a bureau under a

monitor and desktop TV from which wires led to a game console and controller. The bureau doubled as a clothes repository and one drawer contained other random stuff, which included a clipped together sheaf of paperwork.

Carefully, Catrin leafed through. She found bank statements, a contract of employment, a letter of discharge from the Youth Offender Institute in Exeter and one from a parole officer.

But it was Rhys's shout that drew her attention from the kitchen area.

'You'd better see this, sarge.'

She walked through and found Rhys standing over the table, still laid with condiments: salt and pepper, red and brown sauce, vinegar, and mustard. They were significant only because they acted as a scaffolding for the envelope propped up against them.

The envelope had no address and had not been stuck down.

Catrin threw Rhys a questioning glance.

'Is this what I think it is?' she said.

'Only one way to find out, sarge.'

———

'THEY'RE UP HERE, I RECKON.' A male voice.

'Are you sure? I heard a quad drive away.' A second voice, this one female.

'There were two to start with.' The third voice was more assured. Warlow envisaged the shaven head above the mouth it belonged to.

He'd walked around the little clearing to its eastern edge. A thin strip of remaining daylight had condensed into a magenta slash across the sky on the horizon. Warlow crouched and waited. The woman kept up a loud, running commentary.

'There isn't a great deal of light left in the day. We've tracked up the valley here and we know that there is activity up ahead. We've heard quad bikes roaring across the moor like giant insects disappearing into the trees. Could this be where we find answers? Is this the spot where the mystery of the strange activity around Carn Ddu is finally explained? The strange noises, the screams. The possibility that there is a gate here that links our world with—'

Warlow stood up and shone his torch at the lead walker.

'Police, stop there. You're entering a crime scene. I'm going to have to ask you to retrace your steps.'

Someone screamed. Difficult to say whether male or female. Warlow's torch beam picked out Shaven-head who immediately put a hand up against the light. 'Whoa, who are you?'

'Police. We're investigating an incident here. You can't enter this part of the forest.'

'Do you have any ID?' the woman asked. The third person, also a man, directed a torch into Warlow's face, making him hold his hand up against the glare. 'I'll be happy to show it to you.'

'Keep your hands where we can see them,' Shaven-head said.

'What?' Warlow asked.

'You heard. You could have a knife or a gun there. If you reach into your pocket, I'll assume it's an act of aggression.'

'Really.' Warlow stayed calm, though he felt the heat of his temper rise. These were the people who'd been rude at the pub. Now they were simply being idiots.

'Yes, really. We don't know you. You might be a maniac out here in the woods alone. I'd be within my right—'

'To maybe shut up and do as you're damn well told,'

Gil's voice appeared from behind Warlow. 'You've already seen my warrant card. The man you are threatening is DCI Warlow.'

Shaven-head took a step back, both hands up. 'No one's threatening anyone here.'

'Sounded pretty threatening to me,' Gil said, and his smile was all teeth in the torch beam that the third person kept shining at him.

'Now, what the hell are you three doing out here?' Warlow asked.

'We could ask you the same question?' Milton, emboldened by Shaven-head belligerence, asked.

'Mr Warlow has already explained, we're here doing our jobs. Investigating a serious incident.'

'And we're here doing ours. Reporting on unusual activity in a place with hugely significant occult links to the past.' Milton sounded defiant. 'For our YouTube channel.'

Warlow now realised the third person was carrying a camera.

'Great. Look forward to seeing it. But you're still going to have to leave.'

Silence. Warlow wondered if Shaven-head was going to object. No doubt he was considering it. In the end, he did. 'What if we don't want to?'

'Seriously?' Gil said, grinning. 'Nothing would give me more pleasure. We have half a dozen response vehicles on the way. Plenty of room in the back for you three.'

'Where is your car?' Warlow asked.

'About a mile and a half back that way.' Shaven-head pointed into the darkness.

'Then off you go.'

'We might get lost,' Milton objected.

'Temptress,' Gil said.

Thomas appeared at Gil's elbow. 'There's a track fifty

yards to the right. An old mining trail. It'll take you back down to where you've parked, if it's where I think it is.'

'And who is this? Another plod?' Milton asked.

Warlow ignored her. 'Gil, you and Thomas take these charming people to the track. I'll stay here.'

'We'll find out, you know?' Milton said. 'What's going on here. We've heard there are high-ranking politicians involved. That there may be abducted children. Human sacrifice. If you're covering something up, you should be ashamed of yourself.'

'*Arglwydd mawr.* That bloody internet has a lot to answer for.' Gil shook his head.

Warlow looked up to the heavens and sighed. 'Go away and stay away. Please. Let us do our jobs.'

'Some people want the police defunded.' This time, the third member of the gaggle of fools piped up. He had his camera up. Possibly on night vision by now. Baiting Warlow for a reply. And as non-sequiturs went, it was a good one. So, Warlow put him out of his misery.

'I know. Great idea until you actually need them. So long as you ask the mad, the bad, and the sad to play ball, it'll all work out. I'll leave the finer details for you. Meanwhile, we'll do what we're paid to do. Now bugger off.'

He swivelled on his heels, not prepared to give these intruders any more of his time. Warlow had more urgent matters to deal with. The dead were calling to him once again.

CHAPTER THIRTY-TWO

WARLOW MADE it back to Bryn Encil an hour later with blue lights lighting up the night sky the closer he got to the Retreat. Once the circus had their tents up, he was no longer needed to be the ringmaster. Rudi Bidulph and Thomas acted as quad taxis, ferrying personnel back and forth, but by the time Warlow got back, cold and hunger were dulling his senses.

Sigrid had made sandwiches, and he and Gil sat in the rotunda with hot tea and ate before they did anything else. Catrin and Rhys had coordinated the crime scene techs, but when the two younger officers joined Warlow and Gil, they had something they wanted to say.

'When you've finished, sir, there is something you need to see in Jonah's room.'

Warlow had a mouthful of ham and cheese and bread. He put the rest of the sandwich on his plate and then got to his feet. 'Lead on.'

Catrin had locked the door to Jonah's rooms, but she'd left the note out on the little table and the light on.

'What's this?' Warlow asked as he walked in.

Catrin didn't answer. She let Warlow read for himself. The

DCI fished out his glasses and slid them on. He managed most of the time, but reading now was impossible without them, especially in dim light, though driving glasses-free he could still manage. That clever bugger Dylan Thomas ensconced in the converted garage that became an iconic writing shed in Laugharne knew a thing or two. Warlow never stopped raging against the dying of the light. Here literally because only one bulb in the damned ceiling light worked, but there was enough illumination for him to make out the note. Thanks, in no small measure, to the fact that it had been typed out and printed.

––––––

I AM sorry for what happened to George. I didn't mean to. But I did, and that's it. It's been hard up here and when I saw the two women, something bad happened. Like something broke inside me. I knew what I was going to do and I did exactly that. I'm sorry for them too. My actions will cause pain for those close to them, but they are gone and they will not come back. I killed them all and now I have to stop myself before I do it again. No one else is to blame. There is something inside me that grows and grows and has to be fed. Now I have fed it, I feel sick to my stomach. I don't want to feel like that again.

Tell my sister that I think about her.

––––––

HE'D SIGNED one scrawled word at the bottom. Jonah.

'Bloody coward,' Gil said.

Warlow had come across suicide in all its sordid forms. Hanging, jumps from tall buildings, lying in front of moving objects such as trains. Thinking of them now brought up a catalogue of memories he preferred to keep filed away. Jonah's choice of how to end his life fitted the pattern for his age group. As people got older, if not perhaps wiser, their methods changed. Eighty-year-olds preferred poisoning or cutting themselves with sharp objects. But for young people, suffocation or hanging remained the number one option.

He didn't pick up the sheet. But he read it half a dozen times. 'Where would he have printed this?'

'There's nothing in this room, sir. No printer,' Rhys replied.

'Find out if there's an office. There must be one somewhere. See if he had access to it.'

Rhys turned and left the room.

'What do you think, sir?' Catrin asked.

Warlow let his eyes drift over the tawdry little space. A claustrophobic lair if ever he'd seen one. He tried imagining how difficult it might be for any young man confined in this place, in this landscape. Dial in a history of violence and a predilection for sexual predation and the mix might easily become explosive. In that respect, the note made sense. But what he didn't like one bit was the dismissal of the two mispers. He'd confessed to killing them. But not where he'd put them. A cruel omission. But then someone who ended his own life hardly worried about what effect his demise would have on others, despite the sentiment expressed in writing. Warlow suspected the bugger wasn't sorry at all. He agreed with Gil's immediate reaction. If he had done these terrible things, then suicide was indeed the ultimate coward's way out. And not telling anyone where he'd hidden the women, the last twist of the psychological knife.

'At least he can't have taken them far,' Gil said. 'Impossible in the time he had and with no transport. They're here somewhere. We keep looking.'

'Even after he says they're—'

'Even after,' Warlow confirmed Gil's sentiment before

Catrin protested. 'We're going to find these two women. End of.'

No one questioned his omission of the obvious rider.

Alive or dead.

At around 9pm, Warlow called a halt to things. There seemed little point in staying at Bryn Encil any longer. Forensics and the HOP needed to do their thing. 'I suggest an early start and a case review at Carmarthen first thing. But if any of you have time, I'd appreciate some intelligence on this crew of journalists. This Emily Milton and her happy band.'

'They call themselves The Veil, sir,' Catrin said. 'At least, that's what the programme is called. They had a season early on Channel 5. Now it's all on YouTube. And lots of views.'

'Podcasts and YouTube.' Gil shook his head. 'I remember when there were only three channels and the test card. I used to love the test card.'

Rhys and Catrin exchanged puzzled looks.

'It was a static image of a little girl and a clown...' Warlow explained, but faltered on seeing Catrin's raised eyebrows. Plus, he couldn't muster the energy to go into detail. 'You had to be there. Right. 8am. I'm bringing breakfast.'

———

LATER, at Gil's, and prior sandwiches notwithstanding, with a portion of the Lady Anwen's *cawl*, along with a chunk of crusty bread warming their insides, the two senior officers discussed the day.

'What a mess,' Gil said, clutching a late-night cup of tea.

'We could do without the ghost hunters. That's for certain.'

'What's your take on all this bloody paranormal stuff?'

Warlow pursed his lips. 'Am I a believer? Do I think ghosts exist? No.'

'What I don't understand is how people can make a career out of stringing the public along, like this lot, The Veil.'

Warlow snorted. 'There's more than one career path involving stringing the gullible along.'

'I thought you said never to mention politics.' Gil grinned.

Later, alone in the guest bedroom, Warlow texted Molly Staying at Gil's. Hopefully back tomorrow night.

Hopefully?

Developments in case.

Good or bad?

Bad. You're at Gwen's, right?

Yes. But I have to go back to yours tomorrow morning for a change of clothes and college by ten.

Don't forget to lock the door.

He got a saintly emoji in return.

Warlow climbed into bed, weary but with his mind in turmoil. Had they somehow failed these two women? And the simple answer was yes, of course they had. Everyone had the right to live. The right to go about their business. When that right was taken away, or abused, then something in civilisation wasn't working. Even in the quiet, dark, hidden corners of the world. But this quiet, dark, hidden corner was on Warlow's patch. He took it personally.

Such thoughts did not make for a restful night. Sleep,

when it bothered to call, came fitfully and laden with unpleasant images. But what kept him awake more than anything was a conversation he'd had with Rhys just as they were getting into their cars for the off from Bryn Encil.

'Should we inform the relatives of the missing women, sir?'

'Of what?'

'Of their death. Jonah Crosby admitted to having killed them—'

'No, Rhys,' Gil had stepped in. 'We may have to. But it's far better that we find them first. Until we do, we say nothing to the press or relatives. No one else has seen the content of that note yet.'

Rhys had the Audi's driver-side door open. Catrin was already inside. 'But isn't that a bit… dishonest, sarge?'

'I prefer compassionate, Rhys,' Warlow said. 'They'll suffer enough when we find them and they have to ID the bodies. Let's spare them a few hours of pain.'

And so Warlow lay in this strange bed like someone from a Stephen King novel, cursed to absorb other people's pain while they remained blissfully ignorant.

No need to spread that pain. Not yet.

Except that there were always consequences for such actions.

He was up at six. Showered and dressed by half past. As he was putting on his shoes, he got a text from Molly. Thirty seconds later, one from Catrin. Both had the same link embedded in the message.

Fame, at last, was Molly's cryptic missive.

Did you know they were filming, sir? was Catrin's.

Warlow clicked the link. It went directly to a YouTube video entitled The Carn Ddu Project. Big, bold lettering atop the screen.

It was only five minutes long. The first two minutes

were an introduction by Emily Milton. The footage was dark and jerky, the scene a dark landscape with deepening shadows, lit only twenty feet in front of the camera along a trail with trees looming at every angle. At one minute and forty-nine, Warlow heard the same words that he'd heard as he'd crouched in the woods last night, listening.

'There isn't a great deal of light left in the day. We've tracked up the valley here and we know that there is activity up ahead. We've heard quad bikes roaring across the moor like giant insects disappearing into the trees. Could this be where we find answers? Is this the spot where the mystery of the strange activity around Carn Ddu is finally explained? The strange noises, the screams. The possibility that there is a gate here that links our world with—'

And then there he stood, in front of, or rather looming over, the camera lens, his features unclear and distorted in the torchlight.

It was all there, the brief confrontation. Gil and Thomas's arrival. The Veil being escorted away. And then it cut to Emily Milton in a hotel room somewhere, sitting on the edge of the bed.

'I am shaken. Tonight's encounter was scary for all the wrong reasons. We saw activity. A great deal of activity. Quad bikes travelling back and forth and something in the woods. We couldn't be sure because we weren't allowed to get close, but we had eyes on something. A shape, maybe a body, levitating, or hanging in the woods. The police wouldn't say anything, if indeed they were the police. But in all honesty, we were glad to have gotten away from there unharmed. The three men we met, one of whom is a police officer, looked menacing. They didn't want us there. They made sure we left by a different route. One thing is for certain, something terrible is happening in the area. And we believe that Carn Ddu is the epicentre. Perhaps a gate has opened. Perhaps something has come through. A man has been killed. Some people are missing and, as far as we know, the police are clueless. Is that because they are looking for a man when they should look for… something else? I'll be back tomorrow with more. We won't be leaving until we find out the truth.'

Warlow didn't watch it again. He couldn't stomach it. But he showed it to Gil just before they got into the car.

'Is there something we can do about this shower?' Gil asked.

'They're not breaking the law,' Warlow said, though with a regretful timbre to his voice. 'We need to forget about them and get on with what we need to do.'

'What if we come across them again?'

'We'll deal with that when we have to. Now, do you have Rhys's breakfast order? I'll phone it through. Save us a bit of time.'

CHAPTER THIRTY-THREE

WARLOW PICKED up some breakfast rolls from a café on the outskirts of Llandeilo. The Lady Anwen provided an insulated carrier bag, but the aroma of bacon and eggs filled the car on the drive down to HQ.

The Incident Room was already busy when they got there. Uniforms hunched over desktops answering phones and a couple of indexers busy at the back, inputting data. Warlow decided that they'd eat around the one desk, drawn up in a close group. Rhys had the tea ready.

'Right, fresh this morning, breakfast baguette for Rhys, the smoked salmon for Catrin, and bacon and egg baps for Gil and me. There's ketchup in the bag, too. In sachets.' He sent Rhys a pointed glower. More than once, the DC had distributed the contents of such sachets over clothes and documents in the Incident Room.

'Red and brown?' Rhys asked.

'Of course. These are from a high-class establishment.'

As they ate, mostly in silence for the first few bites, Warlow let his eyes drift over the Gallery and the Job Centre. Both were now overflowing. His eye settled on a group of three photographs off to the side under a heading of The Veil. Both his junior officers had stopped chewing as they followed his gaze.

'Right, okay, let's get Nellie out and fed,' Warlow said through his half-chewed bap.

'As in the elephant, Nellie?' Gil asked.

'The Nellie in the room, yes.' Warlow bounced his eyes from Rhys to Catrin. 'The YouTube video. Where are this shower staying?'

'A Travelodge in Cross Hands, sir.'

Warlow knew it. Hidden just off the A40 at a roundabout. Next to a Starbucks and across the road from Aldi and MacDonalds. Some people's idea of a dream weekend package there, no doubt.

'Is that where this Milton woman posted the video from?' A rhetorical question, but Warlow wanted to talk this through.

'Probably, sir.' Rhys nodded.

'Right. Gil is all for throwing them in the sea off the North Dock in Llanelli, but we can't do that.'

'Is there anything we can do?' Catrin asked, dabbing at her mouth with a napkin.

'Not much. It's a free country. So long as they don't get in our way, we can't do anything. The question is, how did they know where to find us?'

'They could have followed us, or they could have tracked us.'

'Tracked us? This isn't the bloody Bourne Ultimatum, Rhys.' Gil had to swallow what was in his mouth quickly. It brought tears to his eyes as he narrowly avoided getting it stuck.

'I did see a guy on a scooter a couple of times. It looked electric. The scooter. So, it'd be quiet. They could have followed us. Or followed you.'

Warlow shook his head. 'Bloody parasites.'

'Popular parasites,' Rhys said by way of qualification.

'Last time I looked, that video had a hundred and fifty thousand views.'

'It's a distraction we could do without.' Warlow bit into his roll.

'The Friends of Light must be having the same conversation this morning.' Catrin slid her gaze over to the photograph of Bryn Encil. 'Bad enough to have one of their staff hang himself. Then to have all this occult, satanic stuff mixed in with it. They'll be having kittens.'

'Black ones, hopefully,' Gil said.

Warlow sent him a wry glance. 'Is that a very tenuous and in poor taste witch reference?'

Gil donned an expression of injured innocence. 'The door was left open and I simply *wand-ered* through it. You didn't leave me any *broom* for manoeuvre there.'

Rhys grinned.

Catrin shook her head.

'Anything come in overnight?' Warlow asked.

Catrin shook her head. 'The post-mortem on Jonah Crosby will be later today.'

Warlow wrinkled his nose. 'I can't spare anyone. Is it Sengupta again?'

Catrin nodded.

'Well, I trust her. I'm sure she'll flag up anything unusual if she finds it.'

'We've had several phone calls from Lucy Pargeter's relatives and partner, sir,' Catrin continued. 'It seems they've seen the video. As has Nola O'Brien's sister.'

'Surely they realise it's all a load of *caca*?' Gil said.

'Under normal circumstances, they would. But I doubt they're thinking clearly now.' Warlow took a last bite of his roll, chewed slowly, and swallowed with relish before getting up. 'First things first. We need to speak to the girls' relatives. Reassure them. They have no idea what Jonah put in that letter. We stay positive for them. We need to reassure them we're putting resources behind finding these women. Let's divide up the calls, I'll take—'

The Buccaneer appeared in the doorway; head bent as per his default stance. 'Ah, Evan, you're here already. Good. A word, please?'

Warlow quickly brushed crumbs from his lips and followed the superintendent out. 'Sorry to spring this on you, but the higher ups have set up a press conference. Green is running it, but they want us both to be there.'

'Me?' Warlow was surprised.

'They want a show of strength. Green will make the statement, but the PR gurus think it's a good idea if your face is on view. After last night's video.'

'You've seen it?'

Buchannan nodded. 'Hasn't everyone?'

'What was I supposed to do, sir?'

'Nothing. I'd have done the same. But they want you seen in the light of day, too. Shed the mysterious figure image. We'll have a quick run through now and then do it. Okay?'

Warlow had no choice here. Better he try to own it than come across like a lamb for the slaughter.

They'd set up a microphone stand outside near the signage at the entrance to HQ. A favourite press statement spot. Warlow stood behind Chief Superintendent John Green, the Buccaneer on the other side, as the senior officer read out a statement.

'I can confirm that a second body has been found in the investigation into the death of George Marsden. You appreciate that as this is an ongoing investigation, we are not at liberty to reveal details until the next of kin have been contacted and informed. As of this moment, we cannot rule out the possibility that this second death is linked to Mr Marsden's killing.'

It was only a statement, but the press were no

respecters of protocol. A voice piped up. 'There are claims of more potential victims. Some missing walkers.'

Green remained measured. 'As I've already said, we can't answer any of your questions as of this time.'

'Detective Chief Inspector Warlow, you were filmed last night. There are reports that these killings may have something to do with rituals. Is that correct?'

Warlow waited for Green to answer. But all he did was half turn to glance over his shoulder. In response, Warlow said, 'No.'

'And you're absolutely certain of that?'

'Some people might want to believe YouTube fiction. I prefer to deal with facts.'

Green raised his hand. 'As you will appreciate, we're in the middle of this investigation, and this is all the time we can spare. Thank you for your cooperation. We need to get back to work.'

The officers walked back into the building. Chief Superintendent Green was a relative newcomer. Promotion from another area had brought him to Dyfed Powys only twenty months ago. Warlow didn't know him that well, but he'd heard good things.

'That went okay, sir… didn't it?' Warlow said.

'At least they've seen you're not an ogre… or a vampire.'

Warlow did a double take before he saw Green's mouth twitch. 'Just get this one put away. That usually shuts them up.' Green took off his hat and he and Buchannan turned left. Warlow took a right.

Exactly like boarding a plane.

———

'How did it go, sir?' Rhys asked when Warlow walked back into the Incident Room.

'It's a press statement. Enough said,' Warlow prefixed the words with a grunt. 'Apparently, they wanted me there to prove that I was human.'

'Big ask,' Gil muttered.

'Did it work, sir?' Catrin came up with a more conciliatory question.

'I doubt it. But the Chief Super seemed happy enough. Still, that's forty-five minutes of my life I'm never going to get back. So, where are we with the relatives?'

'All sorted,' Gil said. 'Sounds like Lucy Pargeter's mother is in the worst state, though.'

'Who spoke to her?'

'I did.' Gil lifted his chin. 'It was all going well until she mentioned that Lucy's horoscope had flagged something up last week.'

'Like what?' Rhys asked.

'That she would get some bad news on Sunday.'

'That's complete BS,' Catrin said.

'Oh, really?' Gil replied haughtily. An image of a fisherman reeling in a big one flashed through Warlow's mind. 'And what sign are you, may I ask?' Gil asked, still with one eye under a raised eyebrow aimed at Catrin.

Catrin shook her head. 'Don't believe in it.'

'I bet you're Taurus.'

Catrin's mouth thinned in annoyance. 'How did you know that?'

'I wouldn't be much of a detective if I didn't, would I? Especially since Craig sent you some flowers in the middle of May which I had to sign for.'

Catrin shook her head.

'How about you, sarge?' Rhys asked Gil. 'What sign are you?'

'I was born on the cusp of Uranus. Messy it was. My poor mother. No such things as caesarean sections in those days.'

Rhys giggled.

Catrin rounded on him. 'Do not encourage him, please.'

'No, my zodiac sign is a unicorn,' Gil said, leaning forward and clicking his mouse to bring something up on screen.

That made Rhys pout. 'I don't think a unicorn sign exists, sarge.'

Gil nodded. 'Newsflash, Rhys. None of them bloody exist. Now, I've just had a prelim report from Povey regarding Jonah Crosby. They found some antidepressants in his room. The rope he used is similar to others found in the woodshed at Bryn Encil.'

'Oh,' Warlow said with alacrity. 'Are we back to discussing actual police work now?'

'That's the trouble with these youngsters. They lose concentration so easily.' Gil kept his eyes on his screen.

'Yes, well, we could do with a more thorough catch-up since you've all been so busy while I hogged the limelight.' Warlow walked to the Gallery. 'Gil, you first.'

CHAPTER THIRTY-FOUR

GIL GOT up and joined Warlow at the map. 'The PolSA is still out there. We've added two dog teams to the search. So far, nothing.'

Catrin's phone rang. She answered and excused herself to take it out in the corridor.

'I suppose the question is, should we consider bringing in cadaver dogs?' Gil voiced this harrowing thought as his eyes drifted over the posted images of Lucy Pargeter and Nola O'Brien.

Warlow shook his head. 'The dog teams need a confined area to work in. We'd need to have better search parameters.'

Rhys looked troubled. 'Are we definitely looking for corpses now, sarge?'

Warlow answered before Gil could, his voice a low, adamant growl. 'No, not yet.' He took a step back to better peer at the boards. 'We should probably wait for Catrin. But on the surface, this all looks a tad too… neat.'

'And tidy,' Gil added.

'What do you mean, sir?' Rhys stepped forward.

'We're back to motivation, Rhys.'

'The five Ps sir? Passion, profit, psychosis, protection, and panic.'

Gil swung around, suitably impressed. 'So, he does listen.'

'Occasionally,' Warlow muttered.

'Are you asking me how one of those Ps fits into this case, sir?'

'Well, I'm not asking you who's going to win Strictly.' Warlow tossed him a side-eyed glance.

Rhys took a big intake of breath and let it out slowly, hands on hips as he concentrated on the boards. 'Well, sir, we know Jonah Crosby was capable of violence. That includes sexual violence. So, that might include passion as in some kind of paraphilia—'

'Para what?' Gil stopped Rhys in full flow.

'Paraphilia, sarge. I read up Jonah's case file. He was in court lots of times. He exposed himself to women before he ever got anywhere near touching them. Do you want the definition?' Rhys reached for his phone.

'No, you're al—' Gil began.

Rhys, enthused, ploughed on without waiting for the sergeant to finish. 'A persistent and recurrent sexual interest, urge, fantasy or behaviour of marked intensity involving objects, activities or situations that are atypical.'

'A pervert in old money, then,' Gil said.

'Anyway,' Rhys went on, 'so his 'p' would be passion. But he's also on antidepressants, so I suppose we can't rule out psychosis, too. Especially if you mix those two things together.'

Warlow nodded. 'Go on.'

Catrin came back in, but with an apologetic hand up as she sat and listened to Rhys do his thing.

'Let's say Crosby visits George Marsden. Maybe he wanted more eggs. George tells him about seeing the women about the place, on the moors, or perhaps they called in on him to get eggs, who knows. All by way of ordinary conversation. Perhaps this triggers something in Crosby. Perhaps he decides there and then to abduct the girls. But now, when it comes to any investigation that would follow, George would naturally remember having told Crosby about the women.. So, Jonah kills him there and then. Cold and calculated. After that, his passion, psychoses, paraphilia ignited, he goes after the women, captures them, takes them somewhere, and kills them. We turn up at Bryn Encil. He has nowhere to go. He's filled with remorse at his actions and hangs himself.'

Warlow turned an appraising glace at Rhys. 'Well done, Rhys. Not bad. All I'd say is that it's too neat and a little too convenient.'

'Oh, no, he's mentioned a "C" word,' Gil said.

'And we all hate the "C" words.' Catrin's voice from behind Warlow made him pivot. 'Sorry about the phone call, sir. I've been trying to get hold of Nola O'Brien's flatmate. I've spoken to the sister, but I ought to speak to the flatmate, too. In case she's a YouTube viewer. We ought to pre-empt what she sees there.'

'"C" words,' Gil said. 'Coincidences, corpse,' he dropped his voice and added, 'canute.'

'Canute?' Rhys asked, leaning in and whispering conspiratorially to the sergeant.

'A term I like to reserve for certain journalistic factions,' Gil whispered back.

'Are they linked to a medieval king, then, sarge?' Rhys sounded interested.

'Not exactly.' Gil's lower jaw slid sideways. 'It's an anagram with a couple of vowels added for the sake of propriety.'

Rhys looked puzzled.

Gil sighed. 'What it is to be an ingenue. Let's just say

that the shaven-headed yob and self-styled minder of The Veil is a canute of major proportions.'

Rhys, mouth open, blinked several times before his eyebrows went up as the penny finally dropped.

'Ah yes, The Veil.' Warlow nodded. 'Who exactly is their hard man, by the way?'

Catrin answered Warlow's question, 'His name is Rory McKay. Ex special forces. Served in Iraq before becoming a self-styled paranormal investigator, the brawn to Milton's brain, according to their website.'

'Have we run a check on him?'

The DS shrugged. 'A couple of run-ins while he was in the army. Mostly brawls. Fancies himself as a hard man.'

'That's all we need,' Warlow said.

'He's been to monasteries in Russia, caves in Somerset, spent nights alone in abandoned asylums. He's the guy that gets to do the dangerous stuff, quote, unquote. Half the time, I suspect he tries to put himself in harm's way in order to appeal to the macho-loving side of The Veil's audience. Women and men.' Catrin grimaced.

'What about the cameraman?'

'Don't know much about him, sir,' Catrin went on. 'Goes by the name of Farhad Hossein. He shortens it to Fad. Parents are Iranian immigrants. He has nothing on the PNC either.'

'So, we have nothing on them?' Warlow folded his arms across his chest and sighed. 'The annoying thing is that we're talking about them when we should be looking in other directions. Being innovative.'

'Think outside the box,' Gil said with a nod. 'I knew a goalkeeper once. He was always thinking outside the box. Worst record in the league.'

Rhys grinned but had the sense not to comment.

Warlow's mobile started up and Led Zeppelin's Heartbreaker drew everyone's gaze. Warlow saw who the caller was and placed the phone propped up on the desk so that everyone could see the screen.

'DI Allenby,' Warlow went for mock formality. 'Nice to see you.'

'Morning,' Jess said. Her eyes flicked up to the Gallery and the Job Centre. 'Oh, my, the boards look pretty full.' ·

'We like to keep busy, ma'am,' Catrin said.

'How is murder week, ma'am?' Rhys asked.

'Not as bad as some weeks I've spent with you lot. I'm ringing to congratulate DCI Warlow on his cameo appearance on YouTube.'

'That's nothing, ma'am,' Gil chipped in. 'He's also going to be on national news this evening.'

'What?'

'I've been press ganged,' Warlow said.

'Oh, very good, very good,' Gil grinned.

'Into a press conference,' Warlow clarified seeing Jess's befuddlement. 'I was Chief Superintendent Green's wingman and had to answer such journalistically astute questions as, did I think the murder was a ritual?'

'Same old, same old,' Jess said. 'I hope you gave a good account of yourself?'

'Spectacular,' Warlow muttered.

'But how is it going, really?'

'Two dead and two missing.'

'Oh my God, I knew it was a mistake to leave you lot alone for more than a few days,' Jess said with a wry smile.

'But you'll be back next week, yes, ma'am?' Catrin asked.

'All being well. But surely you will have sorted this case out by then?' The wry smile doubled down on itself.

'I wouldn't count on it,' Warlow said. 'The mispers have dropped off the face of the Earth. Both phones were found at the scene.'

'Oh, that doesn't sound too good.'

'Plus, the suicide left a note admitting to killing the women.'

Jess said nothing for a good few seconds. When she did, all the banter had evaporated. '*Four* dead?'

'Two definite for now,' Warlow said grimly. 'But the note writer has a known history. He also didn't tell us where to look.'

Jess shook her head. 'That's the ultimate power trip, isn't it? Let the relatives suffer long after I've gone. Bastard.'

It was a good word. A word that summed up how they all felt. Jess wished them all luck with the case and ended the call. When she'd rung off, Warlow turned to Catrin.

'Was your call anything significant?'

Catrin shook her head. 'Still waiting on the flatmate. That was her telling me she'd got my message, but that she was on her way to work and would ring me back then, but there's a tube strike so she could be a while.'

'Right. So, that leaves us with nothing for it but pulling on some threads. See what's wriggling at the end of them.'

And that was what they did. Checking on names, chasing up telephone calls. Waiting for others. But it was Rhys who came up with the one solid idea.

Mid-morning, the DC got up and walked over to where Warlow was checking on Rudi Bidulph's records on screen.

'Lucy Pargeter, sir. She works in recruitment.'

'She does.'

'Well, I was thinking, sir, I have a friend of a friend who does that. Specialises in tech recruitment. Anyway, whenever we've been out as a group, she always has two phones, her own and the work's phone because she gives out her number a lot. You know, ring me any time, etc. And the company she works for doesn't like the work phone being used for anything personal.'

'Meaning what, exactly?'

'Meaning there might be another phone besides the one we found.'

'Is she likely to have taken that with her?'

Rhys shrugged. 'Who knows? But these things can become a habit.'

'Hmm.' Warlow nodded. These were the little things that moved the big things forward. 'Then get on to her employers.'

Rhys got back to it. Ten minutes later, he sat back, put the phone down, and punched the air. 'There is a work's phone. Lucy Pargeter has one and, as I thought, she never used that for personal calls.'

'What if she's left it at home?' Catrin asked. 'Last thing I'd want to do was bring a work's phone with me.'

'There is one way to find out. I'll get on to the provider, see if they can trace it.' He turned back to his monitor.

Slowly, surely, the morning wore on.

CHAPTER THIRTY-FIVE

It was well after two in the afternoon when Warlow took a call from Sengupta.

'Mr Warlow, I'm tidying up my preliminary report. I will, of course email it, but I thought we'd have a quick chat.'

'Always a pleasure to hear from the pathology department.'

Static filed the silent beat that followed until Sengupta said, 'The trouble with you, Detective Chief Inspector, is that I can never tell when you're being serious or not.'

'It's a gift.'

'There, see what I mean?'

But he could sense the smile in her voice. She got down to it. 'Bottom line, Jonah Crosby died from asphyxiation by hanging. The ligature marks are consistent with a fixed knot and, since the body had not been moved – thanks for that, by the way – I can confirm that ligation was from a nylon rope with the ligature point being a tree.'

'So, is there any evidence of spine injury?'

'Are you asking if he jumped from the tree?'

'I suppose I am.' The team had discussed scenarios.

One of which was that Jonah had tied on the rope, stood on the bough, and then jumped. The equivalent of a hangman's drop, being always greater than the victim's height.

'No, no evidence of cervical spine injury. I'm afraid this wasn't quick. You know that falling from a height with a noose is effectively decapitation with traumatic spondylosis at C2. The result is a bilateral fracture through the pedicles of C2 allowing anterior displacement of C2 relative to the body of C3—'

'Slow down, doc,' Warlow said.

'Sorry. That's commonly seen in judicial hanging, still carried out in some countries, and results in spinal cord transection. If it's done properly, it's quick. Jonah's death was not quick. He died of cerebral hypoxia.'

'So, if he didn't jump, what did he do?'

'He may have let himself down, taking the weight of the rope in one hand until he was suspended. But there are other factors. We found some residual undigested tablets in his stomach. We've been able to identify some as fluoxetine. An anti-depressant. Interestingly, some of them looked mashed up, as if he was trying to get them to absorb quickly.'

'We found meds in his room.'

'So, a likely scenario is that he might have overdosed and, when the drugs took effect, and drowsiness may well have been a consequence, he made sure by letting himself down on the rope and slipped into unconsciousness. Does that fit?'

'It might do. Anything else?'

'Significant bruising at the back of his head. I can't quite explain that unless he knocked it as he slid down. Toxicology will take a while. We'll get blood levels then. He has a lot of bruises and cuts on his hands, but I understand he was working outside, chopping and cutting wood. Many of those injuries may be work related. He's lost a couple of nails, which suggests that he might have clawed at the rope. Perhaps by then, he was too weak to reverse what had been set in motion.'

Warlow winced. How many people, at the point of no return, regretted their actions? By definition, he would never know.

'Otherwise, he was a fit twenty-four-year-old,' Sengupta concluded.

Warlow thanked her. Povey's team would examine the tree for evidence of how he'd climbed up it. But in the meantime, Sengupta's scenario sounded the most likely.

He walked out into the Incident Room to relay all this to the team, only to find Gil in animated conversation.

'Yes, I realise that, but we can't stop anyone from posting things on social media. That's not our job.'

Warlow watched as Gil drew the phone away from his ear theatrically, letting whoever was on the other end rant for a few seconds before bringing it back to listen.

'If you think they're doing something defamatory or libellous, that's a matter for your lawyers. I'd suggest you contact them. But I'm sorry, there's nothing we can do.'

Another thirty seconds of Gil listening followed until, once again, he spoke.

'Thanks for keeping us informed and I'm sorry you feel that way.' Gil ended the call and arched his back in the seat.

'What was that about?' Warlow asked.

'The Friends of Light. Though they're not being that friendly IMHO. Rudi Bidulph has sent me a link to another YouTube video posted by The Veil. He's fuming. Says that they're trashing the good name of the institution and we should do something about it.'

'Let's have a look, then.' He summoned Catrin and Rhys while Gil's ponderous desktop slithered its way through the ether to the website link. The Veil's lurid header loaded and then Emily Milton appeared, this time from a point above Bryn Encil looking down. Similar to, but not the exact, viewpoint that Gil and Warlow had parked at the day before. This time, the yard was full of police vehicles and crime scene vans, and once more Emily Milton provided the voice-over.

'Below us is a retreat run by the Friends of Light. A secretive, secular organisation who advocate a holistic and non-scientific approach to curing illnesses. This is woolly stuff, guys. But some big names have bought into it. Some of you may remember Jeremy Burroughs, the comedian who battled alcoholism. The Friends of Light helped him, and he certainly sang their praises for a while before he drowned in his own vomit after two bottles of vodka. Raspberry flavoured if I am not mistaken. There, we think, is where the centre of activity is. We can't get any closer than this, but our sources say that a body has been found and that the death was in some kind of sacred grove, probably involving an oak tree. Now the real question is, was this some kind of sacrificial offering? Rory is here with me to give us his breakdown.'

The camera swung back and showed Rory McKay, shaven head, sunglasses on, dark stubble on his chin. 'The Friends of Light have no religious connections, but then, they've chosen to come to a spot where the presence of pagan activity going back millennia is everywhere. Carn Ddu predates modern history. There are caves nearby with scrawled images on the walls. My point is, if you began a movement linked to pagan beliefs, would you want anyone to know? You're hardly likely to broadcast it, are you? All I'm sure of is that we were here when a body was moved out this morning. Whatever is going on here, it's dark.'

Below them, another car pulled into the yard. Milton dropped her voice.

'More activity. We're going to circle around and see if

we can approach close to the point where we were stopped last night. Keep coming back for more as we dig deep into the mystery of Carn Ddu.'

Somewhere off camera, a quad bike started up, and the clip faded out.

No one spoke for twenty seconds.

'Can't we arrest them for being irritating sods, sir?' Rhys asked.

'No, but let the crime scene manager know they're poking about. Gil, give the PolSA a ring. See if he can get some dogs out to the perimeter of Bryn Encil. That might be enough to scare the buggers off. What time was this shot?'

'This morning, by the looks of it.'

'We all heard the quad bikes,' Warlow said. 'That must be how they're getting around. But the last time I looked, there was no convenient quad bike rental service in the vicinity. So, who is doing the ferrying?'

That gave the others food for thought.

Warlow turned away and swivelled towards the boards again. 'But truthfully, I couldn't care less about the bloody Veil. They're irritating insects that keep buzzing in and out of my face. As far as the case goes, with two deaths, we're wallowing in the mud here. I've just spoken with Sengupta. Crosby died of asphyxiation. He also had an excess of anti-depressants in his stomach.'

'He wasn't taking any chances,' Gil said.

'No. But ring Povey's team. Ask them to examine the tree for signs of how he got up there.'

Once again, Catrin's phone rang. 'It's Nola O'Brien's flatmate, sir. I'd better take it.'

Warlow gave her a thumbs up and she hurried out of the Incident Room as Warlow added, 'Sengupta thinks he climbed the tree and maybe let himself down once the drugs kicked in.'

Rhys grimaced. 'That's… brutal.'

'Hanging yourself is.'

Warlow turned to Gil. 'Did we get any further with George Marsden's computer and those encrypted files?'

'No joy there. I get the odd update from the nerds, and they couldn't access it. But I talked to his publisher again. She said it's likely nothing more than his research. George was a man of habit. Careful. That stuff could have been on there for years.'

Warlow heaved out a sigh.

'What about the search teams? Any—'

The Incident Room door burst open and Catrin stormed in, the phone still to her ear. 'Thank you. You've been most helpful… yes… yes… if you could, that would be brilliant.' She pulled the phone away from her ear and regarded the faces of her fellow officers, breathless from the call and her rapid entry.

'The car. Nola's car. It's outside her flat, sir.'

'What?'

'The Nissan Juke. Her flatmate says it's been playing up and needs a new handbrake. They didn't take Nola's car, they took Lucy Pargeter's.'

'So, we've been looking for the wrong car,' Rhys stated the obvious.

'It's worse than that. I think I know where it was on that Sunday.'

CHAPTER THIRTY-SIX

WARLOW DIDN'T BELIEVE in hunches. Most cases were solved by examining the details. Checking and rechecking reports or bits of evidence, teasing out the lies. But he believed in tipping points in investigations. The discovery of a piece of information that opened another avenue of thought for example. An avenue that made you look in a different direction, or made you look at something you'd seen a hundred times already in a subtly different way. A view that made it shine in the light. Listening to Catrin explain herself now, he got the sense that this might be one of those moments.

'A charity walk, sir. That's why Rhys and I were up in that part of the world. We'd all met at the dam at Llyn Brianne and travelled further east. Y Drygan Fawr.'

A red dot appeared on the map, circling around an area that Rhys was obviously keen to show them with his high-tech pointer aimed, lazily, from where he was sitting at his desk. He looked very smug.

'Tidy. Lovely views from up there,' Gil said. '*Anhygoel.*' Incredible indeed.

'When we got back to the dam, that's when we had the

shout about George Marsden. It's how we got there so quickly. We were almost within spitting distance through sheer luck. But the point is, I was with Craig, and when we got to the dam at the end of our walk, he met someone who knew his dad and knew what Craig did. So, jokingly, he "complained" to Craig, the traffic officer,' once again she used the index and middle fingers of both hands to make air quotes around Craig's title, 'about an erratic driver this man had seen at Soar Y Mynydd that morning.'

'And?'

'He described a red VW.'

Warlow started. 'What does Lucy Pargeter drive?'

'A Golf, sir. Red.'

'*Mynufferni*,' Gil whispered.

'Get hold of Craig and tell him to contact this friend of his dad's. We need more detail.' He turned to the boards. 'At last. A bit of luck. Soar Y Mynydd you said?'

Catrin nodded.

'Rhys, get your coat. We're going up there. Once you get some more information, ring us.'

But Rhys didn't move. His trademark blinks were in full flow.

'What?' Warlow asked.

'Just had an email from Lucy Pargeter's work phone provider, sir.' Rhys had up his phone. 'They've pinged it. They're sending over coordinates.'

Gil threw Warlow a pointed glance. 'Did you check your horoscope this morning? Did it say lucky day?'

Rhys still hadn't moved. 'I'm waiting for the mobile phone company to get back to me, sir.'

'Gil can handle that. Come on. It'll take us an hour to get there. We'll take the Audi.'

Rhys had his coat on within twenty seconds.

———

WARLOW TOOK the call from Craig when they were passing through Llandovery.

'Afternoon, sir.' Craig's voice came across the speaker. 'Here we are again.'

'That's the trouble with having a partner in the team, Craig.'

'Sometimes it feels like I already work for you lot.'

Warlow chortled. Craig had been co-opted more than once to lend his expertise. 'Any joy with your man?'

'Danny? I found him eventually. He's retired but still dabbles with a bit of welding and grinding. He has a garage he uses. Has Deep Purple on full blast usually, so there's no chance of him hearing the phone. Anyway, I found him.'

'And?'

'He remembers seeing the car very well, but it's best I ring you back when you're up there. The roads are a bit spaghetti. Best I talk you through it once you've arrived.'

'Fair enough. I'll ring you once we're at the chapel.'

'I'd aim for that, sir. You'll need to find the junction with the Tregaron road.'

'Tregaron, hear that, Rhys?'

'I've got a rough idea where he means, sir.'

This time, they stayed right of the dam, crossed a cattle grid and up onto the mountain road, navigating the twisting contours of the lake, kale-green ribbons of forestry spreading up from the moorland shores. Warlow had been to Canada, and this place would have slid easily into any jigsaw of the Rockies. The road rose and fell, the views sometimes vast vistas ahead, sometimes invisible around hairpin bends. They met no traffic and saw no living things other than the odd wild pony. When they finally reached the easternmost inlet, they dropped to the shore before twisting away from the lake itself for a couple of miles to the northern tentacle of the reservoir. Rhys then headed west, winding down until they got to a junction with a hairpin bend signposted to Soar Y Mynydd Chapel, and another, straight ahead, pointing to Tregaron. Rhys let the car idle.

'This is where Craig was on about, sir.'

Warlow dialled the number. 'We're here,' he said when Craig answered.

'Good, Danny was heading for the chapel from Tregaron.'

Rhys took the bend and then reversed the car thirty yards so that he was positioned as if he'd come from that direction. Ahead of them, the road now split into three like the forks of a trident. To the left, it climbed in the direction they'd just come. To the right was the road to the chapel. In the middle was a narrower single, straight-ahead track.

'Danny said he was going to turn right to the chapel. It's a four mile out and back jaunt. They'd seen no other traffic all day. As he turned, the VW came up towards him on that chapel road. The road dips so you can't see more than a hundred yards as it curves left.'

Warlow smiled to himself. The advantage of having a traffic officer on board was his encyclopaedic knowledge of the roads. Even these remote ones.

'Got that,' Warlow agreed.

'The car came up and Danny braked because it then took a sharp right.'

'A sharp right?'

'Yep. Not the furthest right back over towards the dam. It took the middle road.'

Warlow stared straight ahead. This track had to descend towards the lake because there was nothing else to the south. Only forest to the left where they'd driven from, hills to the right.

'Where does that track lead, Craig?'

'No idea, sir. Maps show it petering out.'

Rhys had his phone out. 'It doesn't go anywhere, sir. On the map here it runs parallel to a river, the Camddwr, and that leads right into the reservoir.'

'Water,' Warlow muttered in a way that suggested it might be shark infested. 'Craig, this is very useful. I'm grateful for your expertise.'

'No problem, sir. Any time.'

With the call ended, Warlow sat in silence. Rhys had worked with him long enough to know these moments were best left undisturbed. Craig had filled them in on what else Danny had told him. The driver had been a woman and had looked "not very happy". Hardly surprising if Jonah Crosby had anything to do with her, or the car. The obvious next step was to take the middle road and follow to where it led. Get the PolSA to redirect operations because this would be no small task. Warlow glanced across at the map on Rhys's phone. The track followed the eastern shore of this western horn of the reservoir with two miles or more of shoreline to search. They needed to narrow things down.

Warlow reached for his own phone and dialled the crime scene manager at Bryn Encil. Povey's team was still there along with some Uniforms posted at the perimeter of the property, as deterrents for The Veil more than anything. Ten minutes later, he phoned back.

'I have Thomas Seaton here, sir.'

'Thomas, thanks for talking to me. I have a question for you about Jonah. Mr Bidulph told me he sometimes fished in the reservoir and the river. Is that right?'

'He did.'

'Did you ever go with him when he went to the reservoir?'

'Maybe… why?'

'We're up near Soar Y Mynydd and heading down towards the dam. Is there any chance you could come over here? If you came with us, it might jog your memory.'

A reluctant pause. 'We're still busy here.'

'We'd be very grateful, Mr Seaton.'

'I suppose I could. I'd need to clear it with Mr and Mrs Bidulph.'

'Leave that to us. Give the phone back to the officer.'

Five minutes later, the arrangements were made. The crime scene manager spoke to the Bidulphs and Seaton was on his way in a response car.

Warlow looked over at Rhys. 'I don't suppose you brought emergency sandwiches, did you?'

'Well, sir, funny you should say that because my mother did wonder about me... us... the team, that is, having to do so much travelling. She made me a bit of a grab bag. Since we had lunch at HQ, I didn't bother opening it. It's in the boot, sir.'

'Don't tell me there's a flask of tea in there?'

'Oh yes, sir. And ham and tomatoes and tuna and onion sarnies.'

Warlow, for once, was lost for words.

'You alright, sir?'

'I am. Two thoughts strike me. One is why your mother has not been offered an award for her services to the police. And the second is why you are still sitting there instead of getting out and opening the boot.'

Rhys grinned. 'Got you, sir. I'm on it.'

———

IN THE INCIDENT ROOM, Gil had also supplied a fresh brew for himself and for Catrin. The Human Tissue For Transplant box was open. Catrin took a Hobnob, while Gil opted for a Morrison's tea cake.

Catrin raised an eyebrow. 'Don't see those on offer in the box normally?'

'Morrison's leftovers from a birthday party. Not mine, I hasten to add. Good biscuit base, lovely marshmallow as compared with the gold standard, which is a Tunnock's. *Arglwydd,* those Scots can make a bloody teacake. But to be fair to Morrison's, these are bite size and so fulfil the craving with fewer calories. Win, win.'

'I can detect several flaws in that argument, but life is too short.' She dunked and ate, chewed a few times, and then asked, 'What are you working on?'

'Just waiting on the call back from the provider for Lucy Pargeter's work phone. In the meantime, I've been looking up The Veil. McKay in particular. He specialises in surveillance. Were you aware?'

'No.' Catrin frowned.

'There's a thread on one of the blog-thingies where he says he can attach a GPS tracker to a car and remove it with no one knowing it's ever been there.'

'You're not seriously saying he's done that to one of ours?'

'I wouldn't put it past these buggers. I'll mention it to the DCI when I see him. Guaranteed to cheer him up.' Gil took a bite of the mini teacake and seemed to lose focus in a moment of ecstasy. 'You ought to try one. Full marks, I have to say.' His words came out thickly, through a mouth clogged with marshmallow and biscuit. 'How about you? Getting anywhere?'

'Thought I'd run through the Bryn Encil employees list. There are other people there besides Jonah Crosby. I've done two of the hotel staff. Nothing is showing up. Couple more to go, that's all.'

'I wonder how they're getting on up at the dam. They'll be missing this, I know that.' He held up his mug.

Little did he know.

CHAPTER THIRTY-SEVEN

THERE WERE WORSE places in the world to have a Mrs Harries' picnic. What struck Warlow most as he chewed his way through a third triangular tuna and onion with a dash of mayonnaise delight was the quiet. They'd seen no traffic, heard no planes, felt no wind. The day had remained calm and overcast. A day for contemplation while you munched your sandwiches and sipped your tea in a textured, solitary landscape. Artists came here to find the muse. But Warlow's thoughts were focussed only on finding two women.

At last, a response vehicle appeared, winding its way up from the Soar Y Mynydd road. Five minutes later, it went back the way it came, but short one passenger, who now sat in the rear of the Audi. Warlow had kept a couple of sandwiches back, and Thomas Seaton accepted them hungrily.

'Okay, Rhys, let's get moving,' Warlow ordered once Seaton had belted up.

The Audi moved forward along the central stretch of tarmac. A stretch that soon petered out into stone and then packed earth. The river they ran parallel to was not wide and a few hundred yards from the turning, Thomas stopped them and pointed to a right turn.

'We fished here once,' he said.

Rhys parked up and he and Warlow got out. But this was little more than a stream and after just ten minutes, neither officer felt this was anywhere you could easily hide bodies. Disturbed ground here would be easy to spot. Rhys reversed and found the wider track again. They drove on, skirting the edge of another forestry plantation on their left until the road ended at a point where the reservoir proper began and a much wider body of water became visible on their right.

'This looks like a good fishing spot,' Warlow said.

'Can't say I remember being here.' Seaton shook his head.

'But it is accessible,' Warlow observed. Once again, he and Rhys got out, this time Thomas accompanied them. The shoreline of rocky earth and grass stretched a good forty yards north and south.

Warlow turned to Thomas. 'You can stay in the car if you like. We're going to have a quick recce.'

He nodded and walked back.

'Rhys, you go north, I'll go south. It's the last place anyone could park a vehicle without driving blindly into the forest off-road. And there were two women. No point going anywhere where it might be difficult to carry… anything heavy.'

Rhys nodded, his face serious.

Slowly, the officers began combing the shore for any signs of recent activity.

———

GIL TOOK the call a little after five-thirty. Most mobile phone providers had dedicated departments for law enforcement inquiries, and Gil had a working knowledge of how these things worked. Various phone towers received a signal by pinging the phone they wanted to locate. It responded so long as it was on and sent a signal back to the tower. By comparing the strength of the return signal, an estimation of distance from each individual tower was possible. Three towers gave an intersecting position and GPS coordinates. With these, Gil could plot the figures on an on-screen map.

'Bingo,' he said when the little red balloon showed up. Something in his voice drew Catrin's instant attention.

Catrin looked up from her desk. 'What?'

'I've found the phone.'

She scurried around to stare over his shoulder.

'That's at Llyn Brianne. Where's Rhys?'

'Up there somewhere.'

'I'll get him to ping us his location. Hang on.'

She sent Rhys a text. 'Let's hope he has a signal,' she said.

He did. His message came back within seconds. She showed the pinged position to Gil, who flicked from the phone to his screen. '*Iesu*, they're in the right place but on the wrong side of that peninsula.' Catrin held up her phone and took a photo of Gil's screen and texted Rhys.

Meanwhile, Gil was staring at the satellite image of where the phone was.

'Bugger all there as far as I can tell. Just trees at the edge of the reservoir.'

'How accurate is that thing?'

'They say to within a few metres. Four, five maybe?'

Catrin glanced at her watch. 'Then let's hope the light lasts.'

———

RHYS RAN BACK along the shoreline, holding up his hand. When he got near enough, Warlow saw he was holding his phone aloft.

'Gil and Catrin, sir. They've found Lucy's work phone.'

Warlow stared at the image and the two that followed. He turned to peer at the trees behind him. 'We're way off. The phone is on the other side of this forest.'

Rhys nodded, panting. 'On the western arm of the other horn of the lake, sir. Across this strip of forest.'

'Shit. How do we get over there?'

'I thought I saw some access roads as we drove down, sir. Forestry vehicle tracks.'

Warlow remembered seeing rough lines left by tracked vehicles.

'We could try getting through one,' Rhys said.

'No try about it.' Warlow turned and headed back to the car. Seaton looked at them expectantly when both officers got in.

'Find anything?' he asked.

'No. We think we're in the wrong place. We need to get across to the other side of this plantation.'

Thomas shook his head. 'I never fished over that side.'

'Don't worry. In his previous life, Rhys was a bloodhound.'

'Was I, sir?'

'Let's hope you were.'

'What are you looking for?' Seaton asked.

'A phone. We've already traced it. And it belonged to one of the missing women.'

'A second phone?'

'Exactly,' Rhys said, stoked by the news from HQ. 'A work's phone.' His finger reached for the start button, but hesitated. Instead of starting the car, he cocked his head.

'What?' Warlow asked.

'Hear that, sir?' Rhys's window slid down smoothly.

And then Warlow heard it too. The drone of some quad bikes somewhere in the hinterland.

'This is quad bike country, right? Could be nothing.' Warlow wound the window up.

Rhys nodded, but a dubious frown remained.

It wasn't easy to turn the car around, but Rhys managed a ten-point turn and they retraced their route, this time more slowly. Four hundred metres back, the trees thinned out at a point where they'd been culled, and a newly planted area extended to their right. The machines used to cut and move the trees had also made a very rough track, now overgrown with grass, but still visible.

Rhys showed Warlow his phone again. 'According to this, there's a bigger forestry road on the other side, a hundred metres away. I think this is our best bet, sir.'

'Do it.'

'It might not do the Audi much good, sir.'

'Sod the Audi.'

Rhys nodded and turned to follow the rough, uneven track.

The way was rutted. Stunted. branches made some very unpleasant noises against the paintwork. The car lurched, bouncing on its springs, but slowly and surely, they skirted the edge of the denser trees and the way opened until, with a spurt of power, Rhys crested a bank and turned onto a clearer, flatter track.

'Forestry workers must have brought the transporters in as far as here, sir.'

Warlow didn't answer.

The new track wasn't the M4, but it was better than the one they'd been on.

'Sorry about this,' Warlow said, turning to address Seaton in the back seat. 'We have no choice but to bring you.'

'This is unfamiliar territory for me,' Seaton said, hanging on to a roof handle as the car jolted along.

'We don't but bear with us.'

The track ran south for three hundred metres and then petered out into ruts and a wall of newly planted trees. 'I think this is as far as I can take her, sir.' Rhys pulled up.

The map showed the phone location to be directly east, seventy-five metres through the forest and ten or so back from the shore.

'Okay, we walk from here.' Warlow glanced at his watch. After six. Still enough daylight to do what they needed to do. But it would be gloomy under the trees. 'Thomas, mind coming with us? We may need to search, and an extra pair of eyes would be great.'

Seaton nodded. 'I'll be glad to help.'

Rhys had his phone up, heading for the target. They'd gone twenty yards when the DC cursed. Not a hair-raising oath, but bad enough for him. 'Bloody hell. I've lost signal again, sir. It's coming and going. There must be a signal wherever the phone is, but here it's patchy, to say the least.'

Warlow didn't stop walking. 'Doesn't matter. We keep going in a straight line.'

'But it's a phone, sir, we'll never find it.'

'How many yards were left?'

'Fifty.'

'We're not going back,' Warlow said.

The trees were mature and densely packed. Branches crunched and snapped underfoot as the three men made their way through. There may well have been an hour or more's daylight left, but a perpetual dusk existed under the canopy. Warlow kept count of his steps. A rough estimation, but better than nothing. They'd taken forty when he called a halt.

'It's here somewhere. Let's fan out, five metres apart. Eyes peeled.'

They moved in a half crouch, peering at the ground, shifting branches with their feet, sometimes with their hands. When they'd been at it for five minutes, Rhys once again called out. 'Signal's back, sir. But it's only one bar. I've had a brainwave, sir. I'll ring Pargeter's phone now. See if it responds. It must have a signal if it's been pinpointed.'

The sound of more quad bikes seemed louder. But again, impossible to tell where it was coming from.

Rhys pressed some buttons and waited, stepping to his left and then to his right to find the best signal. 'It's ringing, sir, but I can't tell which direction.'

And then Warlow heard it. A standard ringtone. He pivoted. The noise came from behind where Thomas Seaton stood. In a denser part of the forest where a tree had fallen, its shallow base upended. Warlow hurried across and moved around it, only to stop and stare. A mass of branches had piled up, or been placed, over a large object behind the uprooted tree, in a half-hearted attempt at concealment. Though from who exactly out here in the wilderness was anybody's guess.

Not passers-by definitely.

More likely a search helicopter.

They'd have never seen it from the air. Had it not been for the phone, Warlow and Rhys might have strolled right past, too. Someone had gone to a lot of trouble to hide it.

'Found it,' Warlow said. 'And I've found Pargeter's red VW as well.'

CHAPTER THIRTY-EIGHT

The Veil, on two quad bikes, came to a halt and dismounted.

'Where are they?' Milton asked.

'Half a click south,' McKay said. 'They'll have heard the bikes, so we walk from here. Stealth mode from now on, Em. Plus, their car's been stationary for at least ten minutes. I reckon they're on foot, too.'

Milton and Hossein checked their kit. The fourth member of the entourage, the driver of the second quad and the man who provided the bikes, did not dismount. 'Should I stay here then, with the bikes?' he asked.

Milton walked over to him and gave him a perfunctory hug.

'Thanks, Nathan. I don't know what we'd have done without you, mate. Make sure you thank your dad, too, for the loan of the bikes.'

'No worries,' Nathan said, his face flushed and excited. His father had no idea that he'd lent the bikes to The Veil. He didn't need to. Besides, he'd only throw a fit. 'What happens if you find something? I mean, actual demons or something?'

Hossein answered, 'If we do, we record it and we all end up being superstars, man.'

McKay consulted a small device about half the size of a mobile phone. 'We'd better get a move on or we'll lose too much light. The tracker still works. We all set?'

Camera and Milton both nodded.

With that, they walked off into the forest, leaving Nathan Thorley to his own devices.

————

RHYS FOUND the phone in the glove compartment of the VW, under a poorly folded rangefinder map.

'Almost out of power,' he said when he picked it out. 'Lucky.'

'Why the hell would they abandon the car here?' Warlow asked. 'In the middle of all this.' He did a quick one-eighty. 'Craig's contact said he saw a woman driving. So, let's assume they drove here. Why?'

'They were made to, sir?'

'Exactly. So, Crosby wanted to hide the car. But where has he hidden the women?'

'The lake?' Rhys suggested.

Warlow nodded. It made sense. 'It's what, fifty yards that way.' He turned to the east. 'Rhys, call in the troops.' He looked up at the sky and then at his watch. 'But we can't wait. I'd say we have thirty minutes of good light left. Let's make use of it and take a look.'

Once more, they walked through the trees, picking their way along, all the while the gloom deepening. But after thirty steps, the edge of the forest appeared ahead, the gaps between the trees getting lighter as they approached. They emerged onto a grassy strip separating forest from lake. Beyond that lay the water. But in between stood yards of caked mud.

The summer had seen a severe drought in most of the country, and the reservoir levels were low. So low that from where they now stood, a lost world had appeared like skeletons reaching up from a graveyard.

All three men came to a standstill as they took in the remarkable sight. Like a mini-Atlantis rising from the depths, the receding waters had revealed a huddle of buildings, some with four intact walls still, others crumbling ruins. Once, this must have been an entire village. Sacrificed in the name of progress and to fulfil the basic needs of people. Along the shore, to the north, bigger buildings were visible, some of them perhaps never fully submerged even when the reservoir was full. But as Warlow let his eyes take in the sight, he saw a chapel and what might have been a school with a tall gable end and gaps where windows had let in light. Beyond that, lower, longer buildings stretched into the trees. Remnants of a farm or perhaps a mart.

All now high and dry.

It was a grey world that they regarded. The dried mud coated the buildings. Grey clouds blanketed the sky. And further out, the slate-grey waters stood as still as a pond, the keeper of a thousand secrets.

'Sir.' Rhys's voice broke the spell. 'Do you think that they're here somewhere?'

Good question.

Warlow spoke his mind. 'It's as good a place as any to hide something you don't want to get found.'

'Should we split up, sir?'

'Good idea. You take the bigger buildings, the chapel and the school and whatever those other structures are at the north end. I'll do the… street?' He had to search for the word and found it eventually, because now he realised that there was a kind of arrangement to the buildings. A sloping avenue that stretched down until the furthest buildings were completely engulfed by the mud.

'Can I help?' Seaton asked.

Warlow turned to the man. 'Yes. Stay near the shore. I see some smaller buildings between here and the school. Have a look in there.'

Seaton nodded.

'I know there's no need for me to say this, but shout if you find something.'

Rhys and Seaton walked off. Warlow stepped out onto the mud. Some sections remained a darker colour. He sensed that these would be damper patches. Slippery at best, a quagmire at worst. He resolved to stay on the dry stuff. Because where it was dry, the silt had hardened to the consistency of concrete.

As he walked out, he desperately thought about what this place had once been called. He should have known. There was more than one in Wales and more than one that had been, and still were, bones of contention in a nation blessed with bounteous rainfall. Villages drowned to supply water for areas much further away, across the border, where population growth had far outstripped supply. Driving around Wales, especially in the west, painted murals in white on red that said *Cofiwch Dryweryn*, spoke of one of the more contentious projects where the destruction of a community at the behest of a foreign power, an English city council, was grist to the nationalist mill.

Dryweryn had become a rallying call.

But these were fleeting thoughts in Warlow's head. Whatever life had existed in this village had long gone under millions of gallons of water running down from the Cambrian mountains. What he wanted now was for this mausoleum to once more give up its secrets.

Some of the tiny houses he approached were easy to eliminate. One glance in over thigh-high walls showed the caked mud and nothing more. But others stood a couple of storeys tall. These he needed to either climb up, or find an ingress into, so that he could examine inside.

All this he did carefully, and in trepidation. Not only because it was precarious, but also because every time he looked, it was in fear of not finding the two women, but two corpses left by a calculating killer who hoped that the waters would swallow them up. Because, in two months' time, by November at the latest, this forgotten place would once more be buried under the cold grey waters and it would be divers, not Warlow, who would need to fulfil this unenviable task.

Get a grip, Evan, he thought to himself. *You haven't found corpses yet. These women are alive until you do.*

He leant down to look through a window opening at mud level into the space beyond, roofless with one wall already crumbled to nothing but with three walls intact. And there, still attached to a wall and hanging on a nylon string, was a wooden carving.

It read *Cartref.* Home.

But this home held no human, dead or alive.

He stood up and moved on to the next.

————

RHYS GOT TO THE SCHOOL. He turned back, but there was no sight of Warlow or Seaton. Buildings obscured the view. He turned forward to stare further up the shore. He'd head there next. First, though, he needed to look inside this crumbling ruin.

He considered his options. The gable end stood ten feet tall. He walked around to the front, the wall facing the lake, and spied a three-foot gap just above the mud. Probably where the door had been. He wrinkled his nose. It meant he'd need to kneel and perhaps crawl through.

'Brilliant,' he muttered.

In the end, he managed by squatting and sliding his head under, sideways, his hair brushing the lintel and scattering dried mud onto his face and in his mouth. He spluttered and spat it all out and emitted a word he'd never use in front of his mother. Once inside, his eyes were immediately drawn to a jumble of desks piled high in one corner. Why had they left the desks? He stepped across, kicking up grey dust as he did. He studied the Jenga pile. The whole lot was covered by an unbroken patina of mud. No one had entered this room since the waters had gone down. There were no bodies underneath the desks. No need to disturb anything here.

Shadows were deepening as he left the building. He exited the same way as he'd entered and bent at the waist to brush off the patches of dust on his trousers. It was as he walked around the school to make for the large low buildings further on that he heard the scream.

A long, shrill, terrified noise in a woman's voice.

It came from the forest behind him.

Rhys forgot about everything else and turned towards the gloom of the forest. He put his head down and sprinted towards the source of the noise.

CHAPTER THIRTY-NINE

GIL PRINTED off images of Lucy Pargeter's red VW Golf and was adding them to the Gallery when he heard Catrin's exclamation of shock and horror. That she uttered it in a kind of disbelieving whisper made it even more distressing.

'Oh, my God.'

Gil turned to see her eyes glued to the screen.

'What?' he asked, the VW poised under a magnet.

'You need to see this.' She spoke the words without looking up.

Gil strode over and studied the screen and a list of names.

'Friends of Light. The staff at Bryn Encil. I told you I was running checks on them all.'

'And?'

'And this has come up.'

Gil looked at the name, and the death certificate attached to it. 'What the hell does that mean?'

'It means that someone has been hiding in plain sight all this time.'

'You need to get this to Rhys and Evan...'

But she was already on her feet, phone clamped to her ear, waiting, and willing, for one of them to answer the call.

———

WARLOW HEARD THE SCREAM, too. He looked up and saw Rhys running towards the tree line from the ruined school. Quickly, the DCI moved and took a tangential route between the crumbling houses towards where he'd seen the DC cross the divide between lake and forest. But there were bigger patches of wet mud here, and he had to detour around the worst of them. It took longer than he'd hoped. But eventually, he jumped over the final soft patch onto grass, where he paused momentarily to catch his breath and recalculate where he thought he'd seen Rhys last. He looked around for any sight of Thomas Seaton. No doubt he would have heard the scream, too. Perhaps he had followed Rhys, which was not a good thing. Civilians were always a liability in situations like this.

What made him look up the shoreline to the buildings beyond the school at that exact moment he would never know. But it never paid to wonder about these things too much. A movement caught his eye. Something, a shape, crossing the narrow divide between the forest edge and the end building that looked as if it might never be completely submerged, no matter how high the reservoir. That shape, not an animal, but a person.

No, two people.

One hunched over as if pulling or dragging another. And that other moving, too, but not smoothly. As if it was resisting.

Warlow made a judgement call. He abandoned the thought of following Rhys and ran towards the buildings.

———

RHYS SAW MOTION AHEAD. Someone running.

He shouted, but they ignored him.

Whoever it was, they were not running fast because they were lugging a heavy backpack. Rhys put on a sprint. He caught the runner easily and tackled him from behind.

Both men fell and beneath them, branches cracked as they rolled.

Rhys got up first and reached for the baton he'd attached to his belt. He flicked it open and held it up.

'Police. Stay down,' he ordered.

The man ignored him.

'I said stay down.' He stepped forward and pushed the man down.

'No, no, please, we can't stay here. We can't.'

Rhys recognised the voice first and then, as the face beneath him twisted to the side, he recognised The Veil's cameraman, Hossein.

'What the hell are you doing here?'

'Filming. Following you lot. But it's not safe, man. There's something here.'

'What do you mean, something here?'

'Something… I don't know. It came out of nowhere, man. Attacked Rory. Knocked him fucking out. Then it grabbed Em, and… I ran for it, man.'

'Where are they?'

'Back there.' Hossein waved vaguely then started to cry. 'I don't want to die, man. I don't want any of this shit.'

'You ran away and left them?'

'I did.' He was bawling now. 'I ran away and left them because I was shit scared.'

Rhys got up and let Hossein stand. The cameraman kept apologising, like a caught-out child. 'I'm sorry, man. I'm sorry.'

'Head west. You'll come to an Audi. That's our car. Stay there.'

Hossein nodded. For a moment. Rhys felt like slapping him. But fear did all kinds of things to people. He'd already learnt that. You couldn't blame someone for cowardice. Fight or flight was a powerful thing.

'Go on,' he said and watched Hossein trot away.

He found McKay three minutes later by following the groans.

He was lying propped up against a tree, blood streaming from a head wound, holding his left arm up against his chest at the elbow. The wrist of that hand flopped forward. Broken. Useless.

Rhys knelt next to him.

'Fractured,' McKay mumbled.

Rhys nodded. 'What happened?'

'The bastard bushwhacked us.'

'Who did?'

'Some bloke. He sideswiped me from behind. Stomped on my arm as I was down. Farhad ran off, but the bloke… he took Em.' McKay ground his teeth together. 'I need to get up.' He pushed forward and promptly turned to one side and vomited.

'You're not going anywhere.' Rhys quickly fashioned a support for the arm from a fleece he found in McKay's backpack. 'And you have no idea who did this?'

McKay, pale and sickly, shook his head. 'Except… we left Nathan Thorley with the bikes. He could have followed us.'

'Which way did he take Milton?'

McKay indicated with his head.

Rhys got up and hurried through the trees.

———

Warlow got to the building and crept forward. Two-thirds of the roof remained. The rest had fallen in, but the walls appeared thick and solid. Where the render had fallen away, he saw and felt old stone. He walked to the corner and looked out towards the lake and the exposed adjoining outbuildings that the low waters had revealed. These had wide openings and looked as if they had once housed animals. Warlow kept going around the edges of the building, once more on dried mud. He could imagine the reservoir waters lapping up against this wall, though. He could smell the musky damp as he worked his way around towards the far end of this lakeside gable end where another wall led back towards the tree line.

He crept, stayed low, listening, waiting.

At last, his patience was rewarded.

Someone moaned.

Quickly, harshly, that moan was cut off by someone hissing. 'Shut up.'

Realisation, like the first stirrings of an avalanche, shifted in Warlow's head. That voice was familiar. Suddenly, the folly of his and the team's actions felt like a ton of ice falling on his head.

Of course. Of bloody course. And yes, he'd been distracted. As he had been distracted all along by those idiots on quad bikes. The YouTubers searching for a ghost story when in fact, something alive and much, much worse was already amongst them.

His phone buzzed in his pocket.

He picked it out. Catrin was calling.

He cancelled the call and texted her to tell her he couldn't speak.

She texted back the information. Warlow read it and felt his scalp contract. He should have known. Should have realised an hour ago when they'd found Lucy Pargeter's VW.

Warlow walked along the third wall until he got to the last corner. To the side of the building that faced the trees. He peeked but saw nothing. Only a half-open iron door. But his brain kept replaying one phrase.

A second phone.

Those were the words Seaton had used. Which, by definition, meant he must have known there'd been a first phone. Only the police and one other would have known that, since it was the perpetrator who'd thrown Lucy's first phone into the little garden of the Airbnb.

Warlow, hugging the wall, walked to the door, and stepped into the gloomy interior.

'Thomas Seaton, though obviously that's not your real name, this needs to end here. You have nowhere to go.'

A muffled moan to his right made Warlow start and move further in. The place stank of human waste and blood mixed into a vile and unholy perfume. Warlow peered and his eyes adjusted to the gloom. Thomas Seaton had Emily Milton in his grasp, his head silhouetted against the dusky light behind a glassless window. She had silver tape over her mouth and a knife at her throat. Her eyes had the look of an animal near the end.

'Meddlin' bastard,' Thomas said, his accent, now that there was no longer need for any pretence, much broader.

'Who are you, really?' Warlow asked. 'Because you're not Seaton. He's dead and buried in a Glasgow cemetery.'

'You can call me Santa fuckin' Claus for all I care.'

'I think Lazarus would be better, don't you? What's the plan? I'm here, you're here, and soon this place will be crawling with my lot. What then?'

'Nah. That's not how it's going to go. I'm walking out o' here.'

'To where? Unless you can walk over water, there is nowhere to go.' Outside, darkness was creeping up like a panther. Almost with every passing second, Lazarus's features diminished, as if he was melting into the darkness behind. A shame The Veil weren't filming. This would have got them a million hits. But this was no static tableau because slowly, Lazarus inched around, putting himself between Warlow and the half-open iron door.

'Are the girls here? Is this where you left them?' Warlow asked.

'Why don't you ask Jonah?' Lazarus laughed.

Warlow shook his head. 'No. That was all you. It's always been all you. Typing out a suicide note, though.' Warlow tutted. 'That rings all kinds of alarm bells. Schoolboy error there. What did you do, spike his tea? Force him to swallow his bottle of pills and then string him up?'

'Enough talkin'. I'm out of here with this little bitch as insurance. Come anywhere near me and I'll slice her voice box in half.'

They'd moved almost all the way around now. Almost to the door. But from where he now stood, hand clutched around the still terrified Milton, Lazarus couldn't see what Warlow could see; a tall shape outside the square glassless window that Lazarus had been in front of a few moments before. Warlow registered it in his peripheral vision. But he forced his eyes not to flick across. Not to give the game away. Someone was out there. Someone big.

'No one is going to follow you. No one is going to need to.' Warlow's voice was calm, confident. He needed Lazarus to believe him. 'We have people here already. Armed with night vision and laser-sighted weapons.' He hoped he'd said enough.

'Bullshit. Think I was borne fuckin' yesterday. You lot—'

The red dot appeared on the wall to Lazarus's left and swung unerringly onto his head. It shut him up and Warlow quickly raised his hand.

'No bullshit. Let her go, or I drop my hand. That's all it'll take. One movement for your head to be decorating the back of that door.'

'Bastards.' Panic seized Lazarus. He ducked and pushed Milton forward at the same time, lunging through the gap that had once been a back door, turning and heading straight for the dark tree line. Unfortunately for him. The 'armed response team' was waiting. And even though the red laser dot had come from Rhys's whiteboard laser pointer, the rest was accurate enough. He was armed, but only with a telescopic baton, the long legs of a four-hundred-metre runner, and an eye for the tackle. Rhys intercepted Lazarus halfway to the trees and caught him a good one with a thrashing blow from the baton to the left upper thigh, followed by one to the back of the knees.

Lazarus fell with a grunt.

He still had the knife, though. But he didn't once Rhys stamped on his hand.

Warlow joined the DC a moment later, and between them, they had the killer cuffed and subdued within two minutes.

'Shall I charge him, sir?'

Warlow looked back towards the dark building. 'You can. But give me two minutes to find out what exactly that charge will be.'

He stood up and hurried back to the building where Milton, still gagged, had slumped against a wall. Warlow took off the tape from her mouth and her hands. She was crying and clutching at him.

'Okay, it's okay, You're alright. He's gone.'

He felt her shuddering sobs on his shoulder but he pulled her away. 'Stay here. I need to check something out.'

'No, no.' She grabbed at him but he removed her hands gently.

'I need to know what he's done to the girls.'

That quelled her. Warlow put his phone light on. The beam lit up the floor space properly for the first time. Pools of stagnant water dotted the uneven, debris-strewn ground. That it had been some kind of animal pen was obvious from the concrete byres. He walked around a divider and stopped.

His light revealed two slumped forms. One on its side, the other sitting. He swung the beam at the sitting figure.

'Hello. It's the police.'

Sometimes, it truly was a magic word. The sitting figure came to life, and her eyes flew open. Desperate noises emerged through the tape over her mouth. Warlow knelt and carefully cut it free. She, too, was crying, sucking in great gulps of air. Hardly able to talk.

'Are you Nola or Lucy?' he asked.

'L… Lucy. But Nola… is she… oh, God, please tell me she's okay.' They weren't words. Merely barely coherent staccato croaks in the soprano wail.

Warlow went over to the second figure. She didn't move when he touched her. But when he cut the tape to get to the pulse in her neck some of it caught in her hair and, as he pulled it away, miraculously she moaned.

Moaning was good. Moaning was bloody brilliant. Moaning meant she was alive. Warlow let out a tiny 'Hah,' of triumph.

Quickly, he unclipped the spring snaps holding the chain to the wall, unwound the chain from her wrists, and then returned to Lucy Pargeter to do the same.

'Can I help?' Emily Milton stood behind Warlow, wiping tears and snot from her face with a tissue, staring wide-eyed at the scene.

'You can. Stay with these women while I get things organised. Check that they're not injured. Can you do that?'

Emily Milton nodded and went to Nola.

By then, he'd freed Lucy. 'You're okay. It's going to be okay.'

She threw her arms around him. 'Thank you. Thank you.' She pulled back but didn't let him go. 'Who are you?' she asked in a tremulous whisper.

'You can call me Evan.'

CHAPTER FORTY

THOMAS SEATON's real name was Clyde Watson and he had a criminal history stretching back decades. A sexual predator whose wrongdoing began with burglary and fraud but progressed to much worse crimes. Gil gave them the rundown the following morning.

'He's been married three times in the nineties. Why anyone would want to get near him is beyond me, but there it is. He'd usually choose partners much younger than himself. He preferred thin, sometimes emaciated girls. One report I read said that he liked them that way because they looked like children.'

A loud swallow followed this as Rhys downed a mouthful of tea. Better that than spluttering it out all over the floor, thought Warlow.

'In ninety-five, he marries his third wife, a seventeen-year-old called Daryl Pearson. They have a son. He forces her into staying with him by threatening the child while he brings prostitutes home. He likes to choke his partners.'

Catrin doesn't drink her tea. It stands cold at her elbow. Judging by the tightness of her lips, Warlow doubts anything would get past them this morning.

'In ninety-eight, two underage prostitutes are attacked and left for dead in Glasgow. They survive. The details are on file, and I won't go through them now. Clyde Watson is convicted and sentenced. He serves eighteen years. He's already on the sexual offences register for what he's done, but he's also under suspicion for three unsolved murders in the nineties. In 2018, he fails to report to his probation officer. A month later, Thomas Seaton turns up at Bryn Encil. Seaton has a chequered history, too. But his convictions are Mickey Mouse compared with Clyde Watson. As Seaton, he admits to having been convicted of fraud and burglary. What we now know is that Seaton was in prison with Watson, but that he was a poorly controlled diabetic and died shortly after his release. It's likely that Watson stole Seaton's identity and somehow got hold of enough documentation to satisfy the Friends of Light.'

'I prefer you when you're cracking dad jokes,' Catrin said without a trace of a smile.

'There isn't very much good news in any of this, admittedly. But perhaps a sliver of silver lining. Police Scotland are on the way down because they're in the middle of Operation Murray. Five unsolved murders they think might be linked to Watson, including Deborah Sharpe, the eighteen-year-old student who went missing after a music festival in Campsie Fells.'

Catrin nodded. 'I remember that.'

'The DCI, I think his name was Bone, I spoke to says they have a sack load of evidence, including a murder weapon found at Watson's flat.'

'Bone?' Catrin asked. 'Unusual name. But I think I've read stuff about him.'

'Lots to play with there. Name like Bone, I mean,' Rhys said. 'Of contention. Idle. White. Bones, as in the ship's doctor.' He glanced at Warlow. 'Star Trek reference, sir.'

'He sounded pretty competent on the phone,' Gil added. 'Anyway, he's on the way down to interview Watson, and I think he's likely to buy you an enormous bottle of whisky, Mr Warlow.' He nodded at the DCI. 'He hinted at Macallan.'

'Result,' Rhys said. But it was with none of his usual boyish enthusiasm. This word came out gritty and heartfelt.

'What about the women?' Warlow asked.

'Both in hospital, sir. Dehydrated and starving,' Catrin answered. 'But they'll survive. Nola O'Brien has a concussion, a broken nose and a stab wound. But it could have been worse.'

'Yes,' Warlow agreed. 'It could have been a lot worse. And Watson. Is he saying anything?'

He'd let Gil and Catrin speak to Watson and lay out the charges.

'That's the thing about him,' Gil replied. 'He's a no comment artist. Operation Murray has another three missing women they suspect Watson of killing, but they've found no trace of the bodies. He didn't speak at his last trial. But I read something from a psychiatrist that just about sums him up.' Gil shuffled some papers in his hand and scanned through. 'Yes, here it is. He says that "Watson has the reasoning of a four-year-old." Psychopaths like him are stuck in the narcissistic, egocentric belief that a toddler has. They're not to blame for anything, or so they believe. And I know that from personal experience having recently had one of my bathrooms re-decorated with boot polish by a four and half-year old.' He held a hand up to forestall questions. 'Don't ask.'

Warlow turned to Rhys. 'Shame that laser pointer thingy of yours wasn't *actually* a high-powered rifle, eh, Rhys?'

'My thoughts exactly, sir.'

'And the Friends of Light?'

'They've put out a press statement claiming that they are as much victims of Watson's lies as anyone else.'

Warlow shook his head. 'I'll be glad to see the back of this one, that's for certain.' He got up. 'Right, we've all got a mountain of paperwork to get on with. But let's make sure we give this bastard no wiggle room. We dot the i's and cross the t's.'

Everyone nodded.

'What about Nathan Thorley and his dad, sir?' Rhys asked.

'For now, they get the benefit of the doubt about the shotgun incident. Do you want to press charges for what happened to the drone, Detective Constable?'

Rhys shook his head. 'They coughed up. I'm happy.'

'And did we find a tracker, Rhys?' Gil asked.

Rhys shrugged. 'My guess is Hossein removed it when he got back to the Audi, sarge.'

'Then The Veil crew get away with a formal warning for obstructing the police,' Gil said. 'Not that it'll make much difference. Their lawyers are citing freedom to roam and free speech as defence.'

'Then all is right with the world,' Warlow said with a sardonic lilt to his voice as he turned towards the SIO room.

————

On Saturday, Warlow, Molly, and Cadi hit one of the lesser-known beaches. Not exactly off the beaten track but inaccessible by car and therefore off limits for most of the tourists still haunting the Pembrokeshire coast this late in the season. It was a good twenty-minute walk from the car and a hard scramble down. Something the dog managed with ease, but the humans had to be careful about.

'Does she have any mountain goat genes?' Molly asked as Cadi leapt from boulder to boulder.

'No, but she might have had a previous existence as a nanny.'

Molly stopped and stared at Warlow. 'Is that meant to be a joke?'

'I'm spending too much time with DS Jones. My apologies.'

'No, it's okay. That was pretty good, actually.'

They'd brought a chucker and an indestructible ball. Cadi was already doing an impression of Tigger on the beach, bouncing up and down on all fours as she waited for the first throw.

Warlow obliged, and the dog sprinted off to pick up the ball on its second bounce and trot back, pleased as punch.

Molly's phone blipped a notification.

'Is that your mother?'

'Nah, she's on the way, but she won't be back until lunchtime. This is from a mate. Apparently, you're trending on YouTube.'

Warlow's next throw failed badly as he swivelled towards the girl. 'What?'

Cadi, with a look bordering on disgust, ran the ten yards that the ball had flown to retrieve it and drop it at Warlow's feet. This time, he let fly with a good one, and Cadi raced off.

'The Veil. They've posted on YouTube.'

Warlow groaned. 'Not again.'

'I'd have a peep at it before you slag them off. My mate Sara says it's the dog's.'

Warlow, still frowning, stood behind Molly and waited for the video to play. This time, Emily Milton was in her studio. Well lit, made-up with a backdrop of TV and film horror posters.

'Well, guys, do I have news for you today. Just back from our trip to darkest Wales. Rory is in hospital after having been attacked. Don't worry, he's broken his arm but his spirit is still strong. We didn't find any demons. We didn't find the door to another existence. But what we found was a monster. A real monster. I can't tell you the details right now, but I can tell you we were in the thick of it when the police took down a murderer. A murderer who had yours truly by the throat. And I mean literally. Look, see the bruises? In a mo, I'll show you our footage from the edge of the dark dam at Llyn Brianne. The forest where Rory was attacked. The hidden village that rose from the deep. But first, I need to shout out and apologise to the police. My bad, I got that wrong. They weren't in any conspiracy. They were there, hunting just like we were. And their chief hunter, DCI Evan–the Wolf–Warlow, did the biz.'

Warlow's face appeared in the screen's corner. A shot of him half turning. His face serious, his eyes squinted slits into the light. It looked very much like when he and Rhys were at the Airbnb.

'Those buggers were filming us. Me and Rhys—'

'Shhh,' Molly said.

'This is the man who saved yours truly. Actually saved me from a killer. I kid you not. The truth will come out, and I can't wait to tell you guys all about it. But right now, it's still part of a real-life investigation. But what does this mean? Why was a killer in this isolated, desolate part of Britain? Could it be that he was drawn there? Could it be that some force, a dark force, drew him to it? Don't worry, The Veil will keep looking and we will let you all know what we find.'

'*Scheisse*,' Warlow said.

Molly grinned. 'I know what that means. Talk about

flavour of the month. The Veil love you now, don't they? You're their main man.'

'I could do without all that nonsense.'

'Is it nonsense, though? If it is, it's hero worship nonsense.'

Cadi came back and deposited the ball at Warlow's feet, standing back, waiting for it to be thrown again.

Warlow obliged and aimed the throw towards the water for her to have a splash.

'Your mother will tell you the same thing, Molly. There are demons in this world, only they don't have red eyes and horns. They are men and women. Mainly men, admittedly. But they all have something in them. Something that lets them look at the world differently. Look and decide that even though there are rules we must live by in order for us to stop tearing each other apart, those rules somehow don't apply to them. And the consequences of breaking those rules mean bugger all. They've convinced themselves that they're immune from all the little things that make life tolerable for the rest of us. I've just met one of those... beasts. And it leaves a taint. Because he probably doesn't even consider what he's done is very wrong. It's that idea that frightens me. Not ghosts or aliens. It's what can some-times creep into men's hearts and minds.'

He hadn't realised that his eyes had drifted out towards the horizon.

Molly stood, looking at him. 'Are you okay, Evan?'

Warlow twitched a smile. 'Me? Look around you. I'm on the beach with a charming young companion... oh, and you.' He sent her a lopsided grin. 'Things are, how do they say it, hunky to the dory.'

'That doesn't work,' Molly said. 'Doesn't work at all. But the charming companion bit almost did, even if it hurt so much to say you had to hide it in a joke. But I'll take that.' She looked at her watch. 'We're meeting Mum in an hour in the pub. Should we be getting back?'

The ball, let free from Cadi's mouth, rolled once more to Warlow's feet. 'Three more throws and we're off.'

'Deal,' Molly said.

CHAPTER FORTY-ONE

A DIFFERENT BODY OF WATER. A different day.

This time, Warlow stood at the edge of the dark-grey lapping waters of Llyn Brianne. But he wasn't alone. Two other people stood at the reservoir with him. One at his side, the other closer to the water, her feet almost in it. He'd only met this woman an hour ago, but he liked her already. She was attractive, in a made-up kind of way. But that wasn't the reason Warlow had taken to her. He liked her because she'd made the effort to travel two hundred miles plus to be here in this place of tranquillity and desolation out of respect.

Next to him stood Gil, and they both had coats on against the wind that whistled up the valley.

Gil knew the woman only by having spoken to her on the phone. He'd helped with arrangements, too. And now here they were, the three of them. The DCI, the DS, and Celia Robinson, literary agent.

'You sure it's okay to do this?' Celia asked.

'I checked with the environmental agency people. It's fine to sprinkle ashes here,' Gil said.

She nodded, reassured, and held the little urn up.

'Bye, George. Thanks for all the stories. Thanks for your unsung service to this country, too. I will miss our little chats.' Celia spoke in a low, tremulous voice. 'I still don't understand why he was killed.'

They'd never know the whole truth because Watson was unlikely to tell them anything. But Warlow had put two and two together which, the team agreed, sounded like the most likely scenario. It was this he told Celia now. 'One of Watson's victims told us George saw them being driven away with Watson in the car. George might not have made much of it at the time, but if we hadn't found them, if Watson had done what he'd planned, we'd have launched a search for the women. And that search would have meant calling on George as a matter of course because he's a neighbour. He'd remember seeing Watson in a red car with two women. My guess is Watson called on George later, after abducting his victims, perhaps only to engage him in conversation. To find out what and how much he remembered. Unfortunately, you say George had a good memory. That probably sealed his fate.'

'We think Watson might have panicked, acted on impulse. He made no effort to hide what he did anyway,' Gil added.

Celia said nothing more. Instead, she upended the urn. The wind took George Marsden's ashes and blew them out over the water where they settled and disappeared, sinking into the depths. When she turned back to the men, she had a tear in her eye.

'Thank you for coming with me,' she said. 'His brother couldn't come. He's in no state to understand, let alone travel. We are all George has.'

'Indeed,' Gil said. 'Would you like me to sing a hymn?'

Celia half laughed. 'I'm not religious and neither was George.'

'Not the point,' Warlow said. He tilted his head

towards Gil. 'He is in a choir. And this one, this hymn, I think George would like it.'

'Okay?' Celia, still a little unsure, shrugged.

Gil, in his best baritone, lifted his voice and sang the first verse and chorus of *Gwahoddiad*. Of all the hymns that could be sung at Welsh funerals, this was the one Warlow would have at his. Never mind the sentiments, or the need to suspend belief. It was simply a wonderful song. And sung in a chapel, with all the harmonious trimmings, it stirred the heart like no other. There was none of that here at the lake, but Gil could carry a tune. Warlow had no doubt it would be worth a listen. And you didn't need to know the words. Hearing it, even in this alfresco situation, was a way of trapping an emotion.

———

Mi glywaf dyner lais
   Yn galw arnaf fi
   I ddod a golchi 'meiau gyd
   Yn afon Calfari
   Arglwydd dyma fi
   ar dy alwad di
   Golch fi'n burlan yn y gwaed
   A gaed ar galfari

When he finished, Celia, with a mixture of surprise and admiration writ large on her face, was crying openly, tears streaming down her cheeks. 'What's the translation? Tell me, please?'

'No big surprise to hear that this was a Methodist Gospel song from the end of the 19th century,' Gil said. 'Originally, the Yanks called it *I am coming, Lord*. Popular in the trenches in the First World War, so I am told. Google it. Wikipedia has all the answers. This version is one word. *Invitation*. I like ours better.'

'But Wikipedia doesn't have you singing it.'

'True,' Gil said, accepting the compliment.

'That was so nice of you,' she said and wiped away another tear with a finger from her free hand while she squeezed Gil's arm with the other. 'You're right, George would have loved that. He appreciated the authentic in people.' She shook Gil's hand again and then Warlow's.

They walked her back to her car and bid her a goodbye. She left with a promise to send them both a signed copy of one of Bernard Ripley's books.

'Right, then,' Warlow said with a quick glance at the sky. 'We'd better get back to Carmarthen and help Rhys and Gina move in.'

'With a bit of luck, all the heavy lifting will be done.'

'Good point,' Warlow said. 'I dare say we could help with tea-making, though.'

'Great minds,' Gil said. 'I brought the away box, just in case.'

Warlow had noticed the plastic bag Gil had brought into the car. The away box was a cut-back selection of biscuits in a treasured old tin used when the team had to work away from HQ.

'Now you're talking my kind of language,' Warlow said.

They got into the Jeep and drove off, following the river from its source to the estuary where it bled its secrets into the patient and ever-present sea.

A FREE BOOK FOR YOU

Visit my website and join up to the Rhys Dylan VIP Reader's Club and get a FREE novella, *The Wolf Hunts Alone*, by visiting: **https://rhysdylan.com**

The Wolf Hunts Alone.

One man and his dog… will track you down.

DCI Evan Warlow is at a crossroads in his life. Living alone, contending with the bad hand fate has dealt him, he finds solace in simple things like walking his neighbour's dog.

But even that is not as safe as it was. Dogs are going missing from a country park. And not only one, now three have disappeared. When he takes it upon himself to root out the cause of the lost animals, Warlow faces ridicule and a thuggish enemy.

But are these simply dog thefts? Or is there a more sinister malevolence at work? One with its sights on bigger, two legged prey.

Only one thing is for certain; Warlow will not rest until he finds out.

———

By joining the club, you will also be the first to hear about new releases via the few but fun emails I'll send you. This includes a no spam promise from me, and you can unsubscribe at any time.

ACKNOWLEDGMENTS

As with all writing endeavours, the existence of this novel depends upon me, the author, and a small army of 'others' who turn an idea into a reality. My wife, Eleri, who gives me the space to indulge my imagination and picks out my stupid mistakes. Others who help with making the book what it is like Sian Phillips, Tim Barber and of course, proofers and ARC readers. Thank you all for your help. Special mention goes to Ela the dog who drags me away from the writing cave and the computer for walks, rain or shine. Actually, she's a bit of a princess so the rain is a no-no. Good dog!

But my biggest thanks goes to you, lovely reader, for being there and actually reading this. It's great to have you along and I do appreciate you spending your time in joining me on this roller-caster ride with Evan and the rest of the team.

CAN YOU HELP?

With that in mind, and if you enjoyed it, I do have a favour to ask. Could you spare a moment to **leave a review or a rating**? A few words will do, but it's really the only way to help others like you discover the books. Probably the best way to help authors you like. Just visit the book's page on Amazon and leave a few words, or a rating, if you have the time. I've made it easy with country specific links which will take you to the page. Tidy!

AUTHOR'S NOTE

A Body Of Water keeps the team within reach, just about, of their base in Carmarthenshire, but this time a little further North. As well as a nod to the genre, the title here refers in almost the same breath to one of Wales' many dams at Brianne and the secrets the flooding of a valley always hides. The landscape, never flat, lends itself to mysteries around almost every turn. And the silence, the sense of peace and isolation, often attracts people in search of solace, or, occasionally, in order to escape, or hide, from something in their past.

Some inspiration did come from Twm Siôn Cati, and there really is a cave, or at lease two slanting rock faces which narrow into a fissure. Many people have visited this spot, as you will see from the carved graffiti in the stone if you ever go. Whether this man truly had an altruistic streak, or whether the romanticising of a smart thief is a victorian construct—a bit like Christmas—one may never truly know. But it exists, and is signposted. We like our legends in Wales.

Those of you who've read *The Wolf Hunts Alone* will know exactly what I mean when I say that you cannot escape history in this country. And who knows what and who Warlow is going to come up against next! So once again, thank you for sparing your precious time on this new endeavour. I hope I'll get the chance to show you more of this part of the world and that it'll give you the urge to visit.

Not everyone here is a murderer. Not everyone... Cue tense music!

All the best, and see you all soon, Rhys.

READY FOR MORE?

DCI Evan Warlow and the team are back in...

Lines of Inquiry

DCI Evan Warlow believes that murder is a cardinal sin. Even when the victim is a drug dealing, money-laundering criminal. But when a police officer is shot in the same incident at a tranquil beach near Tenby in South Pembrokeshire... Suddenly it's personal. What appears, on the surface, to be a falling out between partners in crime, soon spirals into an operation involving gang warfare and a great deal of money.

And as a motivation for most sins, there is no greater corrupting influence.

But even Warlow is not prepared for what lurks beneath the surface of this most terrible of crimes. The truth, hidden under a tangled knot of lies, will lead him to a terrifying conclusion, and that most dangerous of beings, a killer with nothing left to lose.

Tick-Tock — September 2023

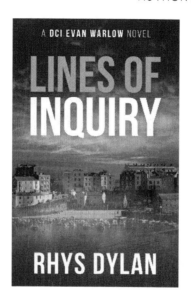

Printed in Great Britain
by Amazon

27789602R00184